THE ROAD BACK HOME FROM HERE

by Janice Broyles

illuminateYA
fiction

Illuminate YA is an imprint of LPCBooks
a division of Iron Stream Media
100 Missionary Ridge, Birmingham, AL 35242
ShopLPC.com

Cover design by Megan McCullough
Interior design by Karthick Srinivasan

Library of Congress Cataloging-in-Publication Data.
Library of Congress Control Number: 2020951557
Broyles, Janice
The Road Back Home from Here / Janice Broyles 1st ed.

ISBN-13: 978-1-64526-279-4
Ebook ISBN: 978-1-64526-313-5

Praise for *The Road Back Home from Here*

Vivid, gritty, and intriguing—this narrative holds you and won't let you go. This is the type of book I was looking for as a teen: realistic, raw, and still clean and something I'd trust I could read and give to my crime-show loving dad as well. I'm excited to watch this author's journey and can't wait for readers to take The Road Back Home from Here.

~Hope Bolinger
Multi-published author of The Blaze Trilogy, Dear Hero Duology, and Sparrow Duology

Janice Broyles writes with purpose and heart, weaving tension, grit, and restoration to create stories of hope. Broyles's work is sure to have an impact on readers of all ages.

~Caroline George
Author of *Dearest Josephine* and *The Summer We Forgot*

Author Janice Broyles takes readers on an emotional and riveting journey as we see the world through the eyes of two young people, trying to escape their demons and make a better life for themselves. It's hard *not* to root for Ellie and Jamison who are thrown together by uncontrollable circumstances, as they both learn the difficult lessons of friendship, loyalty and forgiveness. The Road Back Home from Here is a gratifying read that will lead you on a heart-pounding adventure and keep you guessing until the very end.

~Tonya Ulynn Brown
Author of The Queen's Almoner

Janice Broyles sets the reader on the path called "running" … It's a cat and mouse game from the beginning, which will leave you on your toes or pulling your feet up underneath you as you read on the couch … Broyles has written an action-packed book.

~ Rachel Anderson
Author of *The Puppy Predicament*

Acknowledgements

This book is special to me because it's the first book I ever wrote through to completion. That was fifteen years ago. It's been revised so much that it really is nothing like its initial drafts. Jamison, Ellie, and Mr. Langston's character traits have mostly stayed the same, but that's about it. Even the plot was completely overhauled a time or two! Through it all—every critique, edit, suggestion, and rejection— Jamison and Ellie's story became stronger and more compelling. That said, seeing it come to life through Illuminate YA is a dream come true. And there are many to thank:

First, I acknowledge and thank God, who is my everything. I may plant or water the seed, but it is God who gives the increase. Thank you, Lord, for letting this book develop, grow, and materialize into what it is today. All glory belongs to you.

Thank you also to Rachel Anderson, Linda Egeler, Erin Fanning, and so many other critique partners! You all read this book so many times (and so many versions) and helped me fine-tune it every time. Thank you also to SCBWI and specifically the Michigan chapter for providing me the best conferences and resources needed to improve my craft.

Thank you to Tessa and the Illuminate YA team. Tessa believed in this book the first time she read it and fought for it every step of the way. What an honor to work with such a great publisher and editing team. This includes all of Iron Stream and LPC. Thank you, thank you, thank you.

My family has always been there, both immediate family members and extended family. Your support of my writing endeavors mean a lot to me. My mother, who is no longer with us, loved Jamison's story so much that she took it to work (all 200 typed out and printed pages in a binder) and shared with everyone that her daughter wrote an amazing book. I know Mom is smiling from heaven. She knew Jamison's story would get published long before I did.

I first began writing this book because I wanted to write a fun story that my students would read. Now, all these years later, my students are still my driving force. They help me by inspiring me and challenging my mindsets. I'm better because of them, and this book is better because of their influence on my life.

God richly bless all of you I remembered to thank and those I may have forgotten to thank. Please know my memory isn't perfect, but my heart is full of love and appreciation for each and every one of you.

~Janice

Dedication

Dedicated to all my students—past and present—for teaching me new things and keeping me young.

Chapter One: Jamison

Detroit City

A knock at the door usually meant one of three things. Either the motel manager came by sniffing around for some rent, the truancy officer found out where I was hiding, or Larry had another bag of Mom's next high. I never answered the door for any of them.

This time, the banging on the door woke me up from a sound sleep. I glanced at the digital clock on the motel nightstand. It said 1:37. I sat up quickly, not wanting to have slept for that long. With the curtains closed, the room stayed dark, but currently, tiny slivers of light showed through just enough for me to see Mom still semi-comatose on the far bed.

She looked exactly as I had found her at four o'clock this morning. Completely lifeless.

I moved to her and shook her shoulders. "Mom," I whispered. "Mom?"

The sounds of Family Feud filled the room. I liked to leave the TV on because it drowned out the voices and activities of the motel, but I always covered it so the light from it didn't keep me awake. As I checked Mom's pulse, the laughter from the show seemed out of place.

This had become the new routine. She used to wake up when I tapped her arm or shook her shoulder. But that was before. This past month or two had been different. Scary different. I'd be lying if I said it didn't worry me. Sometimes she would be unresponsive for a whole day. Her eyes would be half-opened too, like a corpse, which freaked me out big time.

Steve Harvey just said something funny on the TV. The audience laughed. The door vibrated with each knock. And Mom lay there.

After I found Mom's pulse, I kept the volume up on the TV, and as quietly as I could, I tip-toed to the door and checked the peephole. Some white guy in a fancy suit stood on the other side of the door. My stomach dropped. Never mess with a white guy in a fancy suit, especially in Detroit.

What had Mom gotten herself into this time?

Then again, it was the middle of an August afternoon. Not that daylight stopped anything in Detroit. I peered again to see if he was alone. That's when I saw him make eye contact with someone to the right of the door. He moved slightly as if to say, Get ready.

He pounded on the door again, and something told me I had mere minutes, maybe only seconds. I moved in overdrive. I went inside the bathroom, stood on the toilet, and removed the plastic we used to cover the small window. Living on the run, you had to be prepared. Mom and I only stayed in rooms with back windows. When we moved in here a couple months ago, we had immediately shoved the window open. Then we kept it open and covered it with plastic in case of emergency. That way it would be easy to escape.

Grabbing her duffel bag, I threw her few supplies and clothing in it, then did the same thing with the handful of clothing I owned.

After I dumped the bag out the window, I took Mom and shook her. "Wake up," I whispered fiercely. "Some rich pimp is here or something."

Her eyes fluttered, but that was it. Sighing, I lightly smacked her on the cheek. I didn't like the idea of hitting her. She was already beaten and smacked too much. Still, it roused her.

"Hmmm?" she said and squinted at me. "Is it time yet?" she mumbled.

"We got to leave."

Her eyes widened, and I sighed in relief. Her blond hair was matted to the side of her face. She still had crusted-on makeup since who-knows-when that was now smeared around her eyes and down her cheeks. But her pupils seemed at least semi-focused. I helped put her arm around my shoulder.

The distinct sound of the lock getting picked seemed to wake her up the rest of the way.

"Did you get my stuff?" she whispered.

"Yes. It's out the window."

"Good boy." She absently patted my cheek while I rushed her to the bathroom.

I helped Mom get onto the toilet. She clumsily grabbed the window. She couldn't muster enough strength to pull herself up and over. These last few months she had gotten so thin and frail, but I'd have to worry later. I pushed on her legs, and she slipped over and out. "Oh, your books," she whispered from outside. "Get those."

Without wasting any time I hoisted myself only to pause. I only had a few books to my name, but they were *mine*. I jumped down, ran to the end table, grabbed the small pile, and headed back to the bathroom.

The door banged open as a commercial of Charmin bath tissue came on. But I didn't stop moving.

"Hold it right there!" a voice boomed.

I practically jumped into the bathroom and slammed the door. I threw my books out the window, then pulled myself out and over. I fell with a thud.

Mom was nowhere around. Then again, with all the drugs that probably laced her system, I understood why. I frantically scrambled around the ground until I found my books and the bag.

"Don't move," the same man said, now rounding the corner.

I spotted the gun immediately. His right hand rested on it. The other guy, the one who'd been hiding from sight, was some big bodyguard type. He even had a shaved head and everything.

Panic surged through my veins. Like a trapped animal, I searched for the easiest escape route.

"You can't run from me," he said.

"I didn't do anything wrong," I said.

"Then why are you running? All I did was politely knock on the door." He said the words very calmly, even straightened the sleeves of his fancy suit jacket. But I could tell he was fit for an old guy. He could probably take out some of my teeth with one solid punch.

What if they grilled me about Mom? Would I crack? What if I had to take a lie detector test? Could I get arrested for aiding and assisting her? I scanned the area. Mom probably hid in the dumpster. But there was no way I could make it without giving her away.

"All I need you to do is answer a few questions. There's no need to worry."

No need to worry? What powder had he been snorting? There were at least five hundred thousand things to worry about at this moment.

"Set everything down, please." He took a step closer to me.

My hands still held the bag and my books. I glanced one more time at the dumpster. The lid shifted slightly. The two men stared me down, but I wasn't about to give away Mom's position. Sighing, I laid everything out in front of me.

"Now what?" I asked, not even pretending to be polite.

The bodyguard, or whatever he was, went to the bag, unzipped it, and dumped it out. Then he began searching.

"Where's Claire?" the older guy in the suit asked.

"I don't know," I said miserably.

"Don't cover for her," he said. "It won't end well for either of you."

"I'm not covering for nobody. She didn't come home last night. I went to look for her, but she wasn't at her normal hangouts."

"Where are those?"

I hesitated for a second. I didn't want to bring trouble to any of the squatters. They were mostly harmless drug addicts or homeless folks.

"Where. Are. Those?" This time he reached for his gun.

"Mostly southside buildings. The old tire warehouse on Cleaver off of Five Mile. Around there."

"Nothing's here," the other guy said, leaving the mess on the ground. "Want me to check the room?"

The older man's cell phone buzzed. He glanced down at it, then swore. "This complicates things. Listen, you need to come with us, peacefully. If you do, no harm will come to you."

"What about my mom? What's going on with her?"

"She took something of mine. As soon as I get it back, I'll leave you both alone. But you need to play it cool."

Tires squealed out front of the motel. Doors slammed shut. "Jamison?" someone called out, pounding on the motel door. The sound echoed through the open bathroom window. "Jamison? Open this door."

I glanced up at the bathroom window, then back to the men.

He seemed to read my mind because he gave me a classic sinister grin. "You have no idea what I'm capable of, Jamison."

"How'd you know my name?" Cold dread filled me. Next time we were alone, I would seriously cuss Mom out. Protecting her from herself was one thing, but now she's bringing in some kind of crime/drug lords or something. Then leaves me high and dry. I don't think so.

"I know everything about you. I know how you've been taking care of your pathetic excuse of a mother since you were just a child. I know that you rarely go to school, yet you manage to pass all your classes. And you only hang out in motels or whatever other ratty place your mother finds. You keep to yourself. Basically, you hide. Isn't that right?"

"No," I muttered, even though it was exactly right.

"Both southside gangs are breathing down your neck." He came even closer. "But, strangely, you're a good kid. Don't want any part of it."

"Stop," I said, feeling creeped out. I opened my mouth to ask how he knew my mom when two men rounded the corner. One was a police officer, and the other one was, "Mr. Langston?"

"Hey there, J-Man!" he said, waving a little too exuberantly. "How's it going, everyone? Looks like there's some kind of party, huh?" He snorted at himself.

Mr. Langston was as out-of-place as a nerdy pasty guy could be in ghetto Detroit. I mean, he currently had on an extra-wide Bart Simpson tie with a suit that might have been in style a couple decades ago. Normally, I ran from Langston. The social worker was intent on taking me from Mom. Even though I was nearly a full-grown man, he still showed up unannounced every couple months to take me away. I'd manage to run, and he managed to leave me alone for another couple months. "Man, I'm seventeen. Seriously. You can stop coming by now."

"You most definitely are seventeen," he said, repeating my words loudly. His nervousness couldn't be any more apparent. Even with the police officer standing beside him. "Yes, but this time is different. We are determined to get you a high school diploma. So, why don't you come with me? I have someone ready to take you in. Someone you'll probably want to meet."

Normally, I'd put up a fight, but not today. If it was between nerdy white guy and scary white guy, it wasn't exactly a fair contest. "Fine," I said too easily.

"Really?" he asked, not hiding his surprise.

"It's our song and dance, Mr. Langston. I'll go with you, then I'll take off." I left out that it got me away from these two thugs intent on hurting me and my mom. I threw all our stuff in the duffel bag, picked up my books, and walked over to Mr. Langston.

"What's going on here?" the police officer asked, pointing to my bag and books, then pointing to the guy in the suit. The older man went to answer, but the police officer cut him off. "I was talking to Jamison."

Everyone looked at me, and I started sweating even harder than I had been. I knew that I couldn't tell the truth. Somehow it wouldn't end well for me or my mom. This guy was trouble in a big way. "They were helping me with Mom. I couldn't find her last night, and they thought they might have seen her."

"And don't worry," the older man said to me. "We'll keep looking. I won't stop until I find her. I promise." He smiled politely at Mr. Langston and the cop.

But I wasn't buying it. If I left now, would they keep looking? It wouldn't take them long to find her in the dumpster. I had to distract them somehow. "Flanigans," I said to him, acting like it hurt me to give out the information. I needed him to take the bait. "Sometimes, after the bar closes, he lets her stay over." I closed my eyes like it hurt so much to think about Mom's extracurricular activities.

Mr. Langston patted me on the shoulder. "How about if we send someone to go and check on her?"

"Please, allow me," the older man said. "She's a friend. Mr. Langston, is it? I'll call you when I find her." They shook hands, and Mr. Langston handed him a business card.

Mr. Langston walked me to his gray Taurus, while the fancy suit guy and his bodyguard got in a fancy SUV with completely tinted windows. They peeled out of the motel's parking lot, and I breathed a sigh of relief.

"You know I'm gonna have to send someone to Flanigans to keep an eye on those two," the cop said. "What does Chit Baltagio want with your mother anyway?"

"Wait. You know that guy?"

"Every cop in Detroit City knows that guy. He owns all the Baltagio car dealerships from here to Canada's border. And that's on the side. What he does most of the time is nearly every crime under the sun."

"And yet, you let him go free," I said, shaking my head. "It's no wonder cops have such a bad rap in the city."

"He wipes his hands clean, kid. That's why I needed you to give me some morsel of info. That way I could at least detain him for a couple hours and annoy him."

"No way was I gonna give anything on him. He's trouble." I looked up and hoped Mom would have enough time to get to safety. "Come on, Mr. Langston, let's get our show going. I need to be checking on my mom soon."

"No can do," Mr. Langston said, walking over to the driver's side. "This time is different."

"Sure." I slid into the passenger seat and propped my duffel bag onto my lap.

"I'm for real." Mr. Langston waved at the cop, then backed out. "When you run away, I always check up on you and your mother. Your mother begs me not to take you. To give her another chance. But this time, she called me. Told me to come here today and pick you up. I was supposed to be here earlier, but I had to wait for an available police escort."

"Back that up a sec," I said, refusing to believe what I had heard. "Mom did what?"

"She called me. Late last night."

My ears rang like someone kept smacking a big bell right by my head. "Did you just say she called you last night?"

"Yes. On my card, I have my emergency cell phone number. I got a call from her about two in the morning. At first I couldn't understand her. I think she might have been crying, or the connection was bad, but she said, 'This is Claire Jones. Do you still want my kid?'"

"What'd you say after that?"

"I asked if everything was all right. And she didn't answer me. She only said, 'You need to pick him up tomorrow at Torch Motel. Do it early.' Then she hung up."

I stared out the window feeling a hundred different kinds of crazy. None of this made sense. Mom wouldn't call Langston, especially at two in the morning. The fact is Mom should have maybe given me up when I was just a kid and could have had a better life, but with all the extra food stamp money and assistance she got with having a kid around, she refused to let me go. Plus, in her weird way, she loved me. She might have been selfish about ninety percent of the time, but every now and then, especially when I was little, she'd lay down next to me and cuddle, and tell me stories. She could tell great stories. All of it sort of became routine, at least when I was younger. The last couple years, her darker days far outnumbered any others. She'd be good for a couple weeks, maybe even try to get a job, then she'd fall down the rabbit hole and binge for a couple months. The first month or so, she'd try to hide it. But then she'd forget to come back to wherever we were squatting at. This last binge had been going on for longer than usual. But that wouldn't push her to call Langston.

But would it push her to get into trouble with that fancy suit guy?

"What's the name of that guy that showed up today?"

"Baltagio. Chit Baltagio."

"Don't you find it strange that my mom would out-of-the-blue call you and tell you to pick me up the day that Baltagio guy comes knocking?"

"She did say that she was protecting you. I thought she meant from, you know, the streets or something."

We pulled up to a stoplight, and I spotted D'Juan at the corner. He walked fast with his hood up, but I could always tell his gait with his slight limp in the left leg. D'Juan tried to act like it was part of his saunter, but I knew that he had some infection in it when we were kids and had to have surgery. He'd been my only friend through most of grade school. But then the reds got him. It'd been different ever since.

Still, I rolled down the window and gave a slight whistle. He glanced up, grinned, and jogged over to me. "Where've you been hiding?" he asked.

"Torch. You'd have found me had ya been looking."

"Been busy. You know that." D'Juan nodded at Langston. "Yo, how long you plan on keeping him?"

All of us on this side of the hood knew Langston. The guy's tried to take most of us at least a dozen times. Some he's taken for good, and we haven't seen them since. Langston thinks he's doing us all a favor, but that's the way most white people work. "Day-Juan, how are you? Staying out of trouble, I hope?"

"Sure thing."

"What's with the hood? Didn't anyone tell you it's August?" Mr. Langston snorted as his joke.

"Trying to hide from you," D'Juan said good-naturedly. "Catch ya' later," he said to me.

"Hey, wait a sec," I called out. The light had changed to green, but Langston waited. "Ever heard of Baltagio?"

D'Juan's expression immediately turned guarded. He gave a slight shake of his head. "Nah, man, ain't nobody talk about him around here." He pulled his hood even further down his forehead and limped away.

Mr. Langston pressed on the gas and kept driving. Both of us stayed quiet for a little while. "He's going down a wrong path," he finally said. "Day-Juan. If they don't already have him selling, he's at least carrying. It's only a matter of time before he gets caught—"

"All right," I said, interrupting him. The last thing I needed was to worry some more. "His name is *D'Juan*. Not Day-Juan. And don't you think I know that? You don't think I know why he keeps his hood down low? So nobody sees the bruises. But right now my mom's in trouble. I don't know what she did, but I got to get to her."

"J—"

"Don't. Don't try and tell me that I need to stay with you, and she called and blah, blah, blah. None of that matters when there's some crazy guy looking for her. He's got a gun, and so does that bodyguard of his."

"What I was going to say was that for once your mother did something *for* you. She was thinking of you. Now I don't know what all is going on, but Jamison, I'm going to honor your mother's request. You're going to a foster home. It's for the best."

"It's for the best? I've been taking care of myself for seventeen years. Whatever, Mr. Langston. You keep telling yourself that." I stared out the window as he made his way up the highway. I itched to do something. Just the thought of Baltagio hunting for her was enough to tempt me to jump out of this moving car. But I had to bide my time. I had to wait until Langston got distracted, then I'd be gone.

Chapter Two: Ellie

Greyhound

There was no going back. No losing my nerve. The tendrils of fear tickled, but I had no time for it. Because if I were to go back—or get caught—No, I couldn't think about it.

I could only move forward.

And I'd planned. I knew this day would come. I instinctively touched my backpack, so full I could barely get it zipped. The rolled up cash burned a hole in my pocket. But I had researched ways to stretch the money, and different places to hide it. So, I had some in key locations. You know, just in case.

I even researched survival skills if I ever got lost in a desert or stuck out in the ocean or in the middle of a snowstorm. I read and reread articles until I nearly went cross-eyed. Everything I needed to live I had with me.

So, why hadn't I stepped inside the bus station? I had already dumped my bike in a place they wouldn't easily find. That meant I was free. Free to walk in the building, buy a bus ticket to anywhere, and start over.

Taking a deep breath, I pushed open the bus terminal's door. Even with my hair braided and shoved into a baseball cap, I didn't want cameras honing in on me. I needed time to get away. Although chances were that Mom would be way too distracted to notice me missing for at least a day or two.

"Next."

I watched as an elderly man shuffled aside. Swallowing any doubts, I stepped forward.

"Where to?"

"Buffalo, Wyoming." After researching least populated areas, Wyoming came up. Good enough as any. I had barely visited any place outside my trailer, so it sounded like a cool foreign country. And I chose Buffalo because they were my favorite chicken wings. Luckily, the lady behind the Plexiglas acted bored and didn't even glance my way.

"That's $139 one way," she said. "Do you need a round trip?"

"No, thank you." I pulled the money out of my pocket, handed her several twenties, then shoved the rest of the money in my pocket again.

She printed some tickets, a receipt, and counted back change. "There'll be three transfers. Make sure you hold on to the tickets, or you won't be able to board. First call for boarding will be in a half hour."

I grabbed everything, nodded, and then moved aside, trying to hide my smile. So far, so good. I had checked bus departure times right before leaving. It's hard to gauge how long it would take to ride a bike fifteen miles, find a place to discard it, and then get here with enough time—but not too much time—to make the bus. I found a spot in the proper terminal and sat down, keeping my head low. I'd watched enough CSI episodes to know that it doesn't take much to locate a person.

All I needed was time. Time to get away. Anything that took too much work lost my mother's interest. If I could get out of this bus terminal and onto a bus, I'd feel a little more relaxed. I glanced down at the faded sweatshirt and ripped jeans I had purchased from the Goodwill. Not my typical outfit, and I kept them hidden until today. Even the slip-on tennis shoes came from Goodwill. Only my socks and undies were mine before my shopping trip, but I doubted anyone would notice them.

I pulled out the TracFone I bought yesterday. It hurt to leave my iPhone behind, especially because I had worked hard to pay for it, but it had a locator thingie. Couldn't have that. As it was, I was tempted to call Lauren, but instead, shoved the phone in my pocket. Too risky. She'd be the first person they'd talk to, and all she currently knew was that I was saving money to buy a car. I had brought a couple books and magazines for travel, but I didn't want to get them out yet. That left staring at the clock as my means of entertainment.

My attention didn't stay long on the clock. I found people-watching much more interesting. Ever since I was little, I would look at someone and wonder their story. Where did they come from? What was their life like? Were they happy?

Across from me, a mother and her daughter split a candy bar. The little girl looked to be around ten. She got some chocolate on her face, and her mom began to laugh. I started thinking up their story. Maybe they were on the run too. No, they appeared to be relaxed and enjoying themselves. Maybe they were going on vacation. But most families didn't take a bus to go on vacation anymore. The temptation hit to pull out my notebook and start writing. I loved taking my made-up stories and putting them onto paper. At least with writing, I controlled the events. And I always made sure the stories ended up with a happily-ever-after. But I didn't want to open my backpack. It was already stuffed to the max.

The brand-new notebook with empty pages would be filled soon enough. Maybe I could buy my own laptop and turn my notebooks into novels. But first, I needed to get out of my own nightmare of a story. I needed my own happily-ever-after.

The piercing sound of sirens filled the station, and I shrunk into the chair, pulling down the cap. Off to my left, two security officers ran past and headed outside.

The mother and the daughter now studied something on the mother's phone. They were smiling and chatting. Maybe it was one of those funny cat videos. They definitely weren't on the run. I leaned forward in the chair to see where the security officers went. They hadn't stopped at me, so I should be fine.

Some guy plopped down right next to me, even though there were lots of available seats in the terminal. "Don't worry," he said quietly. "They're not looking for you."

My blood went cold. From the corner of my eye, I could tell that he was young, but not a teenager. Possibly mid-twenties. He smelled strongly of cologne, probably thought of himself as good-looking, and he currently stared right at me with a smirk on his face.

Think this through, El, I told myself. *He came right to you and had you pegged immediately. He's been watching you.*

I might be a people-watcher, but I didn't like the idea of someone watching me. Especially when I was trying to be invisible.

"I'm Daniel," he said. "But my friends call me Danny. Want a piece?" He held out a pack of gum.

I told myself not to be afraid. I mean, I had read about how these guys would actually look for girls who were alone. Shoot, he even offered me gum, which might be laced with something. But I was probably overthinking something that wasn't nearly as sinister as my imagination let on. Just the same, more than fear, I felt extremely annoyed. My first venture out, my first attempt to leave my past and embrace my future, and this guy shows up?

"No, thanks," I said firmly. Maybe he would get that I wasn't interested in anything from him. Innocent or not.

With a slight laugh, he put his gum away. "So, what are you running from?"

"I'm not," I said through clenched teeth. "Not that it's any of your business."

"Really? Okay. Go and talk to that cop right there."

My stomach nervously flipped. Then I reminded myself that Mom wouldn't even be back from picking up Hank. And if I talked to the cop, I could get this guy to leave me alone. "Sure," I stood up and grabbed my backpack. "I'll make sure to tell him about how you're harassing me."

As I walked away, he said, "I was kidding. You don't have to get up."

I approached the cop. I had to act nonchalant, but it was hard. He raised his eyebrow at me. "Can I help you?"

"Hello, sir, is everything all right? What were the sirens for?"

"Nothing to worry about, young lady. Only a minor situation on one of the buses."

"Okay, thanks." On a whim, I asked, "Do you have any advice for how to handle strange men who approach you and offer gum?"

The cop studied me for a few seconds.

Great. Just what I need. Someone who'd be able to identify me.

"It's probably innocent, ma'am, but it never hurts to be cautious, especially if you're traveling alone."

"Yes, sir."

"Are you traveling alone?"

Be careful, El. "Just to my grandmother's. She'll meet me as soon as I get off the bus."

"Well, take care, then. You should be fine."

There! I thought, as I walked closer to where boarding would take place. *Showed him.* The cop was probably right though. Probably some guy trying to be friendly. I turned to see if he was still sitting in the same spot, but he had left. I scanned the bus station but couldn't find where he went. I couldn't find the cop either. I did a 360, searching the terminal. Where in the world did *he* go? I had talked to him not even a minute ago. Suddenly chills shot up my spine.

"Easy, Ellie," I whispered. "Don't wig out." Not knowing what to do, I waited right at the doors. I wouldn't go outside. With all the buses, it would be easy for something to happen.

And there it was. My first hesitation. Did I really want to go through with this? Was escaping my home worth it?

But that question was easily answered. There was no way I could live under the same roof with Mom and Hank. Mom chose him over me. And I couldn't continue to live in fear.

The intercom announcer interrupted my doubts. "Now boarding Bus number 5176 to Chicago."

The bus pulled up almost directly outside of the doors. I sighed in relief. I wouldn't have to get lost in the maze of buses. And if I walked fast, I could escape the bad guys, if there were bad guys.

Decision made. Nothing would deter me.

Moving quickly, I stepped outside and headed toward the small crowd gathered by the bus doors. The mother and daughter stood in front of me. "Make sure you hold on to your stuff," the mother said. "I don't want you forgetting it on the bus."

"I know, Mom. You've told me a hundred times."

"I think that was only the second time I mentioned it," she teased.

Her daughter rolled her eyes but smiled.

For a moment, I felt jealous. The mother and daughter were obviously close, and they loved each other very much. The daughter even let the mother hold her hand.

I wasn't even sure my mother loved me. At least not enough to believe me or keep me safe.

But more than jealousy, I felt an intense longing. I longed for that kind of relationship. I used to have it. Billy always took care of me. But Billy was gone now.

I tucked the memories away and took my ticket out of my pocket, then hurriedly handed it to the attendant, standing by the bus door. He barely looked at it, arguing with one of the patrons. I took it back and rushed onto the bus. I passed the mother and daughter. The woman made eye contact with me and smiled. But I kept moving, finding a spot near the back by the window.

Once in my seat, I set my backpack on my lap and rested my head against it. This was it. No going back.

As the bus loaded, I studied the people boarding. Hopefully there would be extra seats so that no one sat beside me.

That's when I saw the same guy from the terminal enter the bus. And of course, he looked right at me.

An old woman with big hips and legs waddled down the aisle. "Here," I said, smiling. "Why don't you sit by me?"

Her face lit up. "Oh, thank you, dear." She squeezed herself into the seat and smiled in my direction.

She was no doubt a bottle-blonde who enjoyed putting on way too much makeup, but I felt relief that she sat beside me, so I smiled back. I definitely needed to put her in one of my stories. "Do you need room for your bag?"

"No, no," she said. "I'll keep it right here in my lap. At least for now."

The guy from the terminal asked the person across from us if the seat was taken. But with this lady's girth, he would have quite the obstacle if he wanted to try anything. Smiling to myself, I turned and stared out the window.

Buffalo, Wyoming, here I come.

Chapter Three: Jamison

Escape Plan

I paced Mr. Langston's tiny cubicle. "Too much time has passed," I muttered. "Can you move at any speed other than snail?"

"Please, sit down. You're making me nervous." Mr. Langston glanced up at me from typing into his computer.

"Good. We should be nervous. That Baltagio guy is on the hunt for my mom."

"I already told you that I contacted the police and shared the information. They are looking for her right now. As soon as they find her, they'll pick her up."

"And book her! She's got warrants, and you know that." I fell into the hard, wooden chair opposite his desk and crossed my arms.

"How is that my fault or your fault? If you want her protected from Baltagio, the police station is probably the safest place to be."

I rolled my eyes because the guy had a point, but I wasn't about to admit it. Maybe getting booked and spending a few nights in the slammer *would* actually protect her. But that didn't change the fact that I was worried and I needed an exit strategy. Pronto.

My stomach grumbled loudly.

"You hungry?" Langston opened a desk drawer and handed me a packet of peanuts and a six-pack of small doughnuts. "Here. Why don't I order us a pizza?"

While he placed the call to the pizzeria across the street, I opened the peanuts and poured them in my mouth. I hadn't eaten anything since those Ritz-Bitz cracker packs I stole from the store yesterday. Halfway through shoveling the doughnuts into my mouth, I noticed Langston watching me. "Don't judge," I said with a mouthful.

"I was only wondering if I should order two pizzas."

"I'm thirsty," I said. "Can I go get a drink of water?"

"Sure. I'll get it for you. Stay here." Mr. Langston left the cubicle. He motioned for another social worker to keep an eye on me.

Great. Langston wasn't taking any chances.

Whatever. The moment I could, I'd be gone. I knew exactly where our emergency location was. Then we'd skip town. Maybe a fresh start would do the trick this time. Maybe we could move out of state.

I spotted my name on a folder sitting underneath some papers on the desk. It was as thick as a book. Pages were clipped together, creating this bizarre, semi-organized stack. I looked over my shoulder and didn't see him in sight. Acting like I was stretching, I moved my arm over it, then snatched it quickly. Inside were a bunch of reports. Some of them were really long descriptions of places I lived or conditions of surrounding environment. Some were interviews with teachers and Mom's probation officer. The write-ups weren't too friendly about Mom and me.

Call received concerning young woman leaving child in trailer alone. Young mother works late hours, vows to change schedule to be with child. 12-April-2009

Initial report yields:

Young woman, Claire Jones, age 25, Caucasian, runaway at age 18, one misdemeanor for OUI.

One biological child, Jamison Jones, age 8, Interracial, often left alone, takes care of mother.

Biological father not identified. Mother is unsure, refuses help in contacting anyone.

Mother and son seem to have a co-dependent relationship. This is observation. Psych Evaluation needed to verify the observation. 28-April-2009

Second contact made. Mother and child living in car. Refused child services. Child taken into custody. Subsidized housing and alcoholics anonymous established. 07-January-2010

Contact initiated. Mother and child living in motel. Child taken into custody. Mother promises participation in rehab services. 05-May-2011

Three misdemeanors. Four nights in jail. Child taken into custody. Biological father contacted. No return call. Child runs away. Mother signs up for rehabilitation classes. 21-September-2012

I shut the folder and threw it back on the desk. I couldn't read the rest. An entire folder packed with similar notes. All the times Mom got thrown in jail because I couldn't get to her in time. It even had a couple things about me in there, such as the one time I got caught stealing a bottle of Pepsi. They couldn't get ahold of Mom, so the cops called Mr. Langston. All of it showing Mom and me to be some pitiful partnership. But even more upsetting were the notes about my biological father. Mom told me she didn't know who it was. That she didn't remember the night she conceived me. But the notes said otherwise. The notes made it look like the authorities wanted to find the guy and contact him.

Mr. Langston stepped into the cubicle, handing me a Pepsi. "You like Pepsi, right?"

"How come you got nothing good to say about us?" I twisted the lid and took a swig of the pop.

His eyebrows bunched together, so I pointed at the folder.

"Oh, that's my notes. I try to write down as much as I can, just in case. You shouldn't be looking at it though. That's personal property."

"Just in case what?"

Mr. Langston opened his pop and drank from it, not answering.

"Who's my biological father? Mom said she didn't know who it was. Did you all ever figure it out?"

"Why are you looking at my stuff, Jamison? That's not for your eyes."

"Why not? It's about me, isn't it? Me and my *co-dependent* mom."

Mr. Langston closed his eyes and sighed. "It's not meant for you for this very reason. You are not objective about your situation. It's my job to observe and take notes. That way if anything comes up later, I can go back to my notes and refresh myself on the data."

"Who's my biological father?" I'd wondered about him my whole life. Now, seeing the notes, the curiosity returned.

"Your mother was uninterested in contacting him."

I shook my head, knowing he evaded the question. "You didn't try to find out? I'd think a kid would need his dad."

Mr. Langston darted his eyes, unable to keep eye contact. "You need to discuss this with your mother."

I tried not to get worked up. "All these years she didn't even try to contact whoever was my father? And then to top it all off, she calls you to come pick me up. None of this makes sense."

Mr. Langston took another drink of Mountain Dew. "Family relationships are complicated."

"Family relationship? What family relationship? What's complicated about leaving your kid? First my father and now my mother." I drank from my Pepsi. "Is this guy in jail? Is he into drugs? Don't you think the kid ought to know?"

"I do think kids ought to know. But I'm not at liberty to say. This really is a conversation you need to have with your mother."

"So, he's not the family member that's going to let me live with him?"

"No, but your maternal grandmother is very excited about meeting you."

"My grandmother?" My voice kept raising, but I was in information overload, and I was having a hard time processing. "So, I've got a grandma who has never laid eyes on me, but she's excited to see me. Now. After seventeen years?"

"It's complicated."

"You know what? If you tell me it's complicated one more time, I'm going to pour the rest of my pop over your bald spot that you comb over!"

Mr. Langston's face turned three shades of red in under a second. I couldn't tell if it was from embarrassment or anger, but I didn't care.

"I'm not a kid anymore. I can handle some answers," I said, trying not to yell.

"I get it. But Jamison, I only know so much. And part of what I know I'm not sure is the truth. Your mother has been cryptic about a lot of things."

The lady from the other desk popped her head in the cubicle. "Hey, did you order pizza?"

"Yeah," Mr. Langston said. He stood up and took the wallet from his pants' pocket. "That was quick. How much?"

A delivery man approached the cubicle. It became a little cramped in Langston's tiny office. "Total comes to sixteen-fifty."

"I thought I asked you to wait by the doors?" the lady said to the older man, holding two pizza boxes.

"My apologies, ma'am. I thought I was supposed to follow you." Turning to me, he said, "Here, son, do you mind holding these for a moment?" His gaze lingered for a couple seconds as he handed me the pizza boxes. I felt a wadded-up piece of paper go from his hand to mine. He raised his eyebrows at me until I took the paper and closed my fist around it. He then turned to talk with Mr. Langston and the lady. "I really am sorry, I'll get out of your way."

Mr. Langston handed him a twenty and told him to keep the change. "Let's open up those boxes and eat!" he said to me.

I handed him the pizza and shoved the wadded-up paper into my pocket. My brain warred with my stomach as to what to do. Find a place to read the note or eat? "You know what we don't have?" I asked. "Napkins. I'm going to go get some paper towel from the bathroom. I'll be right back."

"Not quite," Mr. Langston said with a grin. He bit into a large piece. "I'll go get some paper towels. Just no touching my stuff." He left the cubicle and motioned for the lady to watch me again.

Perfect. My chair was out of her line of vision. I opened the paper. I could tell D'Juan's handwriting immediately.

Across the street. Gordy's dumpster. Now.

I read it again, confused. Was he trying to help me run from

Langston? No, that couldn't be it. He had never helped me before. Besides, he knew I had no problem running from the social worker. I went to the window and searched across the street. Gordy's was a big-and-tall shop a few doors down. That's when I saw the hood, the same hood D'Juan was sporting about an hour ago.

"Okay, here's some paper towels," Mr. Langston said from behind me.

My instincts told me that I needed to meet D'Juan. Something was up. Did he have info on Baltagio?

"Eat up." Mr. Langston took a big bite from his slice.

"Thanks, man." I decided to shovel some pizza down my throat. It wasn't like I could just walk down there at the moment. D'Juan would know that I'd have to look for an escape. I sat in the chair again, my insides unsettled. That didn't matter to my stomach, and I took a second slice.

"So, what do you want to know?" Mr. Langston asked, already on his second slice. "And you can only ask questions that I can answer."

"I want to know … I guess I want to know why my mom called you. It doesn't make sense. Even if she got in trouble, she wouldn't call you. And why wouldn't she tell me about my biological father? You said she's keeping all this stuff from me. Why?"

"Well, I already told you what I know about why your mother called me. The only other question I can answer is that she and your biological father made some kind of agreement."

"He doesn't want me to know about him? Wow. What a stand-up guy."

Mr. Langston pressed his lips together. "Jamison, when I first met you, you weren't quite five. But you were so smart that you were going to kindergarten as a four-year-old."

"Everything was fine back then." Back before drugs, when Mom was bright and gorgeous. Long blonde hair and blue eyes that would crinkle when she smiled. We were poor, but happy. At least I was. The trailer we lived in was small but clean. She worked a lot of nights at the bar. At first, she got the neighbor lady to watch me. Until she found out the neighbor lady would shove me in the closet when I was bad. That was when I learned not to be afraid. I realized there wasn't anything in the closet but Mom's clothes. And they smelled pretty. When I was around eight, she started leaving me alone. I'd promise to lock up, and then when she left, I'd make a peanut butter sandwich and go hide in the closet.

"Jamison?"

I snapped back into reality. "What?"

"Thought I lost you there for a sec. Where'd your mind go?"

"To that trailer. Mom left me at night only because the neighbor woman wasn't nice. Then she realized that I wasn't afraid to be there alone. No big deal. You came along and made everything a big deal."

"When I first met you, I wasn't coming to take you away. I was informed that your maternal grandmother had hired a private detective to search for her missing daughter. I was told to come along for the meeting, in order to make sure the child's rights were protected."

"What? My grandmother hired a private detective? Did you pull this from a bad TV drama or something?"

"No, your mother left home as a runaway. Technically, she was eighteen, so it wasn't like we could force her back."

"Stop." A wave of emotion crashed over me. But I didn't like feeling vulnerable. I learned to shut off my emotions a long time ago. They got nowhere. Logical thinking was all that was needed. Now, with all of this information, I felt like I was going to burst into tears, which was crazy. I couldn't remember the last time I cried. "I'm done talking about this. I've got to go."

"Jamison, that's not going to happen."

"To the bathroom. That's all. It's right there. Where am I going to go? I want to talk to my mom more than I want to run away."

Mr. Langston studied me, then nodded. "Okay, but I will be right outside the door."

I marched through the maze of cubicles to the unisex bathroom. The outside doors were on the other side of it. But for now, I would hide in the bathroom.

I shut the door and locked it, then leaned against it. I didn't want to believe Mr. Langston. What did he know about Mom and me? And now he expected me to believe that Mom was some runaway, and some grandmother I'd never met found us when I was little and now wanted me to come live with her.

Sighing, I walked over to the sink and checked out my reflection in the mirror. My light brown skin had shades of gray, and my cheeks looked like sunken craters. My hair stood out all over the place, like an Afro gone wild. Mom told me once that being black and white mixed was having the best of both worlds. Yeah, that sounded nice. Tell that to my reflection which currently reminded me of one of those *Walking Dead* creatures. I washed my face vigorously and my hands, but I suddenly felt embarrassed by my appearance.

I dried off then pulled out the crumpled paper from earlier. I still had no idea how I was supposed to slip out undetected. The bathroom had no windows. Not knowing what else to do, I opened the door, hoping Mr. Langston got called away. Nope. He stood right outside the door.

"All done?" he asked. "I have a few more things to jot down before we take off."

"Um," I paused, wondering how this could work. "Could we go for a walk?"

Mr. Langston immediately looked suspicious.

"Please? I'm kind of freaking out right now, and sitting in your cubicle is like, I don't know, it's like it's closing in on me."

"Jamison, we've been through this before—"

"I promise I won't try to run away."

He raised his eyebrows in apparent surprise.

"Mr. Langston, I'm not asking because I want to run. I seriously need some fresh air. You threw a lot at me."

"I guess I did," he finally said. "Maybe we could take a walk around the block and discuss things as we walk?"

"Thank you," I said in relief.

As we headed out the door, I felt the guilt weigh on my shoulders.

Mr. Langston was a genuine nice guy, but he was also the most gullible guy I ever met. Either that, or the most trusting. And he shouldn't trust me. I've lied to him every time he's picked me up.

"Is this better?" he asked, loosening his tie.

"Yes, thanks again," I lied. The heat clung to me. August in Detroit is a killer, 90 degrees with a bucket of humidity thrown in for good measure.

"You know, for a kid that's been through everything you've been through, you sure are polite," he said with a smile.

I gave a half-laugh, masking the guilt. "Hey, let's cross the street here, so we can walk past the Dairy Queen."

"Oh, I see," he said.

"Just in case." I gave another half-laugh. Man, I was choking! As we started to walk across the street, I asked, "What else did you want to talk about?"

"You were supposed to graduate high school this year."

"What do you mean, 'supposed to'? I missed some school, but I finished all my work."

"According to your school records you missed fifty days last year. Mr. Hershel's been trying to reach you this entire summer. You were a no-show for any of the senior festivities. They were trying to get you caught up."

It bothered me, but what could I do? I couldn't tell him I didn't attend school because I stayed up half the night worried about if Mom would come back alive or not. And sometimes I would have to search her familiar party places and drag her home. Instead I said, "School's boring. But I got most of the online stuff done in the evenings. I didn't know that they didn't graduate me."

"Your test scores were off the charts," Mr. Langston continued. "You scored well past the high school level in reading, writing, and math. Ms. Lewis told me that when you'd show up, you would catch up all of your assignments at lunch, and that you completed your online exams."

"See? I don't see what the problem is." I kept my eyes down the block where Gordy's was at. I couldn't see D'Juan from this angle.

"It's not that easy. You failed gym and choir, and you never showed up to any of your counseling sessions that I had set up the last time we met."

"There are two pointless classes in schools across the country: gym and choir. Forced team sports is a joke. And I don't sing, especially when there ain't nothing to sing about."

"Mr. Hershel said that you would miss every single appointment he set."

"Mr. Hershel is an idiot. I could counsel him. And he smells like stale salami. Even a hungry guy like me thinks that's disgusting. I may be poor, but at least I can afford deodorant." I left out the part that I stole most of it, but that wasn't the point. At least my armpits didn't stink.

"What about your final capstone project? You need it to complete senior year."

I rubbed my forehead, suddenly feeling tired. It had been another long night, and evidently, an even longer day. "If I promise to fix all that, will you please let me stay here?"

"I would. But your mother called me, remember?"

"That's fantastic," I said with fake enthusiasm.

"But I do have good news. With your high test scores and your teachers' recommendations, they're going to let you graduate. You only need to complete your capstone project. Your grandmother's been informed, and she has already set up a tutor to help you finish."

"And if I refuse to go to my grandmother's? I mean, let's be real, I don't even know who she is."

"It's a court order, which means they can send you to juvie if you decide to be too difficult."

"Let me get this straight." Irritation and just a tad bit of desperation leaked into my words. "You're going to force me—against my will—to go live with some stranger who is probably more jacked up than my mom, and if I decide to hit the road, then I'm the bad guy? That is messed up on so many levels."

"Your grandmother is not … jacked up. And if she is, you let me know. Just think," he continued. "If you focused on your schoolwork, you could have a full scholarship to any university in Michigan, maybe even in the country!"

I pretended not to care. Mom often teased me about being a smarty pants and promised if I graduated high school, she would see to it that I went to college and had a better life. Yeah, right. I loved my mom and all, but even I knew that was a promise she never intended to keep. "Do you really think I care two cow farts about college?" I scowled at him. "And I thought you said I wouldn't be at my grandmother's for very long."

D'Juan came into view, spotting me then eyeing Mr. Langston.

"Is that Day-Juan?" Mr. Langston asked.

"D'Juan," I muttered.

"That's what I said. How'd he get over here? We're several miles north of southside."

D'Juan approached us, glancing behind him. "I was about ready to pull the fire alarms. What's he doing here?"

Mr. Langston looked from D'Juan to me, then narrowed his eyes. "I could ask you the same thing. Hey, what's going on?"

"I didn't tell him," I said, ignoring Mr. Langston.

"I can't believe it," Mr. Langston was saying, all indignant. "I *trusted* you. You *lied* to me."

"Oh, stop," I said. "I didn't lie. I needed some fresh air. And I don't mind you coming with me for the company." To D'Juan, I asked, "What's up?"

"Dumpster. And you need to hurry. By the way, this never happened."

"Yeah, okay, got it," I said quietly.

"Promise me," D'Juan said.

"I promise."

He nodded.

"I am so confused," Mr. Langston said.

"I'll be right back." What was I supposed to do with Mr. Langston? Would he let me leave?

"No way, Jose," he said.

"It's only the dumpster around back. I'll only be a few minutes. It might be info on my mom."

Mr. Langston crinkled his nose. "Fine," he sighed exasperatedly. "I'm coming with you."

"Is anybody paying you to be a snitch?" D'Juan asked Mr. Langston.

"Never," Mr. Langston said, indignant. "I am a broke social worker. Would you like to see my bank account? You know what, I take that back. I wouldn't show either one of you my bank account. It might only have thirty-seven dollars in it, but I'd like to keep it."

"Are you insulting us, Mr. Langston?" D'Juan acted offended.

"Yes, I am." Mr. Langston still acted indignant. "Just like I'm insulted to be tricked out here for some kind of meeting. This isn't a drug exchange, is it?"

"Relax," I said, feeling nervous myself. D'Juan still hadn't told me what was by the dumpster. "You're coming with me."

Mr. Langston loosened his big tie again. "Well, let's do this then. I'm hot, and I want that ice cream."

"Take this alley back to right behind Gordy's," D'Juan said. "Blue dumpster."

"What or who am I looking for?"

D'Juan shook his head. "Won't say out here. I gotta go. Take care of you." He limped across the street before I could respond.

I sighed. "Well, come on. Let's go see what this is about."

Mr. Langston hesitated. "Jamison, I'm not too sure I should let you do this."

"You're not 'letting' me do anything. I'm going back there. Whether you approve or not." I started down the narrow alley.

"Do you trust your friend? What if this is his gang's initiation?"

"Your offices are in the nice part of town. Gangs aren't going to be up in here."

The alley opened up to small, rectangular parking lots, directly behind each building. The blue dumpster was pressed up against the bricks between Gordy's and a Cash It Now place. I waited for a car to drive off, then moved toward the dumpster.

"Psst."

Someone waved at me from behind the dumpster. At first, I took a second look because I wasn't sure how any person could fit into the tiny space between dumpster and brick wall. But as I got closer, I saw Mom's blonde head poke out from behind it. "Mom!"

"Shh!" she said, but she shimmied out of her hiding spot and threw her arms around me.

We hugged for some time. I could have hugged her the rest of the day. "I've been so worried about you."

"I know, and I'm sorry." She released me. "For everything." She nodded in the direction of Mr. Langston who had kept his distance from us. He kept pacing back and forth, and looking over his shoulder. "Some things have taken place that change everything."

"Can you explain to me what's going on?" I glanced at Mr. Langston, then turned back to Mom. I whispered, "Why would you call him?"

"Because he's safe. And good. I don't trust many people. Actually, other than you, he's about the only person I know who is truly squeaky clean."

"Okay, but why did you call him? It's not like I need protecting."

Her face crumpled, and she could no longer look me in the eye. "I did something."

"I figured as much when that crazy, rich, white guy came pounding on our door. How'd you manage to get hooked up with Baltagio?"

"Don't say his name," she cringed. "I didn't get hooked up with Chit, but his son, Ray, we've been on-again, off-again for years."

I sighed and pressed my temples. "Let me guess. He had the good stuff."

"Hey," she exclaimed. "He actually bailed us out more times than I care to count."

"Guys like him don't bail women out without getting something in return."

"Listen, I didn't come over here to argue with you. I know that I'm disappointing as a mother. I get it. I can't change any of that at the moment, but none of it matters anyway if they get ahold of you." She grabbed my arms. "Jamison, you're in real danger, and I'm so sorry that I can't protect you. I don't even think you're going to be safe with my mother. Baltagio has a way of finding out *everything*. And to get to me, he's going to come after you."

My stomach did a little flip. "What did you get yourself into?" I asked again.

"It's complicated, and I don't have time to get into the whole story. But I can only think of one answer that he won't expect." She glanced over at Langston, then whispered, "You have to go find Gil Godfrey and tell him everything you know. Then give him the book that has the key. I lost contact with him years ago, but here's his number and address." She handed me a small scrap of paper. "I think the address is current."

I stepped back and looked at Mom like she was crazy. "You want me to do what?"

She grabbed me and pulled me to her. "We don't have time. You're just going to have to trust me. Gil is far enough away that he's not touched by Baltagio's radar. And he'll know what to do. He's a cop."

"I'm not understanding. I go to this guy? Who's a cop?"

"You'll want to meet him," she pleaded. "You've always asked questions about him. Now's your chance."

"Are you saying what I think you're saying?" I was trying really hard not to raise my voice. "Is this guy my—"

"Yes," she said quickly. "And I'm sorry. I should have told you, but I don't have time to explain all the reasons I did what I did. But please, trust me on this. Get to Gil Godfrey. He can help."

"So, then I'll call him and talk to him. I don't think showing up at his door will go over well."

"You're not safe here," she repeated. "I don't even want you making a phone call. If you call Gil and Baltagio gets wind of it, then it blows our only shot. Besides, Baltagio isn't going to expect you leaving."

"I can't handle this," I said, turning to leave.

"Stop," Mom ordered, grabbing me again. "I know this is a lot, but

Jamison, Baltagio will kill you, and then he will kill me. We have to make a move that he doesn't expect."

"So, I'm just supposed to go knock on his door? *Hey, I'm your kid, can you save me from a crazy white guy?*"

"Yes. That's what I'm asking."

"No," I said firmly. "I think going to this grandmother's house sounds better. Considering I never met her either."

Mom watched me, and I noticed she was shaking. "My life is full of nothing but regrets. My addictions have cost me everything." Mom choked back the sobs. It stirred my heart, but not enough to do what she wanted. "I can't lose you. You are the only thing I've done right. I should have let you go years ago. You could have had a normal life. But I couldn't. I would talk myself into getting better."

"It never worked." I spat the words out.

"I know." She shoved a wad of cash into my hands. "It's not much, but it's what I could scrounge up on short notice."

Gordy's back door opened. Mom's eyes widened and she shrank back behind the dumpster. "Minneapolis," she whispered. "2971 Franklin Street. It's the last place he was stationed."

"Well, hello again."

I shoved the money into my front pocket and turned to see Baltagio's bodyguard from earlier step outside the building. He approached me, then shoved me aside. "Watch what you're doing!" I shouted, stepping in front of him. I was the only thing between him and the dumpster.

He smirked, then shoved me so hard, I skidded across the ground.

"Jamison," Mr. Langston said, kneeling down. "Are you all right?"

Both of us heard Mom's yelp at the same time.

"Leave her alone!" I bellowed, jumping up and racing toward him.

In a split second, the bodyguard had a gun pointed at my chest. Mom screamed and clawed at him. "Don't touch my son!"

I took the bodyguard's brief distraction to slam my body against his and tackle him. But it was like trying to tackle a cement wall. He shoved at Mom, but I wrapped my arms around his one holding the gun. His grip on the gun was strong. He kicked me in the chest, and I smacked the ground hard. In the background I heard Langston begging me to get away from the gun, but the wind had been knocked out of me.

The sound of sirens exploded into the air—how had I not noticed them before?—and they seemed to be getting closer.

"It's the cops," Mr. Langston told the bodyguard calmly. I was actually surprised at how calm he was. "They'll be here in under a minute. And I took a picture with my cell phone of you holding Claire while pointing a gun at Jamison. So, I'd let her go. She'll only slow you down."

I recovered enough to see the menacing guy turn his attention to Langston. His eyes were cold and full of fury. "You'll regret that," he said. "That's a promise."

Mr. Langston didn't move, but I saw him swallow hard. What had I gotten this poor guy into?

"I told him to." I tried to cover for the innocent social worker. "When we were coming down the alley, I agreed to turn Mom in. That way I knew she'd be safe. Don't blame Langston. He's only thrown in the middle of this."

"Why would you do that?" Mom asked, all hurt, but I knew she was covering for us too.

"Because I'm tired of all the drama. And this." I pointed to the bad guy. "You need help."

Suddenly the sirens were upon us. The bodyguard grabbed Mom to carry her off, but she moved fast, kicking him in the groin and biting his hand. He yowled and slapped her as hard as he could. As she spun and fell to the ground, he hesitated between her and the door. Eventually, he took off back into the store.

"Mom, are you all right?"

"Help me up," she whispered. "I have to get out of here."

But the cops were already out of the cars.

"There," Mr. Langston said, indicating Mom. "That's Claire Jones, wanted on several counts."

"Mr. Langston? What are you doing?"

"Trying to do the right thing."

I stared at him in shock. And I just covered for him!

"Jamison," Mom called out.

I looked over at her, still processing that the cops were arresting her and that Mr. Langston was a snitch.

"Please, do what I asked," she said. "I know it doesn't make sense, but I'm begging you."

Mom was placed in the backseat of one of the cop cars. I went over to her and placed my hand on the window. She did the same thing. The car started, and I let out a shaky breath. She mouthed, *I love you*, and the car sped off down the back street until it was gone from sight.

I spun around and glared at Langston, who still talked with a cop. Shaking my head, I left him and moved down the tiny alley to the main street. Too much had happened, and my mind spun with all the new information. I had too many questions and not enough answers. What I knew for certain was that Mr. Langston had called the cops. I thought that he had done so when Baltagio's bodyguard showed up, but he couldn't have. He had to have called while I was talking to Mom, which meant he hadn't called them to protect us, he did it to turn my mother in.

"Jamison!" Mr. Langston ran toward me.

This was it. My chance to get out of here. I'd have to hide until I could get the duffel bag out of Langston's car. Because I guess I needed my books. Because I guess I needed to hitch a ride somehow and head to Minneapolis.

Because my mom asked me to, and I'd do just about anything for her.

I took one last glance over my shoulder, saw him closing in, then turned and ran.

Chapter Four: Ellie

Wrong Bus

"Thank you for riding Greyhound. Enjoy your time in Detroit."

I sat up with a start, blinking the sleep from my eyes. For a moment, I forgot where I was. I had slept most of the way, using the nice lady's shoulder as a pillow. But now she was gone, and I sat alone on the bus, other than the driver who was currently standing over me.

"It looked like you enjoyed a good nap."

Who knew that running away would make me so tired? "I'm sorry. I must be a pretty sound sleeper."

"No worries," the older man said with a kind smile. "It happens all the time. But if you don't get off the bus, you'll head to Cincinnati, and I wasn't sure if that was your travel destination."

"No." I got up and slung my backpack around my shoulder. "I'm heading to Wyoming. I think I have to switch buses now to go to Minneapolis." I pulled out my bus tickets to verify.

"Oh, well, first you have to stop in Chicago."

"Isn't this Chicago?"

"This is Detroit." He extended his hand. "May I look at your tickets?"

I nodded and handed them over. "I thought this was supposed to go to Chicago. I double-checked the numbers." I started to second-guess myself. Had I been so nervous that I got on the wrong bus?

"This bus is 5179," he said. "You needed 5176. How'd you get on the bus to begin with? I have to scan tickets before anyone boards."

My mouth dropped open, and I gasped. "I don't know. I handed you the ticket. What do I do?"

"It's not a big deal. One of the clerks at the window can fix this. The worst thing is that you've added a couple hours to your trip."

"Maybe I'll go to Cincinnati," I said in annoyance. "I don't really care where I go at this point."

"You'd still have to change the tickets. I'm sorry, ma'am. But let's get off the bus, and I'll point you in the direction of someone who can help."

As we stepped outside, I noticed the approaching dusk. I felt a chill shoot up my spine, but shook it off. It was my first time traveling alone. At night. But I would handle it. I was glad this old driver decided to help me. I felt a lot more secure walking with someone, especially since the Detroit station was a lot busier than the one in Lansing.

The bus driver took me to the front of the line. "This young lady boarded the wrong bus," he said to the clerk. "She needs to get on a bus to Chicago." He said good-bye and wished me luck.

I kept my head low as the middle-aged woman with about ten earrings on each ear printed out my new boarding pass. She blew bubbles with her gum and acted like she was bored out of her mind. "Boarding is outside terminal six." She highlighted the bus number. "It leaves in fifteen minutes, so you'll need to head that way now."

"Got it." With the new boarding pass in hand, I said thank you and moved away from the desk. I walked in the direction of terminal six, silently kicking myself for getting on the wrong bus.

As soon as I saw the right terminal, I also noticed that same guy from the bus heading toward me. What was his name? Danny? He had another guy with him who had a far more leering look. And his eyes were on me too. Something was going on, and it freaked me out. I could blame it on runaway jitters, but I didn't think so. Something deep down inside warned me. Besides, I knew a predator when I saw one. How normal they looked. How blending in was part of their game. I knew it because I had lived with one.

I scanned the crowd quickly. I needed someone to talk to. Someone who I could fake knowing. But the terminal was full, and most of the seats were taken. I turned fast, pushing myself into the crowd. Looking over my shoulder, I saw the two guys follow me.

This was getting real.

"Don't panic," I told myself, making myself act as nonchalant as possible. I continued to look for anyone who I could strike up a conversation with.

Sitting on the floor, close to the outside doors, I saw a guy—around my age—sitting alone. He looked kind of messy with a huge Afro and a shirt a few sizes too small. If I'd had time, I'd like to write out his story. But no time for that. Steeling myself, I marched right over to him. "I have been looking everywhere for you!"

He looked up in surprise. Wow, he had nice brown eyes. But they were looking at me like I'd grown two heads. "Wh—?"

"Go with it," I whispered. "Please." Then loudly, I kicked his shoe, and said, "Are you going to say hello and give me a hug, or am I going to have to beg?" His expression said he was trying to process what I was asking of him. But he didn't have much more time. I needed him to buy into the game. I gave him a pleading expression and mouthed, *Please.*

He stood up slowly, paused for a second, then gave me a hug. "Sorry," he said. "I didn't know where you'd be."

He had a deep, rich voice, but the guy totally needed a shower. But who cared? He was saving me from creepy guys.

"Well, come on. Where's Grandma?" I took his hand, then turned around to pretend search.

The two men had slowed, but they still moved toward me. I acted like I was totally not bothered. I even acted like I didn't recognize Danny.

As he approached, he said, "Hey look. It's the girl who froze me out."

"Excuse me?" I pretended I didn't know him.

"Danny, from the Lansing bus station. You ditched me. This is my friend, Shazz."

"O-kay," I said slowly, as if to say, *who cares?*

"Who's this guy?" Danny asked. "It doesn't look like your grandma."

I noticed Danny's friend, Shazz, sizing up the guy willing to help me. "It's my cousin Charles. He's taking me to her."

The guy next to me coughed and looked away quickly.

"No, he's not," Shazz said with a jeer. "That's Jamison, sweetheart. Everyone in the southside knows his mother. Ain't that right, J-man?"

"Say something again about my mom, and you'll find yourself with a black eye and a few less teeth," Jamison said real low and cool. "And yes, I am Charles. It's my middle name. Not the one I go by in the hood."

"Sure," Shazz said again. "And this pretty young thing is your cousin? You ain't got no family and everyone in Detroit knows it."

Jamison shrugged. "Like I care that you believe me. Last time I checked you're just a has-been with a criminal record."

"Say that again. I dare you."

"Why don't we give you both a ride?" Danny said, interrupting them. "It seems like Shazz and Jamison know each other."

"Never," Jamison spat out. "I don't know what mess he's in now, but I know all about his side jobs. And I'll pass."

"Always running scared. Too afraid to join. If it wasn't for your buddy, ol' D'Juan, we'd have beaten you into submission or taken you out a while ago."

"Because I want nothing to do with it? My hands are already full, man. That's why I chose to stay out of it. On both sides."

"Everybody chooses sides."

The conversation had completely taken an unexpected turn. Not even the story in my head could have pieced this together. It's my luck that this Jamison—not Charles—guy would know one of the creeps. I heard my bus number over the loud speaker. "Charles, we've got to go." I tugged on his arm.

He seemed to hear the announcement too. "Yeah. It's been real," he said to Shazz. "But don't you be eyeing my cousin."

Shazz made a face, but at least he didn't say anything. The Danny guy watched me with a mischievous grin. Almost like he was enjoying the challenge. Another chill shot up my spine.

Jamison and I headed outside the doors. "What's your bus number?" he asked, since three buses were boarding.

"The one to Chicago." I pulled out the new boarding pass. "5377."

"Really?" He looked over at me and arched one eyebrow. "That's my bus."

"Cool." Though I sort of didn't feel super good about it. This guy obviously came from the hood and knew all about gangs. I might not have felt a bad vibe about him—actually he seemed pretty mellow—but I didn't want him thinking we had to keep up the act once we got on the bus. "Once we're on the bus though, I should be fine."

"Good," he said in apparent relief.

That sort of surprised me. But why would it? I was some stranger who sort of threw myself at him, begging for his help.

"Thanks for back there," I said, as we approached the right bus. "They were following me. I didn't know what to do."

"You thought smart." He sized me up. "I've never met the white guy, but Shazz is already pimping out girls. He's trouble, man."

"Pimping out? You mean like—"

"Yeah, that's exactly what I mean." He motioned for me to go in front of him.

I handed the new driver my bus ticket. "This is to Chicago, right?" When he responded affirmatively, I boarded the bus. Without knowing why, I waited for the guy to check in and join me. Wait a sec, I didn't want to sit next him all the way to Chicago, did I?

I moved toward the back of the bus again, contemplating my options. As I found a spot by a window, I noticed him checking out seats near the front. I felt a twinge of disappointment. I caught his eye, and before I could talk myself out of it, I waved him over. He hesitated again—he'd been doing that a lot—only to head toward the back.

He seemed like a nice-enough guy and having a traveling companion might not make it as boring. Plus, traveling with someone felt safer, and now that I was safely in my seat, I wanted to know about his life.

Why was he at the bus station alone? What was in Chicago for him? But once he got to me, I didn't know what to say.

"I didn't know if you wanted company," I blurted.

"I get a little motion sick," he admitted. "I do better either up front or near a window. Preferably both. No offense."

I glanced up front. They had mostly filled up. "I'm sorry," I said. "How about if you sit by the window? I don't care. It'll be my way of saying thank you."

He eventually nodded and climbed over me to the window seat.

"Are you holding on to the duffel bag?" I asked.

"Yes," he said, turning to look out the window.

"It seems heavy."

"I've got some books in it. What about you? That backpack must weigh twenty pounds."

"Probably," I laughed. "Feels like it anyway. But I didn't want to take a suitcase, so I shoved as much as I could into this."

We stayed quiet for several minutes. He seemed content to stare out the window.

My curiosity took over. Why was he traveling alone to Chicago? Was he running away too? "So, you from Detroit?"

"Yeah. You not so much?"

"No, I live in Grand Ledge. Outside Lansing." I paused, wondering if I should have said that. "But not anymore. I'm moving out to Wyoming."

"Why?"

"Because it's far away from Grand Ledge."

"That bad, huh?"

"You don't know the half of it," I muttered. "What about you? What brings you to this Greyhound bus? Moving?"

"Minneapolis," he said. "To … visit a family friend?"

"You sure?" I laughed.

He shrugged again. "Well, I know I'm not moving. I need to get back. My mother's waiting on me."

"Oh, that's good. I'm sorry that guy—Shazz, was it?—said those mean things about your mom. But I wouldn't take it personally."

Jamison looked out the window again.

Someone up front had brought in fried chicken. My mouth began salivating. I could tell from Jamison's pained expression and the fact that the guy looked seriously malnourished, that he was hungry too. "I haven't eaten anything since this morning," I said.

"I had some pizza a couple hours ago. I was supposed to get ice cream, but that didn't happen."

"Really? Why's that?"

"It's a convoluted story," he said.

"I've got a couple hours to kill."

Jamison looked over at me and smiled. Okay, he would be really cute if he took care of himself. There, I said it. He had these big brown eyes and full lips with two adorable dimples. But I quickly glanced down, my brain betraying me. The last thing I wanted was a guy's attention. Even nice guys. I was damaged goods, and all I wanted was to live my life feeling safe, even if it meant living alone forever.

"How about if you tell me how you got mixed up with the likes of those two guys?" he asked.

"It wasn't on purpose. That Danny guy sat right down next to me at the Lansing station and started asking me questions about who I was running from and why. Really freaky. Like he'd been watching me. I thought I escaped him, but nope. He got on the same bus as me, and then I saw him with that other guy."

"Shazz."

"Yeah. They were coming right to me. I sort of panicked. I got a bad vibe, so I started looking for someone that could pretend to know me."

"Smart move."

"Thanks. Do you think those guys had bad intentions? I sometimes overthink and overreact."

"Possibly," Jamison said with a shrug. "I've been around crime long enough that you don't stick around to figure it out. If you get that little chill up your spine or a feeling that something ain't right. Don't mess with that intuition stuff. Get the heck out. That's what I say."

"Words to live by."

"For sure."

A lady beside us opened up a bag of Doritos. I groaned. "I was going to go buy some snacks back at the terminal, but those two jerks distracted me and took up all my time."

Jamison rested his head against the window and closed his eyes. "Do what I do," he murmured. "Whenever I'm hungry and don't have any food, I go to sleep. Sleep's the only thing that takes my mind off it. Then again, I dream about food a lot."

I tried not to stare, but now that his eyes were closed, I took in how skinny he was. What was his story? Didn't he get some kind of government assistance? My mom did. She was able to buy food every month with a food card from the government. Did that mean this kid was homeless? He looked it.

Feeling guilty, I forced myself to look away. I couldn't get involved with anyone else's business. Lauren used to always joke that I just had to put my nose in people's business and help them solve their problems. "You're always focused on other people's stories. While your own life explodes and burns," she'd say dramatically. She'd been sort of right. What she didn't know was that I had developed a plan for solving my own problems too. It was hard to keep it a secret, especially from her. But I couldn't have anything deter me. The minute Mom told me about Hank's release date, I had started to form a plan. And the plan had been simple: *get out.*

I had already been saving my checks from Burger King. The whole "buying a car" excuse had been legit at first. Mom hated driving me around, and that was when her car worked. Most of the time I walked the two miles to town. So when Mom giddily shared the news that Hank would be coming home, I already had a couple hundred dollars saved up. It wasn't much, but staying under the same roof with Hank was not an option. I had another five months to save every penny I earned. Well, after giving Mom her share, of course. She'd demand half my check. Luckily, I had direct deposit into my savings, so she never knew how much I actually made. As long as I gave her money biweekly to buy her cigarettes and wine coolers, she didn't ask questions.

All the while I kept it a secret. I started reading the Buffalo, Wyoming newspaper online. Checking out the jobs and living situation. There was even a community college nearby should I decide to take classes. But I'd have to lay low for a month and a half. Almost six weeks until I turned eighteen. I hoped that the $1500 dollars I had hidden in various places on my person would last for that long.

Jamison started to softly snore. Not feeling tired myself—I seriously missed my iPhone games—I decided to pull out one of my notebooks and at least write out a story about the mother and daughter from the Lansing station. I partly unzipped the front section of the backpack and yanked out the new notebook and pen clipped to it. As I tried to zip it back up, I lost my grip and the backpack shifted partway onto Jamison, knocking his own duffel bag halfway onto the floor.

"Sorry," I whispered to him. I reached over and carefully lifted his bag to rest on his legs again.

He didn't budge.

I set the bag on his lap, wondering what books he had that made it so heavy. The temptation to look was suddenly upon me. No way. How rude to even consider it.

Focusing on the notebook in front of me, I began to write. But my attention kept drifting back to the duffel bag. The temptation was still there. I glanced over at Jamison. Still snoring. Still not moving.

Maybe it was what Shazz said about Jamison's mother, or maybe it was because this random guy willingly played along to get those jerks to leave me alone, but I was curious about him. Who was he? Why was he on the bus by himself just like I was? And why was he bringing books? Homeless bums don't necessarily make reading a priority, do they? If I was to travel with this guy all the way to Chicago, then I should see what books he likes.

Before losing my nerve, I rested my hand on the corner of the bag. I checked to make sure he still slept, then slowly began unzipping the bag. I'd only unzip a little bit. Just enough to see a book title. I could make out the title from one of the book sleeves: *7 Traits of Highly Successful People.*

Really? I nearly laughed. Jamison looked anything but successful. Oh, well. It wasn't like I could judge.

I gingerly pushed it aside to get a better look at the book underneath it. It was a children's Bible. A really raggedy children's Bible.

What?

I looked over at him, studying him, more perplexed than ever.

Suddenly his eyes popped open and were on me. My hand froze in his duffel bag. I sat still, hoping he wouldn't look down.

No such luck.

"What are you doing?" He yanked his duffel bag and zipped it up.

"It-it-it fell on the floor," I stammered. "That's all. Some items were going to fall out, so I was helping—"

"You're lying," he said, getting worked up.

"N-N-No," I stammered again. Okay, could I act any guiltier?

"I knew it," he said, becoming angrier. "You work for him, don't you?"

I opened my mouth, but nothing came out.

"He really does have his eyes everywhere." Jamison stood up so fast, he smacked his head on the overhead compartment. He climbed over me, holding his head. "I told myself not to help you," he seethed. "Not to trust anyone."

"You don't have to move," I said. "I'll move. That's not fair to you!"

But he had already begun walking up the aisle, searching for an available seat.

"Nice going, El," I said under my breath. I should have just stuck to the notebook.

Chapter Five: Jamison

Trust No One

The bus ride to Chicago seemed to be lasting forever. I didn't necessarily have anything to compare it to, considering I'd never left Detroit before. A movie was playing, but it lost my interest. I wanted to read but couldn't. I wasn't about to take out any of my books in front of these nosy passengers, and I already felt nauseous from the motion sickness. Sleep might help, but I wasn't about to do that again. Thanks to Miss-Drama-Queen-turned-Criminal.

And she just had to be' cute too. Of course, Baltagio wouldn't send some ugly girl. Not that I wouldn't help an ugly girl—I'm not prejudiced like that—but sending a girl who has pretty olive skin, a pretty mix of hazel eyes, pretty lips, and pretty curves, and yeah, what guy wouldn't help out a pretty damsel-in-distress?

But I wouldn't be fooled again.

Mom warned me to trust no one. Other than Mr. Langston, but he wasn't with me. And the jury was still out on that one.

As I sat between two men on the bus, I had nowhere to look and nothing to do, other than replay everything that had happened. After I ran from Mr. Langston, I realized that my bag either sat in his cubicle or in his car. I couldn't remember which place I last set it, but I had to have the bag. The same bag with the book and the key that I needed to take to a guy who might be my father. The father I had never met. What could I do but run back and get that bag?

So, I did. I acted all nonchalant once back in the offices. But the bag wasn't there. It still sat in Langston's car. Nearly groaning out loud, I took a couple more slices of pizza, and moved toward another exit door. And nearly plowed into a huffing and puffing Mr. Langston.

"Follow me," he said between breaths.

"I've got something to do," I whispered. "And I know you called the cops on my mom. No way they got there that fast."

"Follow me." He pushed open the door.

"No. Didn't you hear me? I know what you did. And I'm not going anywhere, other than figuring out a way to help my mom."

Mr. Langston exhaled loudly. "Follow. Me."

For the record, the only reason I followed him was because running with all those state workers in the building would have been pointless. Going one-on-one with Langston would be much easier.

This time we headed to the parking lot. I followed him to his ugly, gray decade-old Taurus. "Get in."

I stopped. "I'm not going with you."

"Do you want to see your mother or not?" he demanded. "I'm taking you to the police station so that she doesn't have to hide behind a dumpster."

"Really?" I asked, feeling hopeful. "But you're the one who called them and turned her in."

"She told me to do it," he said. "When she called last night, she begged for help to get clean. Whatever is going on with Baltagio is finally shaking her up. Today, when I saw you two talking, I remembered our conversation and knew she'd be safer with the police than she would out in the street. And I'm glad I did because it saved both of your lives from that beefcake with a gun."

That's when the enormity of everything hit me. That guy had tried to take Mom. He had pointed a gun at my chest. And now I was in major danger. I sort of crumbled right there in the parking lot. I covered my face, sank to my knees, and tried to even out my breathing. What Mom asked me to do felt impossible. I'd never been out of southside, other than the few times Langston's picked me up, and I'd never been out of Detroit. Now I had to travel out of state and not tell anybody!

Mr. Langston surprised me then. He rested his hand on my shoulder. "You don't have to get involved, J-man. This is her issue. I can take you to your grandmother's. You can finish your senior capstone. Maybe it's time you stop taking care of your mother, and let her take care of herself."

I almost said yes. But I remembered the look on Baltagio's face, the look of I'm-going-to-hurt-you-and-I'm-going-to-enjoy-it, before Langston and the cop showed up to the motel, and I couldn't let Mom face that by herself. And I didn't want to think about what he'd do to me to get to her. I pushed myself back up and swallowed back the anxiety.

Mr. Langston must have known I couldn't walk away. "Let's get you to the police station."

"I ... can't," I said, not looking at him. My brain still buzzed with all the things I had to do.

"Why? She'll be fine. Yes, they'll book her, but I'm sure she'll spend time in rehab."

"I can't tell. Please, you'll have to trust me. There's something I've got to do. Then I'll go with you to wherever."

"Oh, right. The secret dumpster meeting."

"It's for your safety too, Mr. Langston." I leveled my gaze at him then. "I'm sorry you got involved. I hope no one comes for you. That's why I've got to do this."

We stood there for a few minutes. I felt bad because now I realized Mom had been right. Langston was as squeaky clean as they get. He didn't need for me to keep being a headache.

He gave a thin smile and nodded, as if making a decision. "I'll be all right," he said, somewhat shakily. He took out a pen and wrote on a small notepad he kept in his shirt pocket. "This is a number to call me if you need anything. Don't call my cell phone or here. Just in case. This number is to a cell phone I keep at home. No one calls it. So, it should be safe."

"Wait, what are you doing?"

"I'm going to leave my car unlocked, and I'm going to tie my shoe and go back inside. Very slowly. By the time I get to my desk, I'll have to notify authorities that you ran away again."

The truth of what he was doing dawned on me. "You're letting me go?"

"No," he said. "I'm giving you a head start to do whatever you need to do. I have an idea of what she's asking you, and I have to admit, it's probably the only way." He paused, and added, "I trust you, Jamison. I know you think I'm naïve, but I don't think so. I think you're a good guy with a good head on your shoulders. Just be careful. And don't hesitate to call me. I will always be on your side." Then he bent over and began tying his shoelace.

Now that I sat on a bus driving in the dark to go find a guy I'd never even met, I wondered if I should have stuck with Mr. Langston. He would have taken me to see an old lady. I wouldn't mind meeting a grandmother. She might have been a good cook. My stomach growled loudly.

"You hungry?" the big guy said beside me.

I shrugged, embarrassed to answer. Stupid stomach.

"I don't have any chicken left, but I've got the two biscuits that come with the meal, if you want them?" He dug through a fast food bag that he had set on the floor.

I'd been eyeing that bag for the past hour or so. Chicken sounded delicious, but I never refused food. And I liked biscuits just fine. "I appreciate it," I said as he handed me two biscuits and the honey packets that went with them.

"No problem. You look like you haven't eaten in days." He went back to reading some crime novel.

After squeezing honey onto the first biscuit and devouring it, I hesitated at the second one and thought of the girl in the back of the bus. She'd been hungry too. Then I shoved the thought aside and ate the second biscuit.

The more I thought about it, the more I doubted that she worked for Baltagio. Not that I should trust her, but she genuinely looked fearful at the bus station. And she said she came from Grand Ledge.

Still, she shouldn't have been going through my stuff. Probably some runaway turned petty thief. But I wasn't sure about that either. She was too clean. She even smelled like laundry detergent and lotion. I resisted the temptation to turn around and see what she was doing.

The bus pulled off the highway and began to slow down as the bus driver announced that we would reach the Chicago bus terminal in approximately twenty minutes.

Curiosity struck, and I peered out the window, trying not to invade the other guy's space. A portion of the Chicago skyline illuminated the night. Buildings and skyscrapers all nestled together like a band of brothers. But I knew better. If it was anything like Detroit, it harbored felons and pimps and drug dealers and poverty. Yeah, a lot of poverty. The buildings might have been built to act like beacons in the night, but the people in their alleys and on their street corners were never given the same attention.

Sadness descended on me as those thoughts led to my mom, about all the times I had to walk the city blocks one after another, checking her haunts, hoping to find her not too far gone. I sat back, no longer interested in the city of Chicago. It wouldn't show me anything I hadn't seen before.

"Where you headed?" the big guy asked me, as he zipped up his book into his bag.

"I have to switch buses here," I said, trying to evade the question. "That ought to be interesting."

"It's a piece of cake, as long as you get to the bus in time. We're running about a half hour behind."

I could barely sit still waiting for the bus to pull into the station. I had to pee something fierce, and I wasn't about to use the bus's bathrooms. Someone had used one earlier and nearly stank out most of the bus. Nasty.

Eventually the bus pulled into the station. I wanted to jump over everyone and make a mad dash for the restroom, but considering how fast the aisle filled up, that wasn't a possibility. I noticed the girl from the back had somehow managed to push her way up enough that only a few people stood between us. She made eye contact and went to say something.

I turned away. No time for drama. I had enough on my plate, and the last thing I needed was some girl's issues. There was a small part of me that felt kind of bad. I didn't have to be rude. But then I reminded myself of her hand in my duffel bag, and I stayed focused on getting off the bus and getting to a bathroom.

Once in the clear, I hustled. Luckily, a set of restrooms were right inside the door. After I finished my business and washed my hands, I pulled out my bus ticket and checked the time. Five minutes!

I moved fast, heading out of the bathroom and checking the station signs. I pushed through the crowds, hopefully walking in the right direction.

"Bus 6439 to Minneapolis now boarding."

I made it to the doors and saw the line of people outside the bus. Then I let out a breath, thankful I didn't miss it. Without thinking about the reason why, I checked to see if the girl was in line. She was supposed to be on the same bus again, and I wanted to make sure to put distance between us. Or at least that's what I told myself.

But she wasn't there. I did a quick survey of the station and didn't see her. "Not your business, Jamison," I whispered, but the goose bumps along my arms and neck said something different. I scanned the crowd again, this time being thorough. Maybe she was taking longer in the bathroom. Maybe she stopped at the vending machines for a snack.

That's when I saw her. Her cap, that is. Across the station, walking outside the main doors to the general parking lot. And that guy was with her. Walking close. His hand possessively on her waist.

My stomach dropped to my feet.

I had about three seconds to make a decision. Leave her alone, or make sure all was okay. I needed to get to Minneapolis, but could I just walk away? Especially when I knew what that possessive hand meant. I saw bad men do that with my mom. Before I knew it, I started sprinting across the station, pushing past people.

I only hoped I wasn't too late.

Chapter Six: Ellie

Change of Plans

The second I stepped off the bus, I saw him.

I immediately went to find that Jamison guy, but he had sprinted inside. No doubt to get away from me.

Danny approached. He was alone.

"What are you doing?" I asked angrily. "Are you following me or something? Because I've had enough."

"That's the thing with buses," he said, smiling. "They don't travel near as fast as cars. Where's your cousin?"

"He just ran inside to use the bathroom. He'll be out any second."

"Good, that gives us time. Come on."

"No," I said firmly and walked toward the terminal doors.

"Hey, don't be like that." He easily kept up with me. "What have I done for this cold treatment? I was only going to buy you a sandwich or something. I'm sure you're hungry."

"I asked you to leave me alone." I pulled out my bus ticket to check the number. "Now I have to get going. I really hope you find something else to do than stalk me."

He grabbed my arm and pulled me to him, whispering in my ear, "I know who you are, *Elvis Presley*."

I froze momentarily. How did he know my full name? I pushed him away from me. "That's it. I'm finding a cop, and if you touch me again, I'll scream as loud as I can."

Before I walked away, he moved his jacket slightly, showing the gun he had on him. My skin got clammy and I broke out in a cold sweat. My brain kept repeating, *This is bad.*

I tried to think of all the survival techniques to use in this situation, but I couldn't.

"Don't freak out." He smiled as if to reassure me. "I know about your stepfather, and I can help. That's why I need you to come with me."

Hank? How'd he know Hank? And if he knew my stepfather, that made him potentially just as evil.

I scoured the terminal. It was busy, even for it being late. I searched for a police officer or any security official. Then I spotted a uniform by the main door, leading out to the general parking lot. If I could get to him, I could make my move.

"I see your brain working, but you don't understand. All I'm trying to do is to give you options to get away. That's what you want, right?"

"I need to get to my bus," I said, trying to remain calm. "Stop following me."

"Then I'll contact your mother and let her know where you are. I'll also contact the authorities and let them know that you're a drug carrier."

"But—"

"Oh, I know. But it'll be enough to get you turned in and taken home. Back to your sweet family." He stepped closer. "Or, we get a bite to eat, and I'll tell you why I've been following you. I promise it's not as sinister as it sounds." Whispering to me, he added, "I actually want your stepfather behind bars again. Or dead. I'd be okay with that too."

What is going on? My brain screamed. *And who is this guy?*

"Think of it this way," he said. "I'll follow you to the ends of the earth, or you can talk to me now, and then you can be on your merry way."

"I'll miss the bus."

"I'll buy you another ticket. If you want, I'll buy you a plane ticket."

Tears threatened, but I didn't want to appear weak. My insides had turned to knots. Okay, this guy knew my stepfather and didn't like him. Well, neither did I, so we had something in common. Maybe I was taking this all out of proportion. Then again, the guy had a gun, and he made sure to show me. "I just want to be left alone," I said.

"And that can happen. I only ask for a little bit of time."

"Where do you want to go?" I asked. "Can't we sit in here and talk?"

"No, my recording equipment is outside. But there's a diner across the street. It looks like a greasy spoon, but it'll be hot food."

I considered my options. If I ran, and begged for help, then I'd likely be discovered and sent home. Was home better than seeing what this guy was about? No. Then again, I knew better than to trust him. The intercom called my bus number. Before talking myself out of it, I turned and ran in the direction of the crowds, but he must have anticipated it. He grabbed my backpack, yanked me to him, and placed his arm around my waist. I went to twist and yell, but I felt the sharp steel of his gun against my side.

"I love your feistiness," he whispered. "But I tire of your stubbornness. You are coming with me, or you will die. Do you understand? Sure, you can scream and throw up a fuss. I'll fade into the background, and then I'll come for you. Got it, sweetheart?"

My entire body trembled. *This was bad.* Oh God, why did I think I could run away?

He pushed me along, and my feet moved though I wasn't sure how. I thought of Jamison and how he could have been such a help. But no, I had to be stupid and curious and break his trust.

As we headed out the main doors, I tried to make eye contact with the security officer. But he was already looking at me. And it was the same officer from Lansing. He nodded at Danny and smirked at me.

"What do you guys know about my stepfather?" I asked. "And why is that cop here?"

"We run an operation," Danny said, as we walked outside. "Your stepfather owes a ton of money. We couldn't get to him in prison. But now … Now it's payback time."

"He won't pay anything for me," I said. "Trust me, there's no love there."

"Oh, I know," he said. "He told us all about you."

"Hey!" someone yelled behind us. "Where in the world have you been?"

I heard the fast approaching footsteps, and so did Danny. He whirled us around, but he must not have expected someone to grab at me. That's exactly what Jamison did.

Jamison!

My heart exploded in relief as he pulled me to him. "What are you doing?" he yelled at me. "I have been looking all over for you!" Then he turned on Danny, shoving him so hard that Danny stumbled back and fell, dropping the gun. Jamison was fast. Too fast for Danny. He picked up the gun and pointed it at Danny's face. "Go, get a cop," he said to me. "This guy's trouble."

"I don't know which cop is good. Some of them are with him."

"Yell until you find someone who'll listen." Jamison didn't divert his attention away from Danny.

I started yelling for help. I even took out my TracFone and called 9-1-1. I heard Danny pleading with Jamison, but Jamison wasn't having it. And his face was like iron. Fury rippled across his features. Could Jamison actually put a bullet in him?

The security officer from inside ran at us, while drawing his gun. "He's with him!" I shouted to Jamison. "We've got to go!"

"9-1-1, what is your emergency?"

I watched Jamison kick Danny in the stomach, then grab my hand and run. The gun still was in his other hand.

"9-1-1, what is your emergency?"

"Uh, at the bus station," I said while running. "A guy tried to pick me up and kidnap me. Or something. He had a gun and told me to walk outside."

"What bus station?"

"The one in Chicago! Greyhound bus! The guy's name is Danny. He's young and good-looking. Brown hair, blue eyes. And there's a fake cop with him. I'm running right now. Please send cops! Real ones!"

"Stay on the line and walk me through this," the operator said calmly.

"Send cops!" I shouted, then put the phone back in my pocket. To Jamison, I said, "The gun! You still have his gun!"

"I know, but I don't know what to do with it," he said pulling me down another maze of cars. "I couldn't leave it with him. Then he'd shoot at us!"

The idea came to me in a rush. "The bus! It's leaving. If we can make it—"

"Good idea."

"Do something with the gun!"

Jamison emptied out all its bullets while moving toward where the buses were stationed. Then shoved the weapon in his pants' pocket.

"Why'd you empty out the bullets?" I asked.

"So that no one gets hurt," he said in a tone that sounded like one big *Duh!*

But I had no time to say anything more. Our bus was pulling out of the station.

We both sprinted, shouting, "Wait!" to the now exiting bus. But it had already turned onto the main road and hit the accelerator. Jamison chased it longer than I did. I had to stop and catch my breath.

"Let's go back inside." I felt utterly defeated and out of breath. But more than that, I felt exposed. As if being watched. "It's probably safer in there. Then we can get on another bus."

Jamison narrowed his eyes. "I missed my bus," he said in accusation.

My emotions shot in every direction as the reality of what happened and what could have happened landed squarely on my shoulders. I nodded, trying to keep the tears at bay. "I don't know what would have happened if you hadn't—"

"I'll tell you what would have happened." He was getting worked up again. "That frat boy would have had his way with you and then passed you around to all the others. That's what would have happened. He's probably the face of some trafficking or pimping operation. I don't know. All I know is that I needed to be on that bus! I've got my own set of problems to deal with, I can't be dealing with yours!" He paused and tried to even out his breathing.

My entire body shook in terror. I expected some dark van to come at us any second. "Thank you," I whispered, my voice choked up. "I didn't—He came for me, my stepfather ..." I wiped at my face, not wanting to cry, but seriously fearing for my life. "I don't know what to do," I cried. "I can't go home. I can't! But will this guy just follow me forever? He said he would."

"Then we tell the cops." Jamison walked closer. His angry countenance had been replaced with concern and resignation.

"They'll send me home. I'm not quite eighteen. I have to lay low until October third."

"Can't you just stay home and make it work for the next five weeks?"

"No. That Danny guy? He's worked with my stepfather, if that gives you any indication of what's waiting for me. If I get back home, he is capable of—"

"Okay, what you're saying is that you're running from a bad daddy situation. I get it, but if you got out this time, you can get out again in five weeks."

"It's more than a 'bad daddy' situation. It's not the same. My mother's husband—not my father—has been in jail for the last three years, but our lovely state feels that he's safe for society and is letting him out on good behavior." I rung my hands just thinking about it.

"Got it. Well, that sucks."

The simple truth of what he said made me smile. Briefly. "Yeah, it does," I agreed. "Kind of an understatement, given that I am now being chased by some guy who knows my stepfather, and wants his money back."

Jamison grimaced. "Girl, you're screwed."

"Thank you, Captain Obvious." Then I rethought it. This kid just saved my life. "Sorry. I'm a little stressed. Can we go inside now? I feel exposed."

"I don't think that's going to happen." He pointed at the bus station. "They're inside, scouting the place. I saw Danny just a second ago, and the fake cop guy was walking around the bus terminal. We need to find some cover for a while. As it stands, they've lost you, which is good."

"What am I going to do?"

"Well, I've got to be somewhere, so let's lay low, and then we'll go in and get on another bus."

Police sirens sounded down the street. "You've got to get rid of that gun," I said.

Jamison grimaced again, grabbed my hand, and started running down the street in the opposite direction.

"Maybe they can help!" I said.

"I thought you said you couldn't go home?"

"Oh, right."

He led me down a side street. There on the corner a Walgreen's sign lit up.

"What about there?" I asked.

"They have cameras, and that's the first place anyone would check."

"Then where? This isn't the best area."

"I know. Nobody knows ghetto like I do."

We kept running, stopping briefly to catch our breaths, then continued moving. Jamison would slow down, look around in the dark, then make a decision and pull me with him. I wanted to stop, but the sirens still rang through the night.

"What are you looking for?"

"Someplace to squat."

"Squat?"

"You know, lay low, where nobody's gonna come looking."

"I don't want to get too far from the bus station." I tried not to make eye contact with a few loiterers hovering around alleys.

Jamison shook his head. "You're confusing me. Do you want to go back? Then fine. That's what I want to do too. I want to get on a bus and take care of what I have to take care of. But now there are cops, and you're like 'I can't go home' and those two guys are still at the station, and you don't want to go with them. So, please tell me what it is you want, so that I can drop you off and then go and take care of my own business!"

"Listen, none of this is planned," I said. "All I know is I can't go back there right now, but I don't want to go *squat* somewhere either. That's dangerous, isn't it? I mean, there could be drug addicts and stuff. And I've read about Chicago. It's the most dangerous city. More murders than even Detroit."

"Fine, we can't stand out here on the street anyway. They have street cams at the traffic lights and stuff. At least they do in the D."

My stomach gnawed at my insides like a vicious rat. I pressed my hand against it. "Can we sit somewhere and get a bite to eat? Then we can go back?"

Jamison surveyed the street. "I don't know where'd there be food, but point in a direction, and I'll walk that way."

"That direction looks like the start of houses." Dark, deserted homes with spray-painted boards covering the windows. Just the thought of what hid inside sent a shudder through me. "But this way seems cleaned up and, you know, not so ghetto."

"Then we'll go right. Let's see what's down this way." He acted like he had reservations.

"What?" I asked, following him.

"Nothing."

"I'm sorry about all of this." When he didn't answer, I continued, "I only wanted a fresh start, you know?"

Jamison wasn't talking, so I decided not to push it. I felt this mix of guilt, fear, and annoyance, but I also felt grateful he helped me. I couldn't imagine what would be happening to me right now if Jamison hadn't showed up.

We walked by clusters of people here and there. Some glanced our way, one or two seemed to study us a bit longer, but no one said anything or asked anything. Jamison kept his hands in his pockets and his head down, so I followed suit. The police sirens never seemed to end, but luckily, they stayed in the distance.

Suddenly Jamison stopped, and I walked right into him.

"What about that?" he asked, motioning across the street.

Ahmad's Wine & Spirits party store stood at the corner. Several cars littered the parking lot. A few loitered outside smoking, but it was well-lit. Nothing too scary. "Works for me."

We crossed the street. None of the men outside paid too much attention to us. I breathed a sigh of relief. Once in the store, I smelled the single-sliced pizza immediately and nearly started drooling. Jamison must have had the same idea. "Pizza," he said, giving me a half-grin. "About time our luck changed."

The young man behind the counter and plexiglass eyed us then our bags. Jamison nodded in his direction and politely said, "How you doing tonight?"

He didn't answer, only went back to his phone.

"Do you have any money?" Jamison whispered to me.

"Yeah, a little," I said, not wanting to indicate how much I actually had. "Get whatever you want. It's on me."

"I got some cash." He acted insulted. "I was just curious if you did too."

We both grabbed bottles of water and some Gatorade, bags of chips, beef jerky, a handful of protein bars each, and Jamison even grabbed two apples from a small bowl of fruit at the counter.

"I'll go first," I told him, since we couldn't fit it all on the little space of the counter. To the cashier I said, "Can I have two slices of pizza, please?"

"I hope that's just for you," Jamison said. "I'm going to have about four slices."

"Oh yeah, it's for me." I asked the cashier for a bag, which he shoved under the plexiglass. I discreetly took a twenty out of my pocket and paid for it.

As the cashier rang up Jamison's items, the door banged open and a big, dark-skinned man came booming in, pointing at the cashier and nodding with a wild grin on his face. "Shortyyyy!" he exclaimed. "Who's your daddy?"

The cashier grinned back, but he was shaking his head. "Nah, man, I don't want to hear it," he said with a heavy Middle-Eastern accent.

"The Cubs, baby, that's who! Pay up, my man." The heavy man walked over to the counter, standing behind us. The cashier tried to focus on finishing the transaction with us while laughing at the sports jabs of the other customer. "I'm telling you, man, the pied piper has come for you to pay up. I just got my car from the pound, and she's thirsty. Ya know what I'm saying?"

I handed another twenty to the cashier before Jamison could pay. He looked over at me annoyed. "It's the least I can do," I said. I turned to see the guy behind me, measuring me up.

"How *you* doing?" He wiggled his eyebrows.

Even with him flirting with me, I didn't feel threatened. No bad vibes about him. Either that, or I felt safe having Jamison around.

"Why don't you come give this big teddy bear a hug? Don't worry. This teddy bear don't bite."

Jamison took his plastic bag and filled it up with his purchased food. "She's not giving hugs to anyone but me," he said, acting all eased back and relaxed.

The big guy laughed and pretended to hit Jamison in the shoulder. "You dirty dog!" He started laughing. To me, he said, "I'm just messing with you."

I should have been offended or at least bothered by him, but he was so boisterous and good-natured, that I found myself stifling my laugh. Especially because Jamison acted all embarrassed and uncomfortable. "See you later, my man." Jamison made his way to the door.

Moving to follow him, I noticed the two flat screen televisions on the wall to the side of the cashier behind the plexiglass. The bottom one was his security system, but the top television had changed from a commercial to some breaking news. Even though I couldn't hear what was being said, I clearly saw the black-and-white footage of a scene that looked awfully familiar. Suddenly, I felt all the blood drain from my face. Splashed across the television screen was a picture of Jamison holding a gun.

The two men were busy talking. Neither one was paying attention. Which was good. Because they'd have no problem identifying the skinny guy with the big Afro.

Chapter Seven: Jamison

America's Most Wanted

I guzzled the water in under ten seconds and had a slice of pizza down before the girl stepped foot outside. I had to walk away because Big Daddy back there was embarrassing me. I didn't want that girl thinking I thought what he thought. The last thing I wanted was more complications. And God, could this get any more complicated?

Somehow, I managed to get stuck in Chicago. With some girl whose name I didn't even know. And now I had a gun in my pocket. I should get rid of it, but with those guys chasing us, I wanted it for protection. At least pretend protection.

The girl walked out of the store and headed over to me. I chose a wall that hid us somewhat from the main street.

"We're on the television," she whispered. She looked down at the slice of pizza and grimaced. "Suddenly, I'm not so hungry."

"We're what?" I asked. But I'd heard her. I wrapped up the rest of the pizza, no longer hungry either.

"On the television. Breaking news. It's a fuzzy pic of the bus station parking lot, but it's you, holding a gun, and half my profile is in the shot too." She opened her water bottle and drank heartily.

I made myself look away. Now was not the time to develop a crush. Instead, I leaned my head back and closed my eyes. Great. "I got to get rid of the gun."

"You didn't do anything wrong. I'm sure once they review the video, they'll see that."

"No, what they'll see is some white guy walking outside with his arm around his girl. Then, they'll see some black thug grab you and shove the other guy to the ground before pointing a gun at him." Just saying it had me sweating. "I should have just got on the bus and minded my own business." She frowned, and I could see her battle the fear and guilt. I shouldn't have said it. How many times am I going to repeat that she ruined my plans? The apology was on my tongue, but I couldn't say it. Mostly because I meant it. Sure, she was cute and yes, I was able to help her. But it came at my expense. At my mother's expense.

"I don't know what you want me to say," she said quietly. "I've already said thank you. I've already said I'm sorry. If I could change this, I would. But I don't know when he'll show up again. I only know that he will."

"Let's head back to the bus station," I finally said. "Maybe it's cleared out."

"Or maybe they're waiting for you to come back," she said.

Big Daddy from inside had stepped around the corner and to an old Oldsmobile parked not far from us. We made eye contact, and I gave a half-wave as he nodded in my direction. "Whatchya doing around these parts?" he asked. "I know everyone 'round here, and I don't know you."

"Visiting family," I said. "The Browns over on 87th."

"Right." He wasn't buying it. He pointed to the girl's cap. "Are they Tigers fans too?"

I didn't say anything because honestly, he already knew I was lying. Instead I walked over to him, checking out his car. "You just get her out of the pound?"

"That's right," he said, eyeing me suspiciously. "Why you asking?"

The idea formed, and it became crystal clear what the solution would be. "How far can she go?"

"About one block in that direction. That's all I'm taking her."

"What about if I offered you some cash? Would you be willing to take us out of the city?"

His congenial face turned to stone immediately. "What you take me for? I don't even know you."

"I'm just a guy who got lost," I said. "That's it. I need a ride with my girl outside of the city."

"You got lost? 'Cause you sure look an awful lot like that kid who pulled out a gun at the bus station."

"He didn't have the gun," the girl jumped in.

I sighed in exasperation and gave her a *butt out* look I hoped she understood.

"What?" she asked me. "He saw you on the television! How're you going to talk yourself out of that one?"

"She's got a point, man," he said.

"Listen, a guy approached me and pointed a gun at my waist," she began. "Told me that I had to go with him or he would follow me forever. Said that he only wanted to ask questions. But what could I do? A gun was at my waist. Jamison, here—"

Oh my God, did she just give this guy my name?

"I met him at the Detroit bus station—"

And now where I lived. What was next? My Social Security number?

"He protected me from that guy. He shoved him and the gun fell out of his hands, and Jamison grabbed it. That's it."

Big Daddy exhaled slowly. "You know what, I believe you. But it's not my problem, girlie. I just got done with my own mess. I can't be getting involved."

"We only need you to get us out of town," she pleaded with him. "I will pay you and give you gas money."

The guy actually seemed to be thinking about it. Wow, she was pretty good. Then again, she lured me into all of this, so what did I expect?

"I guess there's no harm in helping out a couple of kids," he said. "I need to pay my cell phone bill anyway. How much you offering?"

The girl acted unsure.

"Hundred bucks. Cold, hard cash," he said. "Plus, you fill up the gas tank."

"Are you serious?" I maybe only had a hundred more dollars on me. Mom had shoved a bunch of dirty twenties and tens at me, and it didn't quite come to three hundred dollars.

"The offer's going up to two hundred if you don't decide in two seconds."

"Deal," the girl said, holding out her hand.

He held his hands up, palms out. "Oh no, I don't shake hands. I take the money."

"We'll get in the car, then we'll give you the money," I said.

He looked me up and down. "All right, let's go, but don't you think of starting anything."

"Trust me, that's the last thing I want." I moved to get in the backseat while the girl slid into the front.

She handed the guy several twenties. How much money did she have? He counted them, then stuffed them in his pocket. "Where do you want to go?"

"West," I said, before she could say anything. "Take us west because that's where the bus will go."

He started the car and pulled out of the driveway. "You all gonna share those snacks? Or am I gonna have to beg?"

The girl handed over a bag of barbeque chips. "I'm Ellie," she said to him.

"Charles," he said. "Everyone calls me Chuck."

Ellie turned back to me and smiled. "Charles," she said. "That's what I called you."

I looked out the window and said, "So, you have a name? Nice to finally know it, *Ellie*."

"We've been a little busy." She turned her attention back to Chuck and kept talking.

For whatever reason, it bothered me that she was all chatty and nice with this complete stranger. Maybe that's why she was in the mess she was in! *Oh, his name is Jamison. Oh, my name is Ellie. Here let me throw money at you.*

Interrupting them, I practically growled. "We weren't busy on the bus until you had your hand in my bag, and we weren't busy while we were walking to the store. There was plenty of opportunities for you to tell me your name."

"I'm sorry it didn't come up," she said. "It wasn't on purpose."

"Whatever," I sighed, as we got on the highway. "I don't care." I couldn't get any more involved. A part of me wanted Chuck to drop me off at a police station so I could clear my name. Then I could get back on a bus. Ellie could stick with Chuck. She seemed to take to him.

While they chatted, I busied myself with eating another slice of pizza. Chuck seemed nice enough, but I refused to trust him. Trust no one. I became annoyed at myself for how I wasn't following that core piece of advice. It's how I got into this mess to begin with! For over twenty minutes, as I moved from eating pizza to chowing on my bag of chips, I watched them argue over the Tigers and Cubs. Eventually the city and the surrounding suburbs were long gone.

I didn't have time for this. "Could you drop me off at the nearest police station?"

Chuck looked at me from the rearview mirror. "I don't go near the cops, man. And our deal was to take you out of Chicago."

"Then drive by a station, and I'll jump out of the car."

"What are you doing?" Ellie asked. "That's not our plan."

"Our plan? We don't have a plan. We are not together. I've got my own stuff to deal with, and hiding from the cops now isn't going to help me. You've got yourself another knight in shining armor, so let me do my thing."

"But I can't go to the cops, remember? We talked about this. I can't go home. I know you don't understand that, but try. You have no idea what it was like and what I'll be going back to."

"I have no idea?" All the irritation and impatience rose to the surface. "You don't know jack about me, or about what I'm running from, so get off your moral high horse and stop trying to manipulate me to go along with what works for you. Because you know what? It doesn't work for me."

Ellie stayed quiet, frowning with her lips pressed together.

"Then what's your story?" Chuck asked. "What're you running from?"

Instead of answering the questions, I said, "I know what I don't want to run from, and that's the police. I didn't do anything wrong, and maybe they'll help contact the person I need to contact."

"Listen, I'm not gonna tell you what to do, but it might not go easy with the police. And I'm not hanging out with you two much longer. We've already been on the highway and out of Chicago city limits for a little while. You two need to stick together. Being isolated ain't the way to survive, know what I mean?"

"Thanks for your help," Ellie said to Chuck. "You don't even know us, but you still helped us."

"Well, you paid me," he said. "I'll get off at the next exit."

Ellie glanced at me, that frown still on her face, then turned back to Chuck. "We need to get to Minneapolis."

"No way," he said, drawing out each word. "That's gotta be like ten hours each way. Sorry, guys. I don't mind helping a little, but I've got to get back."

"Right," Ellie said. "I thought you'd say that. What about getting us to the next bus station? I could pay you some more. I mean, I don't have a lot, but I could give you a little more."

Chuck stayed quiet for a minute, then took out his phone, and asked Siri, "Where's the closest Greyhound bus station?" The phone answered by opening up a map. Chuck handed the phone to Ellie. "What does it say?"

"Rockford. About seventy miles away."

Chuck whistled. "That's far. And I've got to work tomorrow."

As I listened to their exchange, I found my eyes starting to droop. Now that my emotions had sort of mellowed out again—it's not like I could jump out of a car on an expressway—the events of the day and all that running had me yawning and sleepy. But if Chuck could drive us to the next bus station, that sounded promising.

"Wouldn't they recognize me?" I asked, making myself stay awake.

"I'm sure they have a visual on me. That's why I need to get to the cops and clear this up."

"With that Afro, anybody'd recognize you," Chuck laughed. "It's like a beacon, man. How long have you been growing that thing?"

"He's right," Ellie said. "Just shave your hair and change your clothes into something a little nicer, and you'd be a different person."

"And how am I gonna do that?" I leaned back into the seat and closed my eyes. I'd be more frustrated, but I was too tired.

Chuck pulled off onto an exit ramp. "This is a good place. They've got a Walmart and a Waffle House. Go get some clippers and stuff at ol' Wally-World, then if you get hungry, ain't nothing better than a Waffle House."

I felt a little deflated. Chuck might have been a complete stranger, but getting to the next bus station sounded promising. Like he'd drive us the seventy miles. What was I thinking? That was far. And it was already nearly two in the morning. My tiredness must make me delirious to think some guy I just met at *Ahmad's* would make that kind of sacrifice.

And now we were being dumped off in the middle of some town between Chicago and Rockford. As Chuck pulled into the Walmart parking lot, I started to quietly laugh.

"What's so funny?" Ellie asked, as Chuck slowed the car by the front entrance.

I rubbed my eyes, which were begging to stay shut. Instead of answering Ellie, I opened the car door. "Thanks for taking us this far," I said to Chuck.

But Chuck's expression seemed concerned. "You two stick together, okay?"

I shut the door behind me and moved quickly into the store. I didn't like the idea of being wanted by the law. So, the quicker I went in and got out, the better. I kept my head down and walked toward men's clothes. Chuck and Ellie were definitely on to something about my appearance. I didn't have a lot to spend though, especially if I was going to buy a ticket at the next bus station.

As I grabbed a shirt from the clearance rack, I wondered if I could get away with stuffing it in my pants. But I couldn't risk getting caught. Besides it was three bucks.

"Here, this looks your size," Ellie said, holding out a black pair of jeans.

"I don't need new jeans. A different shirt is fine."

"Yes, you do. Besides, the fact that it looks like you haven't taken those off in a couple weeks, they're faded blue. These are black. So, they won't be quickly noticed on surveillance."

I glowered at her, completely humiliated at the truth behind her words. I snatched the pants and stormed away from her. Okay, I get it. My clothes were dirty. We only went to the laundromat once a month. The rest of the time I washed my underwear in the sink or tub and made do with the rest.

"Here, let me pay for it," Ellie said, catching up.

I might have refused, but my pride knew I had to save the money I had. I handed her the items and headed outside.

"Wait for me," she pleaded.

But I didn't stop. Once outside, I paused, scanning the parking lot. How was I supposed to get to Minneapolis? I had no idea where we were, and I had no idea how we were supposed to get to another bus station. But the question I was most ashamed of was why I had to get involved with this girl in the first place. Why couldn't I let her walk out with that guy? Then I'd be on the bus, well on my way to helping my mom.

I sat on a blue metal bench, trying to think of way out of this mess. This little strip had a few shops and restaurants. There was a car dealer across the street and a box-style Comfort Inn. That'd be nice. What I wouldn't do for a bed.

On the other side of the expressway, the businesses eventually stopped. But an old highway motel sign stood on a long pole, only half of the sign working. I could see just enough of the motel to see that it had been shut down for a while. Its property was surrounded by overgrown grass and weeds. It looked like something from a horror movie. Probably filled with rats, spiders, and homeless.

Swallowing hard, I rubbed my eyes again. If I lay down, I'd be out. Right here on the bench. So, I opened my bag and took out another slice of pizza that I'd saved. I had kept two slices in the plastic bag. I kept glancing over at the closed motel. I wondered how bad the rooms were. All I needed was a bed.

The Walmart sliding doors opened, and Ellie walked out carrying a bag, a gallon of water, and holding two sodas in her hand. "I didn't know which kind you liked, so pick one."

I took the Pepsi, leaving her the Mountain Dew. "Thanks."

She sat down beside me and started to drink hers.

"What's the water for?"

"Drinking. And cleaning. I feel icky."

"We probably shouldn't sit here." I stood up, feeling even more self-conscious. I normally didn't care what I looked like, but now I was very aware of my ugly and dirty appearance. Especially since Ellie made it clear that she noticed it.

"I know, but I don't know where to go or what to do." Her eyes filled with tears. She blinked quickly, swallowing more of her soda.

"I have an idea," I said. "Follow me." I started walking away, toward the side of the store that didn't have any cars. I walked until the parking lot ended and an open field began. The field led to the expressway. I only wanted to walk through it, to stay undetected from the street lights.

"Good idea," Ellie said. "Are we crashing out here? Too bad we couldn't start a campfire."

"No, not here," I answered. "Over there." I pointed to the darkened motel.

"Oh."

We reached the overpass, but instead of walking over it, I cut across the empty street. I didn't check to see if Ellie was following me though I was pretty sure she was. All I could think about was a bed.

"Are we allowed to do this?" she whispered.

I stopped once we got to the overgrown grass and studied the building. I didn't see any cameras, but then again, it was darker over on this side of the expressway.

"How are we going to get in? I'm sure the doors are locked. Plus, what if the electricity is off? How will we see?"

"I only need a bed. We can deal with the rest when we wake up." I kept walking toward the back of the building, then picked a downstairs room and tried the door. Luckily it wasn't one of those carded lock systems. This was an old lock design.

"Told you it'd be locked," Ellie said.

I bent down and unzipped my bag, pulling out a small pocket knife.

"I can't believe the bus let you travel with that," she said, once she saw what it was.

"It didn't. I took it from the party store." I opened up the knife and began to fiddle with the door's lock. Mom taught me some about locks, but only the basics and only on straight locks. Anything too high-tech, and I avoided it. Not that Mom did. Then again, she'd just smash a window if it was an emergency.

"Where'd you find it?"

"On a turntable near the window. It's only a little one. Almost like a toy. I thought I might need it in a jam."

Maybe it was because I was tired or maybe it was because it was dark outside, but I couldn't get the door to unlock. I kept at it until my fingers started cramping around the little pocket knife. I hated the thought of breaking a window, if I even could. Motel windows were pretty strong stuff.

Eventually I rested my head against the door.

"No luck?"

"Nope," I said, trying not to get annoyed at her. It's not like she could help, or could she? "Hey, go see if any of these doors are unlocked. Who knows? Maybe one is."

While she checked other doors, I stood up and rammed my body against the door to see if I could make anything loose. The thought of beds being on the other side had me near desperation.

"Try this one," she called out several doors down. "It's locked, but it's jiggly."

I went over to her. Sure enough the door jiggled against the lock. I knelt down and tried picking at it. Okay, I must really suck at picking locks because I still wasn't successful. Standing up, I began ramming into that door to see if I could jiggle it free.

"Can I try?" she asked.

"Sure," I said, stepping aside.

"Can I borrow the knife?"

I handed it to her. "Have you ever picked a lock?" I asked.

"Only the ones to our bedroom doors, but those are easy. I'd take a pen point, and click the lock out of place. I used to do that to steal from my older brother. He'd come home with candy bars or bags of chips, and he'd hide them on me. I think he knew I snuck into the room, but he still locked the door."

"You have an older brother? Why can't you go live with him?" I asked, exasperated. "Is he bad too?"

"He's not bad. He's dead."

"Oh."

She turned her attention back to the door. "I think I might have figured it out." She leaned into the door, while maneuvering the knife. Suddenly the door clicked. Ellie turned to me and grinned.

Even in the dark I noticed her pretty smile. "Beds," I said. "Thank God for beds."

We stepped into the stale room, both of us sighing at the same time.

No beds.

Chapter Eight: Ellie

Creepy Motels

Crashing in an abandoned motel put my imagination into overdrive. Straight out of a horror movie. Then again, this entire trip had so far been horror-filled. Why should this creepy, deserted motel be any different?

Even in the dark, I could tell the room had been emptied. I crinkled my nose. The musty smell gave it away. I reached for a light switch. "Please let there be electricity."

"Don't," Jamison said. "We don't know who's around. Someone might call the cops."

But I didn't listen. My day had been horrible, and I felt like my insides were fraying at the seams. An overhead light flickered on. Only one bulb still worked in it, but it was something. Then I saw something scurry into the closet, and I screamed, grabbing Jamison. "There! Did you see it?"

Jamison removed my hands. "Yeah, it was tiny. Nothing more than a field mouse. Chill." He turned the light off. "It's better if we keep the light off."

I flipped the switch again and glowered at him. My fatigue and worry and anxiety were making me extremely cranky. "Listen, I'm keeping the light on. We're in the middle of nowhere. No one knows where we're at. And I want to see what's going to try to eat me. Got it?"

Jamison shrugged and entered the room. "Whatever."

I felt bad for snapping at him, but before I could apologize, my words stalled in my mouth. My heart took a nosedive when I saw the room's condition. Cobwebs, faded carpet that had been chewed through in places, and peeling wallpaper. "I feel like a murderer is going to jump out," I said, eyeing the open door. "Maybe we should find something else."

"Like what?" He extended his arms. "Where are we going to go?"

"We could get a hotel room." I was going through too much cash, but anything was better than this. "There was a nice one across from Walmart."

"How we gonna do that? You need a credit card to book the room. Do you have a credit card, 'cause I don't. And even if we did, that's a perfect way for people to find out where we are."

I could feel the emotions bubbling inside of me. I needed to keep it together. Swallowing back the tears, I pushed, "There has to be something else—"

"There's not!" Jamison yelled, placing his hands on his head in apparent frustration. "We are stuck, okay? What more do you want from me?" He stormed past me, leaving me in the room alone.

With him gone, every emotion exploded out of me. I sobbed, hit the wall, and stomped on the floor. I slumped to my knees and let the anguish take over, my body shaking from fatigue and fear.

"It wasn't supposed to be like this," I whimpered to the room. I was supposed to escape and start over. But the past followed me. And now Jamison was stuck living this nightmare with me. He did the right thing and protected me, yet it was his face splashed across the television screen. A part of me wanted to free him, to tell him to go to the police and clear his name. I wanted to be strong and self-sufficient, but what if Danny found me? Or my stepfather? Images from the past that were tucked away now flitted through my mind as if taunting me.

Rain began to pelt the roof and a low rumble filled the sky. Suddenly I felt very alone. What if he left for good? No, his bag was still on the floor. I peeked outside but couldn't see him. I began to pace the floor, not knowing what to do. The single lightbulb above me started to flicker. "Please, don't go out. Please…"

The lightbulb flickered one last time before burning out.

Chills shot up my spine and goose bumps erupted across my skin. I ran outside, refusing to be in the creepy, dark room alone. Tears came again, but I was done crying. Instead I stared out at the rain and tried to come up with a feasible plan. One that didn't involve mice and horror movie motels. Jamison came around the far corner, and I breathed a sigh of relief. He looked soaked.

"What are you doing?" he asked. He acted mellow again, almost a little sad.

"Lightbulb went out," I said. "I thought I'd wait for you out here."

A small smile played on his lips. "Did you check other lights? If there's electricity in one, there is in others."

"No," I admitted. "I sort of haven't been thinking straight. This place creeps me out."

"Yeah, I get that," he said, looking down. "I'm used to squatting in pretty creepy places. I guess I'm used to them by now."

I nodded, wanting to ask about his past, but it wasn't the right time. Just thinking about Jamison living in abandoned homes and motels made me sad. I might live in a trailer, but I'd lived in it my whole life. It had running water and electricity. I might not be the only person with a sad story.

"About what happened," Jamison began. "I probably shouldn't have yelled at you. I'm just stressed, ya know? My mother needs me to do something that's really important, and I'm behind schedule, so to speak."

"It's fine," I said, wanting to know more but also not wanting to push. This had been the most open he'd been. "I know I'm a problem you didn't ask for. I wish I knew what to do."

"I might not have asked for another problem, but you didn't ask for any of this either. It's not fair for me to take my issues out on you." He finally looked up and met my gaze. "I'll try to keep it cool from now on."

I felt a small ray of hope inside. Knowing I wasn't alone gave me a little more courage. "What you did for me back at the bus station, you really did save my life. I want you to know that. You're …" Should I say the words? I didn't want him to get the wrong idea, but at the same time, with everything that happened, I wanted him to know how I felt. "You're a good guy, Jamison. I don't know your story, but not many people I know would ever sacrifice like you did, especially for a complete stranger."

"Especially for a stranger who likes to go through my stuff," he said with a smirk.

Heat filled my face. "Sorry about that. I was curious, that's all. Mostly I take my curiosity and put it in a notebook."

"You put curiosity in a notebook? Okay, you've intrigued me. How do you do that?"

"I like to observe people and figure out their stories. I write the stories in my notebook. I was going to do that with you. I'd gotten my notebook out and was going to create a story for you, but then, your duffel bag fell, so I picked it up. And yeah, curiosity overruled all rational thought."

"You were going to write a story? About me?"

"It sounds weird, but it's harmless. I like to write stories. That's all. It helps me escape, you know, my life."

The two of us leaned against the outside wall and watched the rain. After a few minutes, he asked, "So, what's my story? What'd you come up with?"

"I never wrote anything down. I was too busy being nosy."

Jamison didn't say anything.

"It would have a happy ending," I said, looking out at the rain. "All my stories have happy endings."

"Good. I'd like that."

"What would be your happy ending?" I asked. "If you could write your own story?"

He didn't answer at first. He was not a big-time talker. But eventually he did answer. "I've always wanted to be a doctor."

"Really?" I tried not to act surprised.

"Yeah, I would want to help the people in my neighborhood. Be a family doctor or something. Write that in your notebook. Write that I become a doctor and go back to Detroit and help everyone."

"Okay, I will. But why can't it happen in real life?"

"People like me don't become doctors. We don't leave the streets."

"I haven't met people like you. I think you're different. If you want to be doctor, I think you should go for it."

Jamison turned his attention on me, and I found myself staring into those big, brown eyes of his and the hurt and pain behind them. There was so much more to his story. And for a moment, I wanted to reach out and hug him and make him feel better, but that moment was fleeting. I had my own hurt and pain to deal with.

Needing to change the subject, I asked, "Where'd you go?"

His gaze left mine, as he turned to watch the rain again. "Scoping things out, making sure we're in the clear for tonight. Thinking about things."

"Discover anything?"

"Nah, it's only us. We'll be fine. And I came up with a couple ideas."

"Really?" My sliver of hope started to grow.

"You have a phone, right? One that's not being tracked?"

"Yes. Do you know someone who could help?"

"I think I do. There's only one person in the world I trust. I even trust him more than my own mother. He might be able to help us."

"If you think it's safe to talk to him, then I say let's go for it."

"Good," he said. "Now let's see if any other light works." He walked into the motel room and started flipping on switches. The overhead light above the sink turned on. So did the bathroom light. He turned on the faucet, but nothing came out. "Looks like water's been turned off."

"That's a bummer," I said. "I was hoping for a shower."

"I thought you bought that water jug?"

"I did, but I'd prefer a shower."

"Luckily for you, we have nature's shower outside," he said in a deep, scholarly voice, pointing to the rain that had started to downpour.

I laughed. "Sure. Right after you."

His face fell. "Yeah, yeah, yeah, I get it. I stink. I'll go first. You wouldn't happen to have any soap, would you?"

"I didn't mean it like that. I only meant that I have never taken a rain shower before."

He peeled off his shirt. "Well, we have those new clothes for me, so it makes sense I go first."

"Here." I opened up the front pocket of my backpack. "It's shampoo and body wash. You'll smell like flowers, but it's all I've got."

Jamison took the shampoo bottle. "Stay in here," he said. "And let's hope I don't get electrocuted." He stepped outside, shut the door, then opened it slightly to drop his pants on the room's carpet.

While he washed in the rain, I searched for anything that could work as a towel. But nothing had been left in the room. I hadn't opened the closet yet, but that wasn't about to happen. I did have a few paper towels from the gas station that had some cheese sticking to them. Jamison had some too.

The door opened and he popped his head in. "We don't have any towels, do we?"

I held up the few paper towels from the pizza. "We have these."

"Aren't those yours?"

"You have a few too, but I didn't want to go through your stuff again."

"It's okay. Save yours. You'll need them. Mine are in the plastic bag inside my duffel."

I found the paper towels and also caught sight of some women's clothes in the bag. I zipped it up quickly and handed Jamison three greasy paper towels. "It's all we have."

"They'll work. Can you please face the wall, so I can dry off and get dressed?"

"Oh, sure," I said, my face warming. "I didn't realize you got completely naked."

"Well, I've still got my underwear on," he said.

I turned and faced the wall, listening to him come inside and shuffle through the Walmart bag.

After a few minutes, he said, "All right. I'm decent."

The new pants and shirt looked nice on him. But his hair.

"Better?"

"Definitely." I tried to think of the right way to say the next words. "I think your hair will give you away."

He sighed. "It's not like we can call a barber at 3 o'clock in the morning."

"I bought some scissors," I blurted, "because Chuck said that it would help with your disguise."

Jamison pursed his lips, then nodded. "I'll do it. Hand me the scissors while you go wash up." He took off the new shirt. "I don't want to get hair on my shirt. It'll be scratchy. Actually, if I can use your plastic bag with mine, I can cover my shoulders."

I helped him secure the plastic bags around his neck, then watched as he began cutting large clumps of his hair and dumping them in the sink.

"Want my help with the back?" I asked.

"Sure," he handed me the scissors and got on his knees. "How's this?"

"I can reach your head now," I teased, and began cutting. "How short are we going?"

"Might as well cut it all off."

"One time I let my brother cut my hair." I smiled at the memory. "I got a wad of gum all stuck in it, and I didn't want Mom to know because I wasn't supposed to be chewing gum. So, Billy cut my hair off."

"How much?"

"He cut a lot. Mom freaked out, and Billy got in trouble. He never did rat me out."

We were quiet for several minutes. Jamison broke the silence and asked, "What happened with your brother?"

I froze briefly, surprised by his question. But I wanted to know more about Jamison. Maybe if I opened up about me—at least a little—he'd share too. "He was hit by a drunk driver, almost eight years ago."

"I'm sorry," Jamison said, and his eyes found mine in the mirror. "I don't have any brothers or sisters, but I've seen my mom face death, and the thought of it … Well, I don't want to think about it."

"Yeah," I said. "He was six years older than me, and we were pretty close. He had just got his license. And then one night, he didn't come home. That was the start of my nightmare."

"Did your parents take it out on you? Is that why you can't go back?"

"It was me and my mom after Billy died. Then she met Hank. He worked third shift, so it was all right for a while. I mean, he'd watch me and make nasty comments, but he never did anything at first. Then, something changed."

"You don't have to talk about it."

"I had come in from playing in Lauren's pool. I was twelve. He started looking at me differently." And Mom didn't believe me when I told her about the first time he came into my room. He denied it, and I was immediately deemed a liar. But I didn't say that part. "I slept over at Lauren's as much as I could. And I'd lock my door. Not that it ever stopped him."

Jamison reached up and grabbed my hand. We stayed that way for a few minutes. Neither saying anything.

"That's when I first thought about running away."

"When you were twelve?"

"My thirteenth birthday, actually. I got certified at my middle school to be a babysitter, and I started watching the kids next door."

"Wait, wait, wait. What does your birthday have to do with babysitting? And what does that have to do with running away?"

He had a perplexed expression, as if trying to put the pieces together, which lightened the mood. I laughed a little, and said, "Never mind."

"No, you've got to tell me now! Don't leave me hanging."

"Fine, but stop interrupting." I said it seriously, but then smiled. "Where was I?"

"Thirteenth birthday. Babysitting. Running away." He threw his hands up when I shot him another look.

"I'm connecting the dots now, so pay attention. My mom forgot my birthday, and I remember sitting on the front steps with my babysitting certificate in my hands, wanting to show her. I waited and waited, thinking that she probably went to go buy a cake or something. 'Cause my mom can't cook. But she never came home that evening. Turns out she and Hank went to the casino. Anyway, the next-door neighbor was this pretty cool lady with three kids. They called her into work that evening, and she saw me on the steps and asked if I could babysit."

"And you had that certificate in your hand," Jamison said. "You were ready to go."

"I guess so, but I never did get birthday cake."

"You were gypped."

"Totally."

"And thus, you decided to run away."

"No, well yes, but not because of my mom forgetting. It was because I earned twenty bucks, and I tucked it away. With the whole Hank thing, I determined to get out of town as soon as I could."

"And he's been released?" Jamison asked, the smile on his face gone.

"Yeah. I couldn't be there. Mom was so excited, and she even told me that I better not ruin it this time. But I never expected this. I never expected Hank's connections to follow me."

"If there's one thing I've learned it's that life's not fair. And that there's a lot of things that happen to us that aren't our fault. We just have to rise above it."

"Is that what you're doing? Rising above Detroit? Helping your mom in Minneapolis?"

"I wish," he said. "It's hard to rise above when responsibility weighs you down. My mom is my responsibility. But maybe one day. I don't know. It's like you said, maybe we can have happy endings, right?"

I didn't answer this time because at the moment all I could think about was escaping. He let go of my hand, and not knowing what else to do, I finished cutting his hair. "It's your turn to open up. I've told you my life story. And I know next to nothing about you. Other than you've squatted before and you're doing something for your mom."

"There's not much to tell."

"Did she remember birthday cakes on your birthday?" I gave him a grin.

"Mostly. At least a cupcake."

I could tell there was more to the story because his expression turned guarded. "What errand are you doing for your mom? Why were you on the bus?"

Jamison studied me in the mirror, then as if deciding to talk, said, "She wants me to go find my father."

"Have you ever met your father?"

"No, he's never wanted me, or at least I think he hasn't, which is what makes this really stressful. I'm just supposed to show up at his doorstep and be like, 'Hey, I'm your kid. Mom needs help.'"

"Is she sick?" I asked, trying to finish up the nape of his neck.

"Sort of. She's a drug addict. She says she's not, but she is. And it's gotten worse these last couple years. Now I don't even know what all she's shooting up." Taking a deep breath, he added, "I miss her. Like who she used to be. You know?"

"Yeah, I get that," I said. "Before Billy died, my mom was different."

We fell back into silence as I brushed off as much of the stray hair as I could. Then I set down the scissors.

"Wow. I feel like five pounds has been taken off my head." He moved his head around, checking the angles. "It feels weird."

"It looks nice." A definite improvement. The short hair made his eyes stand out. But then my stomach formed a nervous knot, and I stepped away. "I think I'll go wash up now."

"The rain's stopped."

"Yeah, I know. I'm going to take the jug of water and try to clean up in the bathroom."

He stepped in front of me and lightly touched my elbow. I pulled my arm back.

"Sorry." He quickly moved away from me, giving us room. "I'm not—I mean, I don't want you to think that I ... Because I won't.

You're safe. At least with me."

Those words made my heart thud in my chest, but I couldn't determine if it was from his kindness or from anxiety at the now realization that I was alone with him in a creepy motel room. "I know rationally that I should trust you. Look at everything you've given up to help me. But sometimes I don't think too rationally."

"Rationality is overrated."

"Really? You seem like a pretty rational person."

"I am. I was only trying to make you feel better." Then he caught my gaze and grinned.

"Ha, ha."

"In all seriousness, can I ask you something without you getting mad?"

"What kind of a question is that?"

"I'm curious if you're sure there's nowhere for you to go? I don't want you to get mad, I'm just asking. What if your mom's worried about you?"

"She probably doesn't even know I'm gone," I said. "And I would have stayed if Hank hadn't been released. He's not a good man. If I can make it to Wyoming, I'm going to get a job and start a life. I have to do this."

"Okay. I only asked because I don't want you to be alone."

"Aren't you alone?"

We held each other's gaze for several moments, as if unable to say any more words. Jamison looked away first. I immediately missed staring into those brown eyes of his. "I've felt alone my whole life. I don't want anyone else to feel that way."

Feeling raw and vulnerable, I pulled out the phone from my pocket and headed to the door. "Did you want to make that call now?"

Jamison rubbed at his eyes and yawned. "I'm thinking that we're relatively safe for the time being. It's the middle of the night, and I'm ready to crash. Maybe I could call him in the morning? I don't know. Maybe I should call him now." He took the phone and punched in the number. After several seconds, he frowned. "He's not answering—

Hey, Mr. Langston. It's me. I've got to talk to you. You need to come get me. There's been some issues, and I'm not on the bus. Why aren't you picking up the phone?" Jamison handed me the phone, acting frustrated.

"It is the middle of the night. We'll try again in the morning."

"What if his line is tapped? Now they have your number."

"Who would tap his phone? I don't think the guys following me know him."

Jamison pressed his lips together. "Never mind. I need to crash. I'll deal with him in the morning."

I looked at the empty room. The thought of lying on the floor freaked me out.

"The little mouse isn't going to bother you," he said. "Trust me. Even rats will leave you alone. All our food is packaged up, so they can't get to it. And we'll use our bags as pillows."

"Rats?" I frowned.

"What are our options?"

"I know. And I'm tired too."

"We'll keep the bathroom light on. That'll scare anything away."

I nodded, then took the jug of water and the shampoo bottle to the bathroom. Even with the spider web in the corner, I shut the door. Then I covered my face and let out a shaky breath. And even though I mostly abandoned prayers after my brother died, I found myself saying another one.

Chapter Nine: Jamison

Unchartered Territory

The sunlight woke me up. At first, I felt disoriented, trying to figure out where I was. Then it all came back to me.

I sat up and scanned the motel room. Ellie was gone, but she left her backpack. I stretched and yawned, tempted to lie back down. But I needed to figure out a way to Minnesota, so I pushed myself up off the floor and went to use the bathroom. The more I woke up, the more I wondered where she was. She obviously didn't go far. And she trusted me enough with her backpack.

But now was not the time to be running around alone. If she wanted to do that, I could have just taken the bus to Minnesota and avoided the headache altogether.

The motel room door opened. "Jamison?"

I felt relief immediately even though I would never tell her that. I stepped out of the bathroom, took some water from the jug and washed my hands. *Act cool.* Actually, I had no idea how to act around her. She made me nervous, frustrated, and intrigued all at the same time.

After last night's conversation, I understood a little where she came from, but she was still a mystery. Then again, the only girl I'd ever really hung around was my mother, and that was different. Way different.

"You probably shouldn't go off by yourself. How would I have known where you went if something happened?"

"I left you a note," she said.

That's when I noticed the bag and carrier of two cups of coffee in her hands. "Coffee?" I asked. "I haven't had coffee in forever." The last time I remember drinking coffee was when Mom and I lived in our own trailer years ago. She would make it, then pour me a cup with hers. She filled it with mostly milk and a spoonful of sugar, but it was one of my best memories of her. Sitting at our small table, drinking our coffees together.

"It's vanilla lattes. They're my favorite." Ellie handed me one.

"How long have you been up?" I sipped at the delicious latte.

"Awhile. I couldn't sleep. Whatever lives in that closet was making noise, and I had a hard time not thinking about that huge spider's web in the bathroom."

"You didn't sleep at all?"

"Maybe a couple hours, on and off, but I woke up and didn't want to bother you, so I decided to go to the McDonalds next to that Walmart." She reached into the bag and pulled out an Egg McMuffin. "One for you and one for me."

"Thanks," I said, touched. "I'm going to try Mr. Langston again first. Where's your phone?"

"I threw it away." She took a bite of her breakfast sandwich.

I swallowed the hot latte too fast and started coughing. "What? You threw it away?"

"You said that someone might be able to trace the call, so I tossed it and ran into Walmart to buy another one." My face must not have hidden my surprise because Ellie added, "I told you I didn't sleep very well. I've been up for a while."

"What time is it?"

"Almost noon."

I groaned. "I can't believe I slept that long."

"It's not like we're going anywhere at the moment. Don't worry about it."

But I did worry. I didn't want us in one place for long. One common piece of knowledge from the streets was that you had to constantly be looking over your shoulder, and if someone was looking for you, never be in the same place for long. "Well, let me have the new phone, and I'll try again. By the way, how much money do you have? You've been spending a lot of it."

"I know," she lamented. "This trip is costing a lot more than I anticipated."

"What are you going to do if you run out of money?"

"I don't know. I guess I better not run out of it." She handed me the new phone. "I haven't activated it yet."

"I'll do it, then give Mr. Langston a call."

She yawned. "I'm going to go sit outside in the sun and eat my breakfast. I don't want to be in this room any longer than I have to be."

I would have followed her, but I needed to talk to Mr. Langston in private. I sat on the floor and ate my breakfast while activating the phone. Eventually I got everything working. I pressed in the numbers for Mr. Langston's special cell phone.

The phone rang, and I hoped he'd answer. And quickly. The quicker he answered, the quicker I could get out of this mess. And Ellie, too. But mostly I needed to help my mom, and sitting in an abandoned motel wasn't going to help her.

I heard static, then a mumbled, "'Ello?"

"Langston?" I said in relief. "I'm so glad you answered, man. I didn't know if you'd be at work."

"I'm not feeling too well," he said.

"What's wrong?" The panic hit me immediately. "Did they get to you?"

"No, no, relax. It's probably nerves and all that. I've been worried about you, and I wanted to be here in case you called. When I saw that I missed your call last night, I felt sick, so I decided to stay home and wait to hear from you."

"I need your help. There was an issue that happened at the bus station."

"What happened?" Now he seemed panicked.

"There was this girl—"

"A girl? You're kidding me."

"It's not like that. Listen, she was in trouble. This guy was with Shazz. Remember him?"

"Of course. Shaquar Smith. Class of 2011." He paused, then stated, "Some of what I'm about to tell you is confidential, but since he's out of the system, I think I can share a little. I'm not one to talk negatively about the kids I try to help, but he was really messed up. His mother did a number on him. He went from one foster home to another but no one kept him. One time a foster parent came home to find he'd cut up the goldfish and set it on the counter for them to see."

"I don't need a play-by-play to know that Shazz is no good."

"Then why are you hanging around him? Are you in Minneapolis?"

"No, that's what I'm trying to tell you, but you got into some long story."

"Sorry. Tell me. I'm listening."

"They were kidnapping the girl. I was going to get on the bus and let her take care of her own business, you know? But I couldn't. I thought about Mom, and how I would want someone to help Mom if I wasn't around. So, I tried to help, and the next thing I know, some white dude named Danny is pointing a gun at me."

"Whoa. A gun? Jamison, all you had to do was get on a bus and let it take you to Minneapolis."

"You're telling me," I complained. "Now I'm stuck with some girl, and we can't go to no bus station because they think I'm the bad guy because I got the gun from the white dude and pointed it at him. Man, it's messed up. I can't even believe it myself."

"I am so confused right now." Exasperation seeped through Mr. Langston's tone. "So, there's a girl and a gun? And a white dude named Danny? Where's Shazz?"

I slapped my hand to my forehead. "Mr. Langston, listen! I need you to hear me. This is serious."

"I'm trying, but this is uncharted territory. Tell me what you need me to do. Should I call the police? Where are you at?"

"We're stuck somewhere outside of Chicago."

"Who's we?"

"Me and the girl," I snapped. "Keep up."

"I need more of a specific location. Then, I'll call the police and send someone to you."

"It's not that simple. The police think I'm the bad guy, remember?"

"So, you explain what happened. I'll give them a heads-up. Besides, if this Danny is a criminal, he's not going to be sniffing around the police station."

I stopped and thought about that. Yes, this would cut me loose. This was good. I could clear my name and finish what I was supposed to be doing. Why I was hesitating? Ellie was on her own before me. I helped her escape Danny. What was I going to do? Did I plan on taking her with me? "What should I do about Ellie?"

"Who? Oh, the girl?"

"Yes, the girl. She's with me. And she's got Danny and Shazz after her."

"She needs to go to the police, too. I don't understand why you haven't already called 9-1-1. You're out of Detroit. I would think Chicago is safe from Baltagio."

"I'll go to the police, but I'm not sure she will. She can't go back home."

"Wait. She's a runaway? Jamison, she needs to go home. This is serious."

"It's not like that. She's almost eighteen. And she's running from a bad situation."

"Give me her name, and I'll write up a report and check into it. If it's an abusive home, we can remove her, but she can't run away."

I paused because I didn't really know her name. I trusted Mr. Langston to do the right thing, but I didn't have that information. And she pleaded with me to not go to the police. She was obviously running from something painful.

"You still there?"

"How's my mom?" I changed the subject. I couldn't let Ellie get into my head. Or my heart.

"She's locked up. Last I heard, she was going through some withdrawals."

"Nothing on Baltagio?"

"Not a peep."

"If I go to the cops, would he find me?"

"I don't think he has all the cops in America in his pocket. Come on, now, be reasonable."

"Okay," I said. "You call the Chicago cops. Tell them I'm in an abandoned motel on the other side of the highway from a Walmart, a McDonalds, and a Waffle House. I'm not sure the city, but it is about thirty minutes outside of Chicago, to the west of it."

"All right. I'll do it now."

I got up from the motel room floor and went to peek out the window. Ellie had placed her sweatshirt under her head and was sleeping in the sun. I felt the unfamiliar tug of longing inside me.

"Thanks." The guilt rose up in me like a tidal wave. I was just going to leave her? No, I told myself. I would tell her about calling the police. I would tell her that I had no other choice. That I had to take care of my mother. I had to get to Minneapolis. Still, watching Ellie sleep restfully in the sun, the guilt nearly choked me. I had to look away.

Chapter Ten: Ellie

Twenty Questions

I felt sunburnt and groggy. The sun had passed over the motel, leaving me in the shade under the small motel awning. Dying of thirst, I got up and went into the motel room to grab a water bottle. I guzzled it down, realizing that I would need to buy some more soon.

After counting my cash, I sighed. I needed to slow down on the spending.

Without realizing what I was doing, I opened up my backpack, found my favorite picture of Billy and gave myself a moment to wallow. Billy smiled at me from the pic, sitting on the dock by the pond we used to play at, holding up a fish as big as his head. What would he think of everything that took place in my life since his death? He would have never let anyone touch me. Mom would have never fallen for the evil Hank, because Billy wouldn't have allowed it, and Mom always listened to Billy.

"Why did you have to die?" I whispered, trying to swallow back the lump in my throat.

I remembered what Jamison said the night before about not wanting me to be alone, but I wouldn't know what to do with myself if I didn't feel that way. "I've felt alone since the moment you were gone," I told the picture.

Glancing around, I became aware that I was alone in the motel room. Alone, as in Jamison's duffel bag was gone. Panicked, I placed Billy's picture safely inside the backpack, then zipped the bag and threw it over my shoulder.

Where did Jamison go?

Why did he take his duffel bag?

How long had he been gone?

The time on the TracFone showed two thirty-five. I had slept for over two hours. He could be anywhere. Not wanting to spend another second inside the pest-infested motel room, I grabbed my Walmart bags with my supplies and headed outside.

I walked around the parking lot, moving fast. No sign of anyone else on this piece of abandoned property. What do I do now? Where do I go next?

Stop and think.

I paused to catch my breath. There was no Wi-Fi on the TracFone, but if I could find a library, I could connect to the Internet. Maybe someone at Walmart knew where the nearest library was. And then what? What could the Internet tell me?

I started marching across the high grass to the underpass of the highway. *Keep moving forward. Away from the abandoned motel.*

"Where are you going?"

At the sound of Jamison's voice, I spun around to face him. "Jamison! You didn't leave?" My emotions were still so raw, and the fear of being alone still so fresh, that I weirdly felt angry at him.

"No." He approached, holding his duffel bag. "I've been waiting for the police to show up, but they never came."

"The police? Why would you do that? You know I said I can't go to the police. You basically did the opposite of what I asked you to do."

"Don't get mad. You were sleeping, and I had to make a quick decision. Mr. Langston gave some good advice. I only need to explain myself, with you as a witness, and hopefully a video that shows more than what the television did, I should be fine. He said that he can find someone to look after you until you turn eighteen, so you don't have to run."

"I don't need anyone to look after me," I said.

"And yet, here I am."

"What's that supposed to mean?"

"It means that you came and asked me for help, remember? Mr. Langston's a good guy. It's okay to admit that you need a little help. Shoot, I need help. That's why I called him. We're kind of in a mess right now, if you haven't figured it out yet."

My anger had yet to dissipate. My attention stayed on his duffel bag. "Why were you all the way in the front of the motel with your bag?"

"I told you. I've been waiting for the police. But they've never come."

"You were going to leave me," I said it more to myself, as the realization dawned on me. "You left me to sleep and stayed out in the front where they could pick you up and leave me."

"What are you talking about? That's not true."

"Then why do you have your bag?"

"Because I was staying out front, and I didn't want to leave the bag for too long. No offense, but I already caught you searching through it once." His eyebrows furrowed together in apparent anger. "And what kind of guy do you think I am? That I would leave you in an abandoned motel?"

"I don't know!" I exclaimed. "I'm confused, okay? Sorry! And why do you think I would be remotely interested in the junk you have in there?"

His face turned to stone. Without saying another word, he went back to where he had been sitting. He set his bag down beside him, crossed his arms, and stared straight ahead.

Even though I felt bad for the words I said, my frustration over the entire situation was getting the best of me. I marched toward him, continuing my rant. "Why are we waiting around here? This doesn't make sense. We could call a cab or something and have it take us to the next Greyhound bus terminal. I'm not staying another night in this place."

"Then go," he said, without looking at me. "No one's making you stay."

"Fine. I will." But I did not really know what I wanted. "How long are you going to wait here?"

"What's with the twenty questions? I said go. Don't worry about me."

"That was one question."

"You've asked at least twenty since you been standing there all angry. Just chill. Do what you need to do. I'm staying."

"Why?" I asked.

He glared at me.

"That was only one more question!"

"Because I'm waiting for the police. I need to be here when they come."

"How do you know they're coming?" He gave me another look. "I'm only asking questions because I'm confused. I don't know what to do."

"I know they're coming because I trust Mr. Langston. He won't let me down."

I sat on the rusty railing beside him. "I can't go to the police."

"Trust Mr. Langston. You only need to hang with a foster family for a couple weeks. It won't be so bad. I might have to do it, too."

"I don't want a foster family. I want to go to Buffalo, Wyoming, and start over. I have it all planned out."

"I had a plan, too. And the longer I wait here, the more danger my mom's in, but the police are my best bet. And they're yours too. The fact is we had plans and criminals messed those plans up."

"What a mess," I muttered, my anger completely diffused. "And all because that guy kept following me."

"Yep. It's a mess."

"I'm not sold about the police, but it's better than being chased by those guys." I exhaled slowly, feeling defeated. "What a bust. I can't even run away."

"It's not your fault. You didn't make Danny and them follow you. They obviously have some beef with your stepdad. But if I keep running, it's going to make me look guiltier. Plus, I have to clear my name, so I can go up to Minnesota."

"Right." I made up my mind. "Then I'll go with you. If you trust this Mr. Langston, then I will too."

The two of us sat side by side for several minutes. I studied his profile with furtive side glances. "You're staring at me," he said, while still looking straight ahead.

"Have you been sitting here all this time?"

"Yes. I don't mind it."

"What if the police don't come?"

"They will."

"But what if—"

"They're coming. Because if they don't come, it means Baltagio got to Mr. Langston. And that can't happen." His frown deepened, and for just a second, his chin quivered.

"Don't worry," I said. "He probably made the call, but the police are trying to find the place."

"I hate when people say that."

"Say what?"

"Not to worry. It's such a dumb thing to say, you know? Of course, I'm going to worry. The police aren't here, and they should be. If Baltagio got to Mr. Langston, it means that he knows where I'm at. Which is bad."

"Give Mr. Langston another call?"

"I did. Twice. But I'm worried that if something happened that the calls—I don't know what to think."

"Then let's go. I'm sure we can find a cab or something to take us to another Greyhound bus station. Or use the phone to call 9-1-1. We can get the police here in minutes. I'm sure of it." I wanted anything but the police, but I also didn't want Jamison to look so desperate. He seemed really worried about his friend.

"Mr. Langston was supposed to talk to them, give them the details about the situation. But what if Baltagio found out and already contacted the Chicago police? This guy has connections. That's why I'm going up to Minnesota. Supposedly, his connections don't go that far, but I don't know about anything anymore. So, I'm sitting here and praying to God that Mr. Langston did what he had to do and the police come."

Maybe in other circumstances I would be relieved that Jamison was just as confused as I was about what the next steps should be, but instead I felt guilt.

"Sorry for all the questions."

He shrugged. His brows were furrowed, and he kept biting his lip.

"I was upset because I thought you left me," I admitted. "I guess I've gotten used to having you around."

He kept looking at the road, but he reached over and gently squeezed my hand.

And I didn't pull away. I didn't recoil. Nor did I when he interlaced his fingers with mine. The feel of his hand in mine was reassuring. So, there we sat, side by side, holding each other's hand, waiting for whatever would happen next.

Chapter Eleven: Jamison

Visitors

The police never came. I wasted a whole day waiting for them. Maybe Mr. Langston couldn't figure out where we were. I wasn't exactly super specific. But how many abandoned motels were there off the interstate? Plus, I was a fugitive. The cops would want to find me.

Which meant only one other possibility, and it made me sick just thinking about it.

"It's probably nothing," Ellie said. She tried to encourage me through the late afternoon and into the evening.

"We should have left earlier today." I stared at the cracker pack that constituted my dinner. I told her that she shouldn't go out without me, and I didn't want to leave my post at the front of the motel. This meant that our dinner consisted of leftover snacks. But I didn't feel like eating anyway.

I was tempted to call D'Juan, but he didn't have the kind of power to help. Plus, I didn't want to tell anyone else about my location.

Ellie grabbed her notebook. "Let's write up a plan."

"Why?"

"Because having a plan helps."

"I should have never called Mr. Langston. I should have called 9-1-1 to begin with. Or, we should have left first thing this morning." I began pacing the motel room floor.

"That's not coming up with a plan."

I shot her an annoyed expression. "I did have a plan. It didn't work.

We're still here."

"Okay, so we come up with another plan. How about we leave first thing tomorrow morning? We call a cab to take us to the next bus station."

"Do you know how much cabs cost? They're not cheap."

"Maybe we can ask someone to drive us? That sort of worked."

"I need to call the police." It was the only way. "I need to explain what happened, and hope they haven't been touched by Baltagio. They could help me get to Minnesota." I stopped pacing and glanced over at Ellie. She stared at the floor, her pen no longer in her hands. "The police can help. I don't see how else we can do it."

"I don't mind paying for a cab," she said. "We'll take it to the next bus station."

"My picture is probably plastered at every bus station."

"But you look so much different now."

"Why are you willing to gamble with my life, but you won't even consider going to the police about your situation? If this Danny guy knows your stepdad, then it's probably enough to get you out of the home for good."

"Bad guys are good at lying. And when that doesn't work, they always have a backup plan. Trust me, I endured him for years before someone finally believed me. And now? They're letting him right back into the home."

All right, she had a point there.

"There's got to be a way to get you to Minnesota, find the guy you're looking for, and then get me on a bus to Wyoming."

"How much money do you have left?"

"Enough for a cab," she said. "I even got a number from one of the newspapers at Walmart."

I looked out the window. Maybe we should leave now. Darkness made it easy for me to hide, but it made it easy for the other guys to hide too. And Ellie wasn't too good with the whole hiding-in-darkness situation. She refused to turn off the motel bathroom light. "Call a cab and see if one can pick us up at Walmart some time tonight."

Ellie called the number.

While she talked with the cab company, I stepped outside to do a quick check of the area. Deep inside, I knew something happened with Mr. Langston. I felt frazzled and my normally calm sense was jumpy and paranoid. Scanning the abandoned field beside the motel, I whispered, "What did you get yourself into?"

Ellie approached behind me. "The earliest they can be there is eight a.m. tomorrow morning. Should we sit at the Walmart bench and wait for it?"

"I don't know." I turned to her. "Normally, I have it together, but this is uncharted territory, as Mr. Langston called it. I've never been out of Detroit, and I don't know what to do now that I've found myself in this mess. I need to go to the police and somehow clear myself, but what if it doesn't work? I can't be much good to my mother if I'm in jail. And then there's you. If I go to the police, what will happen to you?"

"If I could just get to Buffalo, Wyoming, then I'll be okay. No one expects me there. No one will think to look there. Then I can start over. I can live a quiet, safe life without a stepfather and whoever else comes with him."

"We probably shouldn't sit out in the open," I said. "Let's head over to Walmart first thing in the morning. Does that thing have an alarm?"

"I think so."

"I guess we'll get up first thing and take a cab. Let's hope nothing happens before then."

Not knowing what else to do, I headed back to the motel room and prayed we weren't sitting ducks.

Once we were both inside, I locked the door as best I could. Seemed silly, they could break in with or without a lock.

"Want to play some cards?" Ellie asked.

The question caught me off guard. "Cards?"

She took out a deck of cards from the front pocket of the backpack. "Since we don't have a television or anything else for that matter, I thought we could play cards."

"Cards?" I asked again. "Why would we do that?"

"I just told you. We don't have anything else to do. I've already written in my notebook, and I have to give my creative brain a break. A girl can only write so many stories." She began to shuffle the deck.

I pointed my thumb toward her backpack. "What else do you keep in that thing?"

"Not much. I couldn't take my iPhone with me, so I took my mom's cards. I love playing solitaire. Billy taught me how to play poker, but I don't remember much."

I went and sat on the floor, my legs spread out in front of me, debating between playing cards or lying down. My eyelids felt like bricks were pushing them down, not to mention my head felt weird. Being out in the sun all day made my eyes and skin hurt. I still held Langston's number in my hand. My brain waged a battle with what to do next.

"Earth to Jamison."

"Sorry. I've got a lot on my mind."

"We have a plan. Tomorrow morning. Super early. We take a cab to the bus station, and then we're back on track. We might as well pass the time." She kept shuffling.

"I need something to take my mind off everything, so sure. Let's play some cards. All I know is War and Go Fish."

"War, it is!" She dealt.

As we played cards, Ellie asked, "If you could go anywhere in the world, where would you go?"

"Oh, we're playing this game too?" I teased.

"I'm only trying for light conversation." She flipped over a card. "Ha! War!"

We flipped the next cards until my king beat her three. "Hand it over." I counted the cards I won and placed them in my pile. "I don't know," I said. "I want to get out of Detroit."

"But you said you wanted to be a doctor in Detroit."

"I want to get out, then go back. On my own terms."

"Got it. For the record, I think you should become a doctor." She dealt the cards again. "You would be good at it. You're all mellow and stuff."

"First, I need to finish my senior capstone project, so that I can technically graduate."

"Ah, yes. Gotta love those senior projects."

"You had one too?"

"Yep. I had to do a presentation on my past, present, and future. What's yours about?"

"I don't really know. I wasn't paying attention when they gave out the instructions." We laughed and caught each other's gaze. I quickly looked back at my cards. "Your turn. What do you want to do with your life?"

"Mine isn't as noble as yours, but if I got to choose, I'd be a country singer."

"What? I thought you'd pick author or something."

"I want to do both," she said, as she laughed.

"Can you sing?"

"No, not at all."

Both of us started cracking up.

I lasted another few rounds of War, but Ellie saw me yawning and decided on a tie. "We both win," she said, and put her cards away.

"Let's hope so," I said, lying down and resting my head on my duffel bag.

Ellie placed her backpack near mine but not so close that it was awkward. She hesitated before resting her head on her backpack. "Did you ever throw away that gun?"

"No, I have it in my pants," I said. "I took it from my old pair and put it in the pocket of these. Just in case."

"What were you going to do if the cops came?"

"Give it to them. It probably still has Danny's prints on it."

"I never thought of that."

"I should probably get rid of it. If we're going to the bus station tomorrow, I can't have it with me."

"That'd be a good idea."

I closed my eyes but before I drifted off, I said, "Thanks."

"For what?"

"For taking my mind off things for a little bit."

"No problem. Here's to tomorrow being a good day."

I awoke to the cold barrel of a gun pressed into my temple and the smell of cologne hitting my nostrils. The same scent from the bus station.

"Don't do anything," Danny whispered. "Or we'll kill her and make you watch."

I opened my eyes to the sun peeking through the curtains and Shazz standing over Ellie, pointing a gun at her head. Ellie, thankfully, was still sound asleep. A million thoughts spun through my mind, but I couldn't act on any of them. Not yet.

Mr. Langston must be in trouble. That's the only way these guys found out where we were. My stomach flipped at what that meant, and I felt the urge to throw up.

"Get up," he whispered in my ear. "Slowly. No sudden movements." Danny stepped back.

The gun in my front pocket seemed to be on fire, and my fingers itched to grab it, but there were two of them, and they were armed. I'd have to bide my time and wait until I could have the advantage.

As I stood up and reached for my duffel bag, I made eye contact with Shazz. His gaze bore into me. His lips pursed, and his eyebrows slightly raised. I knew he was trying to tell me something, but whatever he wanted from me wasn't going to be good either. I moved toward the door, Danny following me.

Before stepping outside, Danny quietly said to Shazz. "And no touching. I get first dibs."

My stomach rolled.

"Remember our deal," Shazz responded, just as low.

Ellie stirred, then stretched. When her eyes shot open, they immediately zeroed in on me. "Jamis—"

"Not a word," Shazz ordered, pressing his gun to her temple.

I caught the look of sheer terror on her face before Danny shoved me hard out the door. So hard, I stumbled and fell face first.

"You don't need to be looking at her any more. Not unless you want to pay for your time, and after, of course, I'm done with her."

Danny implicating that Ellie was his property—and what that meant—got me riled up. I went to grab the gun. Until I saw the three guys standing outside a van just in front of us. I also noticed another vehicle. Shazz's black, pimped-out Thunderbird. And D'Juan leaning against it.

D'Juan?

"Hold him," Danny ordered one of his guys.

I tried to move toward D'Juan, but Danny's entourage had already grabbed me. I struggled against them for a few seconds, then stopped. I couldn't take down all of them. I needed to conserve my strength for when it mattered. I briefly closed my eyes and prayed for that chance.

That's when I felt Danny's fist slammed into my gut. The pain doubled me over, but the two guys holding me yanked me upright. Danny sailed a second punch to the other side of my ribs, exploding my insides like dynamite. I crumpled like a limp sack, dropping my full weight into the support of the gorillas on either side of me.

"That's what you get for not minding your own business," Danny ground out, then spit in my face.

"This wasn't the deal," D'Juan said, pulling out a gun and pointing it at Danny. "Let him go, or you're dead."

Danny hesitated.

"I said, *let him go.*" D'Juan took a menacing step closer to Danny— so close I could see his second gun pointed at the guy to my right. One pointing at Danny, and the other pointing at the guy to my right. I would have wheezed out a thanks, but it was hard to have gratitude when a couple of your ribs felt broken.

The motel room door shot open. Shazz shoved Ellie outside. Her hands were tied at the wrists, and a nasty-looking gag was crammed into her mouth. As soon as her wide, terror-filled eyes landed on Danny, she squirmed and struggled to get away.

"Release him and take her," Danny ordered.

I dropped to the ground as soon as they let go. The pain robbed me of my breath.

Shazz stepped over to me. "All right, we cool?" he said to Danny. "You got yours, and I got mine."

Danny barely acknowledged Shazz. "Get out of here," he said to us. "I got my prize."

As he ran one of his fingers down Ellie's face, she squirmed and kicked him in the shins. He grabbed her by the neck, and I opened my mouth to protest. Her horror-filled eyes pleaded with me.

"Leave her alone," I said through clenched teeth.

"We're done," Danny yelled at Shazz. "Get him out of here, before I break the agreement and put a bullet in his head." To his men, he said, "Put her in the van. We've already wasted enough time."

"Stop," I shouted, but Shazz and D'Juan had already grabbed me and started dragging me to the car. "Guys, come on. We can't let this happen."

"Shut up," Shazz snapped. "If we didn't have to deliver you to Baltagio, I'd have let him beat you some more." He shoved me into the back seat and made sure I saw his smirk.

Ellie's muffled screams echoed across the parking lot as they manhandled her into the van. I threw open the door, desperate to help her, only to be shoved back inside by D'Juan.

He got in the front seat and turned to face me. "What kind of mess did you get yourself into?"

"Please, man, that girl is in trouble. I've never asked you for anything in my life. But this."

"She's not our problem. If we don't get you back before tonight, we're all a bunch of corpses." D'Juan's expression shifted briefly to one of fear.

"What have you got *yourself* into?" I asked, reversing the question. "You working for Baltagio now?"

"Listen, I didn't ask for this. You know that. But Baltagio's not someone to mess with.'"

Shazz got into the driver's seat.

The van had already started to pull out.

"Shazz, I'm begging you. Whatever you want from me, consider it done. But we can't let Ellie go with those guys."

"What do I care? I've got a bunch of Benjamins waiting for me."

Before I could talk myself out of it, I blurted, "Listen, I promise I'll join. I'll be initiated, but I've got to save her. Give me this, and I'll do what you want." I couldn't believe what I was saying, but I could still hear her screams in my head. "I'm clean, and that'll open up a lot of doors for you. No one in our neighborhood would think I'd run the bags."

Shazz's hand halted on the ignition.

"He's right," D'Juan said. "He could be a runner. No one'd suspect him. That's leverage, man."

Shazz started up the car. "He's as good as dead if Baltagio wants him."

I'd played the game a time or two; I'd do it again. Nothing appealed more to us street spawn than money. And Shazz more than most. But I had to keep my cool. D'Juan especially had to believe me. "No, he wants my mom, not me. He only wants to use me to get to her. If you guys play it right, Baltagio will keep me alive. Everyone knows I'm squeaky clean."

"With Jamison running for you, there won't be no competition. Talk about some coin." D'Juan rubbed his thumb against his fingertips as if he could feel the money already. "With him off everybody's radar, you might have a chance to grow out of Detroit."

"If I do this, I own you." Shazz studied me in the rearview mirror. "Do we have a deal?"

Cold slivers of panic moved along my spine, but what other choice did I have? I might have been willing to leave her, but that was when I thought she could keep traveling on her own and was relatively safe. She wasn't safe anymore, if she ever had been.

"No one hurts Ellie," I said, deciding my fate.

"Deal." Shazz revved the engine and said to D'Juan, "We'll make it quick."

D'Juan took out his gun. "Tires?"

"Yeah. I never liked Danny anyway." Shazz peeled out of the motel's parking lot and followed the van onto the freeway. "There can't be witnesses. Chicago traffic will end our shot. We have to do it now before any morning traffic."

I sat on the edge of my seat as Shazz followed the van. D'Juan checked around and rolled down the window. He leaned out, aimed and fired one shot.

The tire popped, and the van started swerving.

"Other tire," Shazz ordered. But D'Juan had already fired, and the second back tire popped.

"My man!" Shazz whooped, smacking D'Juan's shoulder as he got back in the car. "No one's a better aim, brother!"

Shazz got up behind the van as it started to pull over. Right at the edge of the road, as it still swerved to steady itself, Shazz drove alongside it. "Front tire, bro."

D'Juan went to fire another shot, but Danny's guys had caught on and started to fire back.

"Quick man!" Shazz screeched.

D'Juan had no time to aim. The van plowed into the side of the car as he fired another shot. Their driver's window shattered and suddenly the van was rolling side over side down the embankment.

Shazz pulled over, cursing. "They better not have messed with my paint job, or I'm gonna kill them all." He turned back to me. "I swear you better be worth it, or I'll put a bullet in you myself."

But I was already out of the car. Shazz or D'Juan easily caught up, and each of us slid down the embankment to get to the van. It had settled upside down against some trees.

"I think the driver's down," Shazz said.

From outside the van, a gunshot blasted through the air. The three of us ducked but kept moving.

Danny came around the van, holding up his hand. The other arm was wrapped around his chest, and there looked to be a gash in his head. "What are you doing?" he yelled.

Shazz pointed a gun at him. "Jamison made me an offer I couldn't refuse. Now give us the girl."

"Go get the girl," D'Juan said to me. "I'll cover Shazz."

I kept moving toward the van, pushing past the pain in my ribs. "Ellie?" I called out.

Her muffled response came from the back of the van. I pulled at the upside-down door, and it slid halfway open. The two men in the driver and passenger seats were knocked out—or worse—but the third guy held a gun at Ellie's head. He'd been hurt but still held her tightly. I pulled the emptied gun from my pocket and pointed it at him. "Let her go."

"I don't think so," he said.

Ellie slammed her elbow down against his groin. As he writhed in pain, she scrambled away from him and shoved him hard. He sprawled awkwardly on the roof of the upside-down van, revealing a bloody gash across his pants leg.

I held my hand out to Ellie. "Hurry!"

She crawled toward me, but the guy grabbed her leg. Ellie kicked him in the face while I pulled her to me. Together, we stumbled backward, falling onto the ground. She began to shake violently, the sobs taking over her body.

"It's okay. I'm here," I said quietly. Danny could round the corner of the van any minute. I tried to steady my shaky hands enough to free her of the gag and untie her hands. The instant she was loose, she threw her arms around me, crying into my shoulder. I felt nearly as relieved, but we weren't clear yet. "We're not exactly safe," I whispered. "Danny's alive, so stay down."

Ellie nodded and wiped at her face.

Holding her hand, I led her quietly around the corner. The scene stopped me in my tracks.

D'Juan stood over Danny *and* Shazz. Both of them were down. I looked from the two bodies on the ground to my childhood friend.

D'Juan acted shaken, but his gaze was clear when his eyes found mine.

"What happened?" I asked.

"You're not the only one who wants to escape. Now come on, we need to get out of here. The police were probably already tipped off." He bent down, got the keys from Shazz's pocket, turned and headed toward the T-bird.

Chapter Twelve: Ellie

Third Wheel

I lay in the back of the car, trying to pull myself together. But I couldn't stop shaking. Jamison kept telling me that it was over, that I was okay, but the fear had already sunk its teeth into me. Especially because Jamison's friend said that Danny wasn't dead.

I listened as Jamison asked, "Wait. You didn't kill them?"

"What do you take me for?"

"You just shot down a van. Then you're standing over two bodies. What am I supposed to think?"

The friend shook his head, but he was smiling. "Were we not in the same Sunday School class? Thou shalt not kill, bro." He made a sign of the cross, then looked pointedly at Jamison.

"Sorry," Jamison said with a laugh.

I could only see the side of Jamison's face from where I lay, but his smile looked relieved. My heart, on the other hand, still banged in my ears from the terror-filled morning.

Don't think about it. But I couldn't help it, reliving the scene over and over.

Jamison turned and gently patted my shoulder. "It's over. You're all right."

I took in a shaky breath, and with Jamison's gentle touch resting on my shoulder, I found a normal heart rate.

"You were going to give yourself up to Shazz? To be a runner?" the driver asked Jamison.

"I said what needed to be said."

"Well, thankfully, you had me there."

Jamison gave my shoulder one more squeeze before turning around to the front. "I'm glad you had my back. Thank you."

"Brothers forever," the driver said, holding out his fist. Jamison bumped it.

As I watched the exchange between Jamison and his friend, the terror from earlier morphed into something else. Extreme gratitude? What would have happened if Jamison hadn't somehow gotten his friend to help me escape? I never had someone who would do so much to protect me, at least since my brother died.

Billy. I closed my eyes and drew in shaky breaths, missing my brother so much it hurt. Tears leaked onto the backseat, but I couldn't stop the flow.

How did my life go so wrong? How did I end up here? Suddenly, my stomach flipped. *Don't get sick,* I told myself. *You're already acting like a damsel in distress.* And I hated being this way. I hated that my simple plans to hop a bus to Wyoming had turned out so horribly wrong. I hated knowing that I had ruined Jamison's plans to help his mom.

That paled in comparison to what just happened. Now I knew how much my life was in danger. The terror tried to resurface. So, I blinked back the tears and watched Jamison up front.

Jamison's friend kept talking, oblivious to my internal battle. Which was fine. If it was too quiet, I might lose it completely.

"Shazz had me go over to Danny to make sure he didn't do nothing crazy. He wanted us to throw him in the trunk and maybe hold him for ransom. Whatever. That guy is always about money. Then the idea came to me, and I saw a way out. It must have been divine intervention because I've been praying about my life for years now. Ya know? I don't want to end up in jail like every other brother from the block."

"So, you knocked out Danny, then Shazz?"

"Yeah, basically. Danny already had a head wound, so I smashed it with the butt of the gun. I know, I know, not pretty, but I needed him out. Then Shazz came over and was like, 'Good idea.' Before I could talk myself out of it, I smashed the butt of my gun against his temple. Two-packed punch."

"When they come to, they're not going to be happy."

"Call the cops on them," I said, forcing myself to sit up. I was done lying down. It was time I follow a plan to help Jamison. And, maybe, like he said, the cops would help me steer clear of Hank. "We need to do it now while we have a chance at getting them." I took out my phone.

"Shazz has been evading arrest for some time," the friend said as if in thought. "I bet Danny has evidence in his van to arrest him. Yeah, yeah, good idea. Call the cops and make it anonymous."

"You'll have to get rid of your phone though," Jamison told me. "We probably should have gotten rid of it after I called Langston."

"We'll get another one," the friend said.

I nodded and, without talking myself out of it, called 9-1-1. "Hello, I'm calling because there was a big accident on I-90 heading east to Chicago. I think I even heard gunshots, but I'm not sure. Can I be connected to the local police station?"

After I hung up from talking to the police dispatcher, I felt a little better. "Do you think they'll get to them in time?"

"They're knocked out cold," the friend said. "I think we'll be okay."

"Here," Jamison said. "Can I have the phone?" I handed it to him and he threw it out the window.

"Now that that's out of the way, you going to introduce me to your lady friend?"

"This is Ellie," Jamison said. "And I only met her two days ago."

"I'm D'Juan," D'Juan said, smiling at me from the rearview mirror. "I can see why J-man took a liking to you."

Jamison hit his friend in the chest. D'Juan only laughed.

"Thanks for everything back there," I said, not knowing if I entirely trusted D'Juan, but still feeling relieved that I might be out danger. "For helping Jamison and all."

"J-man and I go back. Way back."

"To Sunday School?" When they both acted surprised, I added, "I overheard you talking about it."

"That's right. Even further than that, but yeah. We both were the only two who showed up regularly. Even though this guy showed up for the food and snacks." He pointed at Jamison.

"Ha, ha," Jamison said sarcastically. "And you showed up because Sister Tina was pretty."

D'Juan shrugged. "The Lord works in mysterious ways. What can I say?" To me, he asked, "So, what's your story? Where you coming from? Where you going?"

"I'm from outside of Lansing," I said, making myself engage in conversation. "Getting out from a bad situation, that's all. Heading to Wyoming so I can start over again."

"How'd you get messed up with Danny? That guy's pretty evil. His whole organization is in cahoots with Baltagio."

"He followed me, I guess. I'm not sure. My stepfather owes him a lot of money, so he said that Danny could use me to pay off the debt." I shuddered as I remembered Danny's words from the van.

You're mine. Until the debt is paid, and even then I might not let you go.

Jamison reached back and took my hand, giving me a reassuring smile. "It's all right. We called the cops. We're safe."

I nodded and smiled back at him, but I couldn't mask my fear. He kept his hand in mine, and even though I liked the warm strength of his fingers as he squeezed my palm, I pulled my hand away. I didn't want anyone touching me right then. Instead I leaned against the window and thought of my brother.

Suddenly D'Juan grabbed Jamison in a head squeeze and rubbed his short hair. "Where'd it go?"

"Will you drive?" Jamison laughed.

D'Juan took the wheel again. "It looks good. Is she why you're all cleaned up and sharp?"

"We thought it would be like a disguise. How'd you know where we were anyway?"

"I guess Baltagio hunted down Danny after that bus station surveillance tape last night. Told him he was looking for you. Danny told him all he wanted was the girl. I heard all that from Shazz."

"Shazz was with Danny."

"Yeah, he works with anyone if it comes down to money. Baltagio found out and told Shazz to bring you back alive and with the key. If it doesn't happen, then—well, you know. Shazz told him about our friendship, then picked me up last night and told me I had no choice. But I wanted to go anyway. After he told me about the surveillance video, I was worried about you. I thought you might need my help."

"I appreciate it," Jamison said. "But if Baltagio finds out you double-crossed him—"

"He won't. I know your mom took that key. And I also know it could totally bring down Baltagio. So, we need to finish this little quest you're on. Where'd your mom tell you to go?"

"To find my father. In Minneapolis."

D'Juan glanced over at Jamison with a look of disbelief. "What?"

"Yep. Supposedly this guy can help. She feels he's the only one who won't be touched by Baltagio."

As I listened to Jamison and his friend, the guilt settled on my shoulders. If he had never helped me, he'd already be in Minneapolis with his father.

"And you left the light on!" D'Juan teased Jamison. "Really? That's like a beacon."

"I know. I tried to get Ellie to turn it off, but there were mice in our room."

"Yeah," I said, feeling guiltier. "Sorry about that."

"Do you think we need to get off the main highway?" D'Juan asked.

"The car's not stolen until Shazz says it is," Jamison said. "And I don't think he's talking right now. But how long we gonna drive before a break? It's been about two hours. I'm hungry and I've got to use the bathroom."

"Me too." I still felt sick.

D'Juan took the closest exit.

"There's nothing here," Jamison complained.

"What's that?" D'Juan said. "It's a gas station *and* a restaurant. We need gas. Do you all have some cash or are we doing a drive off?"

"I've got a little bit," I said, unzipping the small compartment I kept some in. But it was gone. All of it. "Where is it?" I panicked. I still had enough to get on my feet, but not if it had been stolen!

"Did you put it somewhere else?" Jamison asked.

"No, it was right here," I said, holding back my emotions. I refused to be a crying mess anymore, especially in front of Jamison. But my money was gone, and I couldn't stop it.

"Is this it?" D'Juan asked, pulling my small roll of bills out of his pocket.

"Why'd you take her money?" Jamison snatched it from his hand and gave it back to me. I kept quiet, holding the money in my hand while trying not to get more upset.

It's right here. And you're all right. Deep breaths.

"No, I didn't," D'Juan was saying. "Shazz dropped it in the console when he got into the car after the motel. After I left him off the highway, I put it in my pocket."

"He must have taken it while I was sleeping." I shoved the money in another zipper compartment, relieved to have it back. I had some money in other places, but this was my largest roll.

D'Juan pulled up to a pump. "Gas and grub," he announced, getting out. Then he poked his head back in the window, looking at me. "And it looks like you're paying."

"I've got some more cash left." Jamison opened the door and slid out. He still held his arm protectively over his ribs and winced when moving wrong.

I opened my door and followed him inside. "What happened before I woke up this morning?"

He kept walking. "First, I woke up with a gun pressed against my temple. Then Danny forced me outside where he proceeded to thank me for intervening at the bus station." Jamison stopped just outside the bathrooms. "What'd they do to you?"

I shook my head, shuddering. "Luckily he didn't have time to do anything other than tell me all the things he was going to do with me. It would have been worse if they'd got me to wherever they were going."

Jamison's mouth set into a deep frown. He went to reach for me, then dropped his hand. "I'm glad that didn't happen."

"How'd you get Shazz to go along with rescuing me?"

Now he shrugged. "Nothing, really. Don't worry about it. It all worked out."

This time, I reached for him. "It had to have been something important to get someone like Shazz to change his mind."

"I couldn't let anything happen to you."

"Thanks for having my back. I hope I can return the favor someday."

"Yeah, maybe. I'm tallying up my bill. Be prepared," he teased.

D'Juan stepped out of the bathroom. "You two just going to stand there?" He moved past us and into the store.

"So, you and D'Juan have been friends a long time? Reminds me of how close I am to my friend, Lauren."

"Yeah, we go way back."

"Do you trust him?"

"Maybe before today, I would have questioned his intentions, but I think he's like us. Now if you excuse me, I got to use the facilities."

"Me too." I left him for the women's bathroom. While inside I washed my face and neck, reminding myself that everything was fine. D'Juan seemed to genuinely like Jamison, and he did give me back the money. I wanted to relax, but my nerves were still tripping.

I stepped outside the restroom area and noticed D'Juan leaning against the wall, waiting for me.

"Everything all right?" I asked. "Where's Jamison?"

"Seeing if they have any ace bandages or something to wrap around his ribs."

"Oh."

He stepped closer, studying me. After what seemed like too long of an awkward pause, he said, "What's your story anyway? Why you all of a sudden show up in his life?"

"I …" I stumbled over what to say. His stare-down wasn't helping. "I ran away, but I didn't get very far."

"How'd you get messed up with Danny? He's crazy, man. Crazier than Shazz. And he's got ties to Baltagio. The same Baltagio that's looking for my friend."

"Danny was following me almost from the beginning. I don't fully understand why, but it has to do with my stepdad owing him money. He just got released from prison. That's why I had to get out of there."

"What was he doing time for?"

"Child molestation," I said, my mouth becoming dry.

D'Juan raised an eyebrow. "You?"

"Yeah. It was supposed to be five to eight years, but he got out in four for good behavior."

"Listen, I'm gonna keep my eye on you. You better be telling me straight."

I nodded. "Thanks for helping us. Today could have been so much worse."

"Let me explain something." He jabbed a finger at me. "I did what I had to do for *him*. That's it."

I instinctively shrank back from his finger. My nerves couldn't handle any more aggression. "I'm sorry. I didn't mean to mess up everything. I don't know what else to do."

"Once Jamison has your back, he'll always have your back."

"I've learned that."

"My goal is to get him where he needs to go. That's it. Got it?"

His intense stare bored into me, and I ran a shaky hand across my face. "I only need to get to a bus station. Once we get to Minneapolis, I'll take a cab. I won't bother him anymore."

D'Juan finally stepped back. "As long as we're straight. Protecting him is my mission."

"Jamison said you two have history."

Now D'Juan gave a small smile. "J-man has been my only real friend. And he was there for me. After my older brothers forced me to join Shazz, it was bad. I'd been beaten up and left for dead in the street."

"Your brothers did that?"

"They had a part in it. I couldn't get help. That's the initiation. To show I could do it. I nearly died and would have if J-man hadn't of showed up. He's good. I mean in here—" he pointed to his chest. "He don't deserve what he's been dealt with in life, but he's still good."

"I know."

"Do you?"

"I have never had anyone sacrifice so much to help me. Ever."

Jamison appeared from around the corner. "What are you two doing? Let's get some food and get out of here."

"Did you find the Ace wrap?" D'Juan asked, moving toward his friend.

"Nah, I'll be fine though."

I followed them to the other side of the station where the truck stop diner was. It smelled of grease and burgers, but my stomach wasn't having it. I would wait in the car, but I refused to be alone if I didn't have to be.

The three of us slid into a back booth.

"Do I want lunch or breakfast?" Jamison asked, looking at the menu and rubbing his hands together in apparent anticipation.

"Both," I said, seeing how cheap the prices were. "We can take a meal to go for later."

When the weathered waitress stopped by the table, Jamison and D'Juan ordered like they hadn't eaten in days. Eggs, bacon, hash browns, pancakes, and toast, then burgers and fries and large sodas to take with them. I ordered a soup.

"Not hungry?" Jamison asked.

I shook my head and looked away.

"Hey, they're gone. D'Juan did us a favor. Take a deep breath."

I nodded but couldn't look at either of them. I felt like I would shatter into thousands of pieces. *Hold yourself together*, I ordered.

After the waitress left with her notepad full of our large order, D'Juan poked Jamison in the arm. "Remember the after-church dinner?"

Jamison smiled and cringed. "Don't bring that up."

To me, D'Juan said, "We were at church because they was having an after service meal. A lot of the block showed up for that. Well, J-man wanted to check out the food, so during Sunday School we both acted like we had to go to the bathroom. But we snuck to the fellowship hall."

"They had a long spread of desserts lined up," Jamison added. "It was too tempting."

D'Juan laughed. "We ate and ate. All of Sister Telly's blueberry pie was gone."

Jamison tried to laugh but stopped and held his rib.

The waitress dropped off their sodas and my soup.

Jamison drank from his, then clarified, "Missionary Baptist always looked out for the neighborhood kids. The pastor felt like he was the dad we never had."

"Yeah," D'Juan agreed. "The two of us would get picked up by the church bus even when our moms weren't with us."

"That church kept me fed," Jamison said. "They'd drop off bags of groceries and would check on Mom."

"Is that why you have a children's Bible in your bag?" I asked. "Was that from the church?"

D'Juan and Jamison became very quiet. They drank from their sodas, and neither one of them gave me any eye contact.

"Did I say something wrong?"

The waitress set down all their breakfast plates loaded with food. "When do you want the burgers?"

"Can they be put in to-go boxes, please?" I asked.

When she left I noticed the two guys started devouring the food. But neither one was talking.

I sipped my soup, but I couldn't keep up with how fast they were shoveling the food in. Like two starving kids.

My life might have been horrific, especially in my early teens, but when my brother had been alive, life had been content. We always had food and a roof over our heads. Mom had lots of boyfriends, but she never kept them in the house long, and even so, Billy took care of me. But from the looks of it, there was more to these two than I fully understood. When I mentioned the children's Bible, Jamison actually grimaced. Not from his ribs either. More like the pain from a bad memory.

The rest of the meal was awkward. Both of them ate without speaking. I finished my soup more confused than ever, but I knew not to press a topic. If they didn't want to talk, I wasn't going to push them.

I took the bill and went to the counter to pay. The waitress handed me two bags full of to-go containers. The two guys were whispering to each other when I got back to the table. Talk about feeling like a third wheel. Especially when I evidently said something that I shouldn't have.

"I'll be by the car," I said, then turned and left them still in the booth.

I wasn't outside long before Jamison walked out of the restaurant to join me.

"Where's D'Juan?"

"He saw a display of TracFones. He thought we should get another one."

"Good idea." I paused, then added, "I'm sorry for upsetting you in there. I'm not sure what I said, but evidently I shouldn't have."

"It's not a big deal. I'm not mad." He scanned the area around us before saying, "Pastor Steve was killed about three years ago. It's hard for D'Juan to talk about."

"That's horrible."

"It's not only that, it's"—he scanned the area again—"It was D'Juan's older brother that killed him. Pastor Steve was visiting church folk. D'Wayne, that's the brother, he was in the passenger seat searching for one of the grays. I don't even remember what it was about. The gangs always hate on each other. Anyway, Pastor Steve got in the line of fire. D'Wayne's doing maximum life."

"Did D'Wayne go to the church too?"

"Occasionally. We all did as kids."

"How much older?"

"He was eighteen and tried as an adult."

The store bell jingled as D'Juan stepped outside and headed to us.

"And to answer your question inside, yes, Pastor Steve gave me that Bible." Jamison didn't say anything more, only nodded in D'Juan's direction, then slid into the passenger's seat.

D'Juan still looked grim. His mouth was set in a deep frown, and he wouldn't even look at me. "Get in the car," he ordered, before getting in himself.

I slid into the backseat and rested my head against the car door again. I couldn't worry about Jamison's friend. I had my own issues to overcome.

D'Juan started the car and pulled out onto the road. We drove in silence for several minutes before he said, "I have to tell you guys something, but I don't know how to say it."

"Out with it," Jamison said.

"There was breaking news on the television in there. It showed the crash scene."

"Anything about us?" Jamison asked. "Or this car?"

"No," D'Juan said. "It showed the messed-up van."

"Good," I said in relief. Then I saw D'Juan wasn't done. He had his lips pressed together and was squeezing the steering wheel in frustration. Nearly cringing myself, I asked, "What?"

"Out with it!" Jamison snapped.

"They found a body. A dead body." D'Juan looked at me through the rearview mirror. "I'm sorry, Ellie. There was only one body, and it was Shazz. I didn't kill any of them. So, I don't know what happened when we left."

"But I saw Danny on the ground." I began to tremble.

"The guy in the van was still alive," Jamison sighed in exasperation. "His leg was bust, but he could have still made a call."

"Before the police?" I said in a panic. "Why didn't we think of that?"

"And they know we took this car," Jamison said quietly and in resignation.

"There's still time," D'Juan said. "Minneapolis is only four hours away. Danny was messed up. There's no way he jumped into another van to follow us."

"True," Jamison said, looking back at me and grabbing my hand. "He's going to need medical help. That gives us some time."

I swallowed back the bile and took in a shaky breath. "When is this nightmare going to end?"

"We need another car," D'Juan said. "That'll help throw them off our scent."

I leaned my head against the window and closed my eyes. The food threatened to come up as the fear came back with a vengeance. Danny's words in the van replayed in my head. I shivered in revulsion thinking about what he said he wanted to do to me. And to think Hank had taken part in their trafficking ring before meeting my mom.

"He needed a place to hide from me," Danny had told me while in the van. *"So, he found a desperate woman. Now I can see why he couldn't resist keeping his hands off her daughter."*

Jamison took my hand. I nearly jerked it away, but the concern on his face stopped me.

How long was I going to drag him from his own responsibility? From what he told me and from what D'Juan said, Jamison had his own issues to deal with. All of this running was because of me.

"I think it's time I go to the police." I choked on the words, knowing what that meant. But maybe Lauren could let me stay with her for a couple months. Maybe I could take my money and get a place to hide out for a couple months. Would Danny follow me there?

"Let's get to Minnesota," D'Juan said. "We're not that far. Once we get there, we'll figure things out."

"I can't hide behind Jamison forever." I shifted my focus to him. "It's not fair to you. You've got your mom and your own life to think about. And if it's go back home or go with Danny, home would be slightly better. At least I could maybe talk some sense into my mother." I knew that was impossible. She adored Hank, even more than she loved her daughter. But at home, I only had to worry about the evil stepfather. I didn't have to worry about being passed around like a party favor.

Jamison watched me for a few minutes, neither of us knowing what exactly to do. He finally said, "Last night, I told Mr. Langston to bring the police. You stayed and waited with me. So, I'm going to stick by you. You don't have to choose one nightmare over another. Somehow we're going to get out of this mess."

"Jamison, I don't know."

"We're in this together," he declared. "The end."

A tear of relief escaped, as my heart seemed to expand inside my chest. My face heated from the strong emotions that at the moment were greater than the fear inside me. As D'Juan drove down the highway, all I could do was stare into Jamison's eyes, and relish in the gratitude of not having to go down this road alone.

"Talk about being the third wheel," D'Juan said under his breath.

We laughed, and the moment moved passed us. But Jamison didn't let go of my hand, instead interlacing his fingers with mine.

And this time, I didn't push his hand away.

Chapter Thirteen: Jamison

The Road Less Traveled

I held the new Tracfone in my hands but hadn't yet called the number. A day after I called Mr. Langston, Danny and Shazz both showed up at the motel. D'Juan didn't think that Mr. Langston had anything to do with it, but he wasn't entirely sure. A part of me couldn't believe I would even doubt Mr. Langston's loyalty, but I still hesitated.

"How did Baltagio know I was in Chicago?" I asked D'Juan.

"Shazz, I think."

"Yeah, he was with Danny at the bus stop." Mom had warned me that Baltagio had eyes everywhere. I thought she had been exaggerating, but evidently not.

"This Danny character is new to our hood."

"Did you show up together? At the motel?"

D'Juan acted uncomfortable. I wanted to trust him, but I found myself questioning his loyalty too. Was he leading me directly to Baltagio? But why would he do that? And why would he knock out Shazz and Danny, if he was going to turn around and hand me over himself? Could he be motivated by money? Did I have a price on my head?

"Tell me what you know," I demanded. "You and Shazz and Danny and his group all miraculously show up at the same time. Why?"

"All I know is that Shazz told me to go with him because he thought you'd come back easier with me there. I don't know about Danny or all of them. But Shazz seemed to know they were going to be there. He didn't act surprised or anything."

"And he didn't tell you?"

"J-man, I swear it. I don't know the answers. But I'm glad it happened. Not because I wanted you to be in danger or that girl…" he pointed in the back to Ellie who had fallen asleep leaning against the window. "But I saw an opportunity, and I took it."

"Yeah," I said quietly. D'Wayne and Shazz had led the group who initiated D'Juan. They hadn't asked. They hadn't given him any warning. They only yanked him from his bed in the middle of the night, tied him up and gagged him, then took him to an alley where gang members took turns beating him. If it hadn't been for me deciding to go to school that morning to get some breakfast, he'd have probably died out there. D'Wayne had been home, and that monster must have had a flash of conscience because he told me where I could find D'Juan. He warned me not to take him to the hospital. I nearly did anyway, but I knew if I did that, the gang would kill him for failing the initiation, and I'd probably be killed for helping him fail. "I'm glad you did what you did back at the accident. If it hadn't been for you, we'd be at Shazz's mercy."

"I couldn't let you give yourself to him," D'Juan said, visibly emotional. "You have no idea, man. When you said that you'd do whatever he wanted to save the girl, I ain't never felt that kind of fear before, at least not since a long time. Someone like you don't belong in no street war."

"Neither does someone like you."

"Unfortunately for me, I had older brothers who didn't give me a choice."

"But now the world is yours," I said.

He stayed quiet, so I stared at the phone again and contemplated calling.

"How long you gonna let her hang around?" he finally asked, talking low.

"I don't know," I said. "But I've got other things to worry about. Like meeting my biological father for the first time."

"About that ..." D'Juan looked uncomfortable again.

"I don't like you keeping secrets from me," I said in annoyance. "I know you're not saying something important."

"It's about your mother."

My heart seemed to skip a beat, and the back of my neck exploded in goose bumps. "Tell me."

"She's had a long history with the Baltagio family. She's been on and off with Baltagio's son."

"Yeah, she told me that."

"For a long time. Like eighteen years long time."

"Okay," I said. "A long time. Why you acting like that's a big deal?"

"You've never wondered why none of the gangs been knocking on your door? Come on, man, they pulled me from my bed. How many nights you been alone 'cause your mom's out doing her thing? How many times could they have easily grabbed you?"

I had no idea. On our block boys joined the red brotherhood. It wasn't a question of whether or not they wanted to. They weren't really given the option out. So, why had I been left alone? And why had Shazz been practically salivating when I offered to join in order to save Ellie?

"Why are they not touching me?" I asked. "There's a reason, right?"

"It's something with Baltagio's son, Ray. You've met him."

"Ray? As in the same Ray that used to live with us back in the trailer? The same Ray who got Mom partying too much and then left us? That Ray?"

"That's Ray Baltagio," D'Juan said.

"What are you saying?" I began to get defensive. How had I not known that was Ray Baltagio? Maybe because my mother kept it from me.

"If I tell you, you can't get mad at me. I'm only telling you what's known around town."

I didn't say anything because I couldn't promise that I wouldn't get angry. "If it's about me or my mom, I deserve to know."

"True." D'Juan exhaled slowly. "No one was to lay a hand on

you. There has to be a reason. The only thing that makes sense is your mother's connection with Baltagio."

Dread poured through me. I thought of Chit Baltagio at the motel and how he knew stuff about me that a stranger wouldn't know. "I'm not related to them. If that's what you're implying," I said, then I repeated it. "I'm not. Mom would have told me. And Ray, the Ray that used to live with us, barely gave me a second glance. And if he was taking care of us, why were we so poor? He couldn't put us up somewhere nice?"

"The guy's got a wife who is a high classy broad. I think he keeps your mother on the side and throws her the good stuff."

"What are you saying?" I demanded. "I don't like you talking about my mom like this."

"I didn't say anything, but it is what it is. Neither one of us got to pick our parents."

I felt sick. Mom had been keeping all of this from me? "It doesn't make sense. She told me to go to my biological father in Minneapolis. I saw Langston's notes. Some guy named Gil Godfrey."

"Did she actually say the words, 'biological father'?" D'Juan asked. When I didn't answer, he continued, "That's why I said that it's rumor. It's the talk on the street. I don't know what part of that is real and what's not. Somewhere there's some truth."

"You know what I found out from Langston?" I didn't wait for him to answer. "I found out that I have a grandmother."

"Well, technically, we all have grandmothers."

"Yeah, but this one wants to meet me. I guess Mom ran away when she was young, and she hasn't ever talked to her mother."

"Somewhere you have a normal, white grandma, and yet you grew up between 4 and 5 Mile on Detroit's southside."

"I know. Mom didn't tell me about this Gil Godfrey either. It makes me wonder what else she's kept from me." We passed a highway sign that highlighted Minneapolis being forty-six miles away. "We're almost there."

"What's the plan? Knock on this guy's door and say, 'Hey, what's up? You don't know me, but I might be your kid'?"

"Something like that. Mom thinks this guy can help."

"Either that or she doesn't expect to live, and she wants you to meet your father in case you need some help after she's gone."

I stared at him in horror as the realization of his words dawned on me. "You think that's the reason?"

"Stop looking at me like that. I don't know."

"Mom's in jail, awaiting trial. Langston said she's in there. Alive."

"Okay, okay, what do I know? But get real, all right? Stop living in dreamland. You know that if Baltagio wants your mother, a jail cell ain't gonna keep him away."

"No, I don't know that. The first time I met the guy was the other day. Obviously, there's been a lot going on that my mother neglected to tell me about!" I raised my voice, which woke Ellie up.

"Everything all right?" she asked, stifling a yawn.

Neither one of us answered.

Ellie tapped my shoulder gently. "What'd I miss? You seem upset."

I still didn't respond because of the emotions rolling through me. Normally I kept it altogether and never lost my cool, but the last couple days had sent my head into a tailspin. The underlying emotion—the one I tried not to think about even though it kept bubbling to the surface—was betrayal. All these years my mother dragged me around from one roach-infested place to another. I took care of her, missing school and free meals because I had to go find her and make sure she was alive, hiding out in dingy motel rooms so that the street gangs wouldn't harass me. And all this time I had other family? And the guy who was chasing me might also be the one protecting me?

"Take this exit," I said to D'Juan. "I need to get out and get some air."

He didn't question me. He pulled off the highway and into another gas station. "I'll fill up while we're here."

While Ellie handed him another twenty, I opened the door and left them behind. Walking to the back of the building, I punched Langston's number into the new phone. He would have some answers, especially if I was any relation to Baltagio. If he answered the phone.

Langston picked up on the first ring. "Hello?"

"Hey, it's me. What happened? The police never came, and you didn't answer the phone!"

I heard Langston sigh in relief. "Thank God," he said. "I have been worried sick. Your other phone number doesn't work."

"Yeah, we had to get rid of it because we didn't want anyone tracing it to us. But we had it for two days. Long enough for you to call me."

"I sent police out, and they said no one was there! Then the next thing I know you're wanted in connection to Shazz's death."

"Whoa! What was that?"

"It's everywhere, Jamison. The kid with the gun at the bus station is the one the police are looking for in connection to the death of two black men."

"Two? How is there two?" My world started spinning. I leaned against the grimy siding of the gas station.

"One is Shazz, but the other one I don't know who it was. Some big guy from Chicago."

My mouth dropped open, and I nearly dropped the phone. "Chuck?"

"His first name was Charles, but I'm not sure his last name."

"He's dead? As in *dead*?"

"I'm pretty sure. Jamison? Talk to me. You've got to tell me what's going on. I can't help you if I don't know."

"Danny, that guy I was telling you about—the one trying to kidnap Ellie—he showed up at the motel this morning. He held a gun to my head before giving me to Shazz. Then Danny took Ellie in a black van. I talked Shazz into helping me rescue Ellie in exchange for me working under him." I paused, not wanting to give up D'Juan. "I didn't kill Shazz. I swear it. The other guys did. They got in an accident, and I went to help Ellie."

"What an absolute nightmare," Langston said under his breath. "You need to turn yourself in. I'm serious, Jamison. This is real. You have warrants out for your arrest."

"What about my mom? I got to get to this Godfrey guy and give him the key. I can't come all the way out here and not complete it."

"Are you there? In Minneapolis?"

"Almost. I'm in Minnesota now. We're not too far from the city."

"I don't know." His tone became high and pitchy. "I'm confused with what the right thing is anymore. Turn yourself in, only to let Baltagio go free, or keep going and try to convict a known crime lord?"

"Why are you talking weird?"

"I'm not." He coughed, and his voice went much lower. "I'm not. I'm just nervous. And worried."

"Give me his number."

"Who? Godfrey?"

"Yeah, I'd call him right now if I had the number. That way if anything happens, at least he's tipped off. Could you get me the police station's number?"

"Are you sure you want to do that? The police will arrest you upon contact."

I had yet to stop shaking from the news that Chuck—the nice guy who drove us so far—suffered because of me. The emotions that threatened before were so close to the surface, I had to rest my hands on my knees and take short breaths until my breathing evened out. *No tears,* I reminded myself. *Tears get you nowhere. Use logic. Think strategically.*

"I found his number," Langston said into the phone.

"Whose?"

"Godfrey's. I didn't know I had a recent one." His voice was all pitchy again.

I felt the warning. "You have Godfrey's number and yet you allowed me to go on this trip? Something seems off, Mr. Langston."

"I-I just found it. Look at that. Right here. I think you should call him."

"How do I know you're not working for Baltagio, and you're giving me a wrong number?"

"You're going to have to trust me." He rattled off the number while I committed it to memory. "I have to tell you one more thing. You're not going to like it, but you need to know."

"What?" I gritted teeth, trying to keep the emotions at bay.

"I got a call this morning that someone paid your mother's bail. Obviously Baltagio can't just walk in, and we don't recognize the guy who picked her up, but it's no doubt someone working for him."

"My mom's gone?"

"Yes," he said. "I'm so sorry."

I hung up on him and pressed my eyes shut with the palms of my hands. Mom was gone from the jail? Picked up by some guy? Suddenly the emotions erupted, and I pounded my fists against the gas station's cement wall. "NO!" I yelled, not caring who heard. This couldn't be happening. My entire life unraveling, and I had no control over any of it.

Ellie placed her hand on my back. There were no words spoken, but her presence was somewhat of a comfort. My rational mind knew that since I met her, my life had been doubly complicated, but since this morning's horrible events, I felt that I had someone in this with me. Sure, I was grateful for D'Juan showing up, but Ellie was different. I would do whatever I could to protect her. It might make things more complicated, but it also made sense.

I composed myself, then turned to her. Before I knew what happened, she wrapped her arms around my neck and hugged me. The hesitation was brief, as I wrapped my arms around her. We held each other until D'Juan joined us.

"I take it you called Langston," he said.

"Yeah." I reluctantly released Ellie. "I'm wanted for Shazz's death."

D'Juan shifted his gaze and didn't say anything. He already knew.

My fists now throbbed and bled, but not bad enough to take my attention off D'Juan. "Why didn't you tell me?"

"What point would it make? We have to finish what we set out to do. It's the only way this is going to end well."

"You're being accused of murder?" Ellie's eyes teared up. "I won't let that happen. We'll tell them everything."

"If we're still alive," D'Juan muttered. "Make no mistake. We're playing their game right now. If we don't play our cards right, we're going to be buried six feet under before tomorrow morning."

"No," I said, thinking logically again. "We've got a wild card they're not expecting. Mr. Langston gave me Godfrey's number." I punched the numbers into the phone and turned on the speaker.

The other end rang and rang. I almost gave up hope until someone answered. "Detective Godfrey."

My brain froze. On the other end of the line was possibly my father.

"Who is this?" he demanded.

"Jamison," I blurted. "Jamison Jones. I'm Claire's son."

The other end of the line stayed quiet for several minutes.

"Listen," I snapped. This wasn't about to be a father-son moment. "Mom is in big trouble. I don't know what's going on, all I know is she said to find you and give you Baltagio's key. Now she's gone. Someone got her from the jail cell. You're the only one she trusted for me to give this to."

D'Juan interjected. "Tell him we got people hot on our tail."

"We're in trouble," I said. "We didn't do anything wrong, I promise. But I've got to get to you before they get to me—"

"Where are you at?"

"The Mobil gas station about forty-four miles out of Minneapolis. We're headed north."

"It was exit ninety-seven," D'Juan said.

"Exit ninety-seven," I repeated.

"Stay tight," he said. "I'll be there in under thirty."

I ended the call and actually smiled in relief. "He's on his way."

D'Juan and Ellie both smiled. "And he's police?" Ellie asked.

"A detective."

"And he's just going to show up?" Ellie asked. "Has he ever met you?"

"No, but he recognized my name. I could tell."

"You're off the hook, man," D'Juan said. "I'm sorry about not telling you everything I saw on the television. I didn't want to upset you more." We stayed quiet for a few minutes before D'Juan asked, "Did you hear anything about your mom? She's out of jail?"

"She's gone. Someone got her out."

D'Juan's mouth set into a deep frown, and he scrunched his eyes closed like it pained him to keep them open. "We ain't never gonna be free. None of us."

"Do you know something I don't know?" I asked him. "I can tell Godfrey when he gets here. You don't think anyone'd hurt her?"

"Not with you at large. But it ain't good."

"It had nothing to do with me, right?" Ellie asked. "I would hate to think something happened to your mother because of me."

I thought of all Mom's secrets and all the bad choices she'd made in life. "No. Mom's situation has nothing to do with you. I did find something out though. I think Danny hurt Chuck."

Ellie's face fell. "I know," she said. "He told me in the van that that's how he found us. They went into the party store to see if any kids were in there, and the cashier let him see the surveillance."

The relief from contacting Godfrey was short-lived. The grief that someone got hurt trying to help us was winning out. "He died because of us?"

"Danny's evil," she said. "He told me that the fat guy paid a high price for helping me out."

"And when were you going to tell me? Why am I finding stuff out after the fact?"

"A lot happened. It wasn't on purpose. I promise."

D'Juan looked from me to Ellie then back to me. "Who's Chuck?"

"A guy we met at a party store not far from the bus station in Chicago," I answered. "Ellie paid him to drive us out of Chicago."

"Wow. I mean, that makes sense. They'll mess up anyone who gets in their way." D'Juan fidgeted, no longer looking me in the eye. He peered over his shoulder to the front of the gas station. "Listen, since we got some time to kill, I'm gonna sit in the car and wait it out there. I'll leave you two alone."

He walked away, and I knew exactly what he was doing. And I couldn't blame him.

"Is he all right?" Ellie asked. "He's acting strange."

"He's gonna take off."

Her eyes widened. "Why? Should we stop him?"

"Why do you think? Do you think D'Juan's going to be safe? Even if he goes with Godfrey, he'll pay a price at some point. Criminals like Danny and Baltagio never forget."

"And he heard about Chuck."

"It clicked. Chuck helped us, and he got hurt. D'Juan helped us, and if he gets caught—"

"It won't end well for him," Ellie finished my thought.

I started walking back around the front. "I'll be right back." I saw her doubt. "I promise. I only want to say good-bye." As I came around the front, I saw my bag and Ellie's backpack set on the curb close to the doors. D'Juan had already started the car. He saw me as I approached his window. Judging by the redness of his eyes, this had to be a tough decision for him.

His window already down, he said, "You know I always have your back, right?"

"I know."

He sniffed and rubbed his eyes, trying to compose himself. "This is the only chance I have. To get away. If I don't get out of here, I'm dead. I'm probably already dead."

"I know. I'm not mad, D. We wouldn't have got as far as we are now if it hadn't been for you showing up."

He nodded. "I just want a life where I don't have to look over my shoulder all the time, you know? They can't find me. If they do—"

"I swear I will tell no one that you helped me. As far as anything goes, I knocked out the two guys and stole the car."

"Danny saw me. He's gonna know I did it."

D'Juan was right, and it made the fear all the more real. I wasn't only trying to protect myself, but I wanted those I cared about to be protected too. "Remember when we were young, and we'd watch those TV preachers?"

"Yeah," he laughed softly. "Creflo Dollar and T.D. Jakes were always back-to-back. I remember we'd place our hands on the television set and repeat after them."

"I think I've been saved one hundred twenty-seven times."

D'Juan laughed again. "For sure. 'Better be safe than sorry.' That's what you'd say."

"You wanted to be like them," I said.

"A preacher." D'Juan shook his head. "Maybe not a preacher, but a black man in a nice suit with all that confidence. Those were pipe dreams, my friend. Now all I want is to get past my twentieth birthday. And that's still two years away."

"You don't have to be a preacher, but don't give up. Drive and don't stop until you're safe. Start over. And then find me one day and tell me how great your life turned out."

"I'm a dropout with nothing to my name but a stolen car. It's about survival. That's all it has been, that's all it will be."

"Nuh-uh," I said. "I'm not buying it. I don't understand why all of this is happening, but one thing I've learned is that God has protected us, man. Both of us should be dead, but we're not. And if I had to meet Ellie so that you could get out of Detroit and have this opportunity, then don't you dare waste it. Set yourself up somewhere safe. And do what you have to do."

He stayed thoughtful for a few minutes. "I have an auntie somewhere near Cleveland."

"Then there you go."

"How am I gonna get there? I got to get rid of this car."

"Take a bus. No one's going to be looking for you there." I grabbed what little money I still had in my pocket and handed it to D'Juan. "It's a little over eighty bucks."

D'Juan got out of the car and gave me a quick hug. "Stay alive," he said. "I want to hear that you made it out too."

"Deal."

When he slid back into the car, I shut the door. "See you on the other side?"

"Amen," he said, then he put the car in drive and left me staring after him.

Chapter Fourteen: Ellie

Stranded ... Again

I stayed back as Jamison watched the fading black Trans Am turn onto the highway and eventually disappear from view. Even though Jamison had said that someone was coming to get us, I still felt unsure and anxious at D'Juan leaving us behind.

Jamison made his way over to me. He looked grim. "Do you ever get a feeling ..." He stopped and pressed his lips together.

"Yeah, all the time," I said. "Like right now I have a really bad vibe. I don't know why, but it's there."

He nodded like he felt it too.

"Why'd he leave us? And why'd you let him?"

"He double-crossed Baltagio. Completely changed the plans to help us escape. If Baltagio catches him, he's dead."

"Then wouldn't the police help?"

"That's what I don't get. Why didn't he go with us to the police? He knows something, and he didn't share it."

"If he knows something, why wouldn't he tell you? You're his friend."

"I don't know," he said. "But he is hiding something, that's for sure. I felt that I needed to go along with it. I needed him to believe that I was all right with him taking off."

"So, you don't trust him?"

"Yes and no. I want to trust him, but I have too many questions and things aren't adding up. It doesn't matter though. I don't want him dead. That's why I let him go. I'm hoping that he really is gonna start a new life somewhere."

I didn't respond because I knew Jamison wanted to believe the best about his friend.

"What do you think? Should we stick around for Godfrey?" he asked.

"Why is he coming all the way down here?"

"I don't know. I thought that was strange too. I mean, he's never met me. It seems weird that he'd be so willing to accommodate me. He didn't even ask a lot of questions."

"How'd you get his number?"

"From Langston."

"And you trust Langston?"

"Yes, I do. But I don't know. Something wasn't right. What if they got to him? The more I think about it, the more I feel like the only thing I should go on is the address my mother gave me. Why send me all the way here if Mom knew Langston had his number?"

"Maybe she didn't trust him."

"She said he was squeaky clean, but then she told me to trust no one."

"Then we trust no one. You remember the address?"

He closed his eyes. "Twenty-nine seventy-one Franklin Street."

"With everything we've been through, it's better to be safe than sorry."

"I agree." He smiled.

"What? What'd I say?"

"I used to say that when I was a kid. Better to be safe than sorry." He surveyed the landscape and his mouth set into a frown. "There's nothing out here. How do we get there?"

"I like it when you smile," I said, before realizing what I said. "I mean, you frown a lot, but your smile is nice." My face felt hot, no doubt from mortification.

His mouth twitched into a half-grin. "Interesting time to hand out a compliment."

"Well, you know, considering that this little adventure we're on still has the potential to end horribly, better now than never."

"Look at you dishing out all these clever sayings."

"Okay, stop. We need to come up with a plan that doesn't end in kidnapping or death."

"You're right. So, I won't tell you that I think you have a nice smile too. I'll wait until later."

Heat rose on my face again and I tried to suppress the smile.

He became serious. "We got to move quickly. They'll be here within ten to fifteen minutes. I'm sure the cashier saw me saying good-bye to D'Juan, so whoever shows up is going to know that we are stranded." He kept glancing at a small burgundy Saturn sitting by the dumpster in the back.

"What are you thinking?"

"I hate to do it, but we could ..." He pointed at the car and looked back at me as if to gauge my response.

"Now's not the time to question what's right or wrong, especially when our only other option is going to be scary worse."

"True." He grimaced. "But I hotwire a car about as good as I pick a lock."

"What? I thought you were a thug," I teased.

"Nope. No thug's life for me. But come on. No one's here. If we're gonna do it, we gotta move." He made his way over to the car and checked the door, which opened easily. He sat in the driver's seat and fiddled underneath the wheel. I didn't want to say I questioned his ability to hotwire a car, but I wasn't entirely confident.

I scanned the gas station and saw the back door that led inside the building. The idea started to form. "Hey, Jamison—"

"Shh," he said, focused on the car.

I left him at the car and went to the door. It was propped open slightly with a stick. I slipped inside. The tiny back room was empty. A sweatshirt hung on a coat hook, along with a purse. Without making a sound, I eased toward the items, then began searching the purse. No keys. On a whim, I reached inside the sweatshirt pockets. Jackpot.

I darted from the backroom and placed the stick back in the door. Jamison now knelt on the ground, his body inside the car, his head looking underneath the driver's wheel.

I jingled the keys. "Will these help?"

He peered at me from under the steering column, then stood up. "Where's your faith in me?"

"Are you driving, or am I?"

"Maybe you should. Technically, I don't know how to drive."

I set my backpack in the backseat and slid into the driver's seat. "I can't believe I'm stealing a car," I said, as Jamison got in on the passenger side.

"Don't drive in front of the gas station. Drive through the grass here. It looks flat enough."

I followed his directive, my hands shaking now that we were actually stealing the car. The field beside the gas station was bumpier than expected, which didn't help my nerves. "That girl's gonna get off her shift, and be in for a surprise."

"We'll return it," he said. "We only need to go forty miles north."

I pulled onto the road, driving past the gas station to get to the expressway. The little Saturn's engine vibrated as I pressed on the gas. "It doesn't like to go past fifty," I said over the muffler.

"We just need to get forty more miles," Jamison repeated.

He must have had a lot on his mind, so I let him think while we headed up the highway. My stomach stayed in a knot. There were a hundred different ways the situation could go bad. Just thinking about Danny still out there made me more nervous and scared than before, but I had to keep it together. Get to Jamison's dad's. We had a goal. It could get done.

But then what?

"What if that really was your father that you called?"

"I don't know. I guess he'll show up at the gas station and figure out that I'm not there. But the more I think about … I don't know. I guess what it comes down to is that I made a decision. The police didn't show yesterday when I needed them to, and then Langston didn't answer his special cell phone number both times I tried to call him. Yet, today he picks up on the first ring."

"Would he double-cross you?"

"No, but I couldn't risk it. Not after what I saw Danny do to you. We've got to get to safety. And with D'Juan taking off, and Langston acting weird on the phone … I don't know. There's so much I just don't know. So, our best bet is to go the address my mom gave me. That's the plan."

"And when we get there?" I avoided the other question I wanted to ask. What did that mean for me? At some point soon, he would be at his destination. And me? I clenched my one fist, digging my nails into my palm. Stay calm. Don't get Jamison worried about you.

"You okay?" He had been watching me.

"All things considered, no, not really."

"At least you're not wanted for murder."

"That doesn't make me feel better." I glanced over at him. "This entire situation is like worst-nightmare material."

"Yep, so we keep moving forward." Jamison paused. "Things could be worse. Think about it. What if Shazz hadn't agreed to help rescue you? What if D'Juan hadn't have been there?"

"I know, but what about Chuck? He didn't deserve whatever happened to him."

Jamison stayed quiet for a moment. "I have to believe that these guys are going to get what's coming to them. I don't know how or why, but it'll happen. Until then, we do what we know to do."

"Like steal?" My voice raised slightly. "I know you've been taking stuff from the different gas stations. I know D'Juan stole the TracFone. Shoot, we just stole a car! What if karma comes back to get us?"

"I haven't been stealing. Well, not regularly, at least. This car was the first major thing I took on this trip. As far as D'Juan, it's possible. It's about survival. I don't like it, but stealing sometimes has to be done."

"Oh," I said, feeling bad for making the accusation. "But you have stolen before? Like at stores?"

"Yes, unfortunately. I don't like to. I tell myself I'll pay it back when

I get a job."

"How come you haven't got a job? There's got to be some in the area."

"Sure, there are, but taking care of mom takes a lot of time. I started working at Chicken Shack and lasted about a month. That was during one of Mom's good times. But then she never came home. I had to start a shift, but she wasn't at her usual hangouts. So, I got fired from that one. I lasted about three weeks bagging at Jonny's local grocery store."

"Bummer."

"I decided to wait."

"Wait for what?"

"Wait for an opportunity. I don't know. I keep hoping Mom will change, and I can have a normal life. But maybe it's too late for that."

"Why?"

"Mr. Langston told me that Mom's out of jail. That means that she's in danger. And I'm not there to help. I don't know what I'll do if something happens to her."

"You're doing the right thing," I said. "You're doing what she asked you to do."

"Tell me something about you." Jamison changed the subject. "I've got to think about something else."

I frowned, surprised by his request.

"Come on, let's stop talking about bad things. Who are you, Ellie? I know you left your mother because she likes bad guys. I know a little bit about your big brother. I know you saved a bunch of money because I've been tempted to steal it a time or two. I know that you can drive. And that you're smart. And that you don't like mice. And that you want to be a country singer, even though you can't sing." He paused, then added, "And I know that you write stories, and you especially want a story with a happy ending."

My heart started to beat loudly in my chest. He knew all that about me? And he thought I was smart! "Wait a sec. You were thinking of stealing? From me?"

"The first time we met. On the bus. And in the motel room. I investigated a little. But I didn't take anything. I couldn't bring myself to do it. Besides, you were acting so guilty I knew you'd give me the money if I asked."

"True." We grinned at each other, and I noticed his dimple. I looked away fast. "Um, something about me? My name is Elvis. Elvis Priscilla Presley. With one 's', not two."

"Really?"

"Yep."

"That's a strange name for a girl. Your mom's an Elvis fan?"

"She likes country. My brother was named after Billy Ray Cyrus."

"I can see why you go by 'Ellie.'"

I playfully smacked his arm. "Be nice."

"Okay, okay. Do you watch any shows?"

"I mostly work. At Burger King. I was saving up money to get out. As soon as I heard that Hank was approved for an early release, I knew it was time."

"It has to be hard to leave your mom."

A part of me missed the mom in my younger years. Not that we had been close. My father decided that drinking, gambling, and other women were far more fun than a wife, small son, and newborn baby girl, so for most of my early years, it had just been Mom. But she had never been close or affectionate to me. She had adored Billy. I always wondered if she blamed me for my father's leaving. And after Hank got convicted, she never spoke to me anymore unless it was to give her my money.

"It's not hard to leave her."

"Some people shouldn't be parents," Jamison said.

"No, they shouldn't," I agreed. "Sometimes I want to have kids, so that I can be the kind of parent that I never had. But then I get scared. Like what if I'm as bad as my mom? What if that meanness is in me?"

"I may have just met you, but you're not mean. As far as my goals, I want to have three kids. One boy and two girls."

"Really? Why three? And why only one boy?"

"I don't know. It's just what I see for myself. When I'm daydreaming."

"What else do you daydream about?"

"Well, I don't really have time to daydream anymore. But I can tell you that I think a lot about going to college and becoming a doctor. Then I'm going to buy a big house on Detroit's rich side, and build a clinic in the southside. I'm gonna offer free healthcare. In my dreams, that is."

"How's it gonna be free? There's operating costs and stuff."

"I don't know." He laughed. "God'll provide. Anyway, it's just a dream. I don't even know if I'll graduate high school, let alone go to medical school. I've got that stupid capstone project."

"It's simple. If you want to graduate, graduate."

"It's not that simple. I'm up half the night making sure Mom gets back. I missed a lot of school."

"Don't miss school."

"Then I don't sleep."

"Jamison, it's okay to put yourself first. If your mother isn't back in time—"

"What? Leave her squatting in some dump? Her body laced with drugs? When she wakes up, she doesn't know where she's at half the time. I've got to take care of her."

"She couldn't stay put for school nights?"

Jamison looked at me like I had just sprouted three heads.

"I'm just saying that your mother is choosing to go out, but you need to choose to finish school. You'll be glad you did."

"I don't need an after-school lecture, okay?"

"Please don't get upset. I didn't mean …" My tongue got tangled.

"You didn't mean what? To leave my mom out on the streets to die while I get some shut-eye?"

"It's not your fault she's on the streets."

"Does it make it any less my responsibility? Do you think I enjoy walking the streets, searching for her? Or that I have to carry her back to wherever we're staying at the moment because she's usually passed out? Trust me, I hate it. I hate every second of it. I hate that I have to give my own mother baths, and that I have to feed her sometimes or she won't eat. I hate that I don't have any life or friends or extracurricular activities! If it wasn't for D'Juan, I'd have practically no connection to the outside world! It's all about her. *Claire*." He spat out his mother's name in anger.

This time I reached for him. I took his hand in mine. "I wasn't trying to be critical."

"Ever since Pastor Steve died, I wonder each night if it's the one that I'm gonna find her dead. I try to stay back. I try to show her how angry I am at her. But it never works. I didn't pick my life, but she's it. And now she's gone from jail, and I have no idea where she's at. And I'm not there to help her."

"You are helping her. Doing what you're doing now. We're going to this Godfrey guy, and we're getting help."

The siren made both of us jump.

The cops. Right behind us. Lights flashing. Sirens going.

"Oh my God. We stole this car. We're going to jail. Or it's Danny. And he's gonna take me."

The panic in Jamison's eyes said enough. He turned and stared at the cop car as if trying to figure out what to do.

"I can't outrun them in this!" I yelled.

"I'm wanted for murder," he said, oddly calm. "I'm going to jail."

"No! I'll tell them everything. Or I can keep driving." The little Saturn sputtered as if protesting. "This can't be happening. We're almost there. We almost made it."

"We don't have a choice," Jamison said so quietly I nearly missed it. "We're busted. Pull over."

I didn't listen to him at first. I kept driving while wracking my brain for a solution. There had to be some way to escape. But there wasn't. This car couldn't go any faster. And the cop car had somehow materialized into two, with one riding beside us.

"Pull over," Jamison said again. "It'll get uglier if we don't."

"What if it's Danny?"

"These guys don't look familiar. I think they're legitimate cops."

I gripped the wheel tightly and tried not to hyperventilate. I slowed down and pulled over. Jamison's expression was completely neutral, not showing any emotion, but his left eye had a slight tic.

"I'll tell them everything. You won't get in trouble."

"I can distract them, and you can make a run for it. That way you don't have to go with them. I don't want you be forced back to your mother's house."

"I'm not leaving you. You haven't left me."

Four police officers surrounded our car. One said, "Please step out of the vehicle."

Jamison unbuckled his seat belt, showed the officers his hands, and then opened the door.

"Move slowly," the cop ordered.

Another cop knocked on my window with his knuckle. "You too. Step out slowly and keep your hands visible."

By the time I stepped outside, two police officers already had Jamison pinned to the car and were searching him. One had Jamison's face smashed against the hood.

"He didn't do anything wrong. Please, this is a big misunderstanding."

The cop beside me was much gentler than how they were treating Jamison, but he still patted me down and recited my Miranda rights.

My heart sank to my feet as I watched them manhandle Jamison to the backseat of one of the squad cars. "He didn't do anything wrong," I pleaded again.

But no one was listening.

Chapter Fifteen: Jamison

Gil Godfrey

I kept my mouth shut the entire trip to the cop station. Ellie wasn't with me. They shoved her in another vehicle. Even with all the charges against me, I still hoped she'd be okay.

My rational mind said that I hadn't done anything wrong. That all I had to do was explain myself and let the evidence do the rest. It didn't help that they found the gun on me, even if it wasn't loaded. I squeezed my eyes tight and tried to think logically.

I had to give them my bag. It had the book that had the key.

Where was the bag? I opened my eyes and looked behind me. Was it still in the Saturn?

"Sit still," one of the cops ordered.

I turned to face the front, not looking at either of them. I knew better. Never look a cop in the eye.

All I had to do was wait until they started asking questions, then I would ask for Gil Godfrey. He'd come, wouldn't he? But I wasn't even sure he knew my name. I'd have to name-drop my mother. And if I got a phone call? I'd call Mr. Langton. He'd know what to do. No. Not Mr. Langston. He'd given me the wrong number. I was sure of it. Was he being bribed? Tortured? He sounded weird on the phone. But if I didn't call him, who could I call?

I thought of Mom but found myself getting more upset. Of course, I had no way to get ahold of her.

Great. No bag. No book. No key. No Langston. No Mom.

I bit down on my lip, breathing through my nose.

The police car pulled into the station, and the guy in the passenger seat got out, opened my door, and told me to walk with him. A few parking places away, Ellie was getting pulled out from the backseat of the other cop car. We made eye contact. She wasn't even trying to hide her terror. She called out to me, but the cop with me yanked on my arm.

"This way." He pushed me through the doors.

I'd actually never been in a police station. I avoided them. But this station looked straight out of a movie. Rows of desks behind a tall, Plexiglas counter. A set of heavy, double doors were to the right of a rectangular sitting area. And everything was beige or blue. And tacky.

The cop pushed me through the double doors, and we began walking down the stretch of desks, all the way past another set of doors, and into an enclosed interrogation room.

"Sit. Someone will in shortly." He handcuffed me to the table.

"Gil Godfrey," I blurted, staring at the mirror in front of me. It had to be one of those see-through walls even though I couldn't see anything but my reflection. "May I speak to Gil Godfrey, please?"

"Just sit tight." He shut the door.

I rested my head on the table and created a conversation in my head that I'd have with my possible-biological father. I couldn't decide if I was more nervous for being arrested for murder and whatever else they thought I did, or if I was more nervous that I might be face-to-face with the man who abandoned me and my mom. Then I imagined Ellie in one of these rooms, nervous and scared. I imagined taking her hand and interlacing her fingers with mine, reassuring her. I imagined the warmth of her hazel eyes on mine. It was silly to think that anything would ever come of us. Once this was taken care of, I'd be back in the D, and she'd be—where? Would she head to Wyoming?

"Stop it." The words echoed. Ellie didn't deserve to live in poverty. She deserved so much more than I could give her.

The door opened, and I jumped as if the cop had walked in on my imagination.

"A little jumpy?" He set a cup of water in front of me. He was an older white guy with a thick gray mustache and droopy eyes like he hadn't had decent sleep in the last thirty years.

I downed the water in one gulp. "Thank you. May I speak with Gil Godfrey, please?"

"We've contacted his precinct." He sat across from me. He had a file with him full of paperwork. "Until then, let's talk."

I nodded, hoping that he'd believe what I had to say.

He took out the surveillance shot of me pointing the gun at the Chicago bus station. "That's you?"

"Yes, sir. But it's not what it looks like."

"What does it look like?"

"It looks like I'm pointing a gun at a guy."

"And that's not true?"

"No, it's true. But it's his gun. And he was pressing it against Ellie's back. I shoved him, and the gun fell. I picked it up and pointed it at him. I wasn't going to shoot or anything. I was just trying to protect Ellie."

He showed me a picture of the gun with an evidence tag on it. "This is the gun found on you."

"Yes, but there were no bullets. I emptied them. I didn't want to hurt anyone. I only wanted to have it, just in case."

"Just in case what?"

"We have some bad guys chasing us, sir. I know it sounds like a bad western movie or something, but it's true. Having a gun—even one with no bullets—is like having a little layer of protection."

"Who's chasing you?"

"Well, there's this guy named Danny. I don't know much about him other than he looks like a frat boy. About six feet two, brown hair, slicked back. Last time I saw him he had on a dark blue polo shirt. He's been after Ellie this entire trip. He's messed up. Tried to kidnap her at the bus station and at the motel."

"Why is he trying to kidnap her?"

"Because her stepfather owes him money?" I tried to remember what Ellie told me. "Her stepfather was released from prison, which is why she took off. She couldn't be living with him after what happened between them. But I guess he had dealings with this Danny guy, and he told Danny that he could have Ellie as payment."

"You're talking human trafficking."

"Yes, sir, I am. It's been scary. And that's only her side of things. I've got my own issues. Which is why I need to talk to Gil Godfrey."

The cop sat back and watched me for a minute. "What's your story? How long have you known this girl?"

"I've known her for three days. We met at the bus stop in Detroit. My mom needed me to go to Minneapolis to find Gil Godfrey. He's the only one she trusts. Anyway, Ellie came up to me and asked me to play along that we were together. Danny was there at the station. So, I acted like I knew her. Then we both got on the bus and headed to Chicago. I was going to leave her alone, but then I saw Danny leading her out of the station. That's when I shoved him, and that's how you got that surveillance picture."

The cop placed a picture of Chuck in front of me. He had been badly beaten, but he looked alive. "Is he alive?"

"You know who this is?"

"Yes, his name is Chuck. He helped us get from a party store in Chicago to just outside the city limits. He's a good guy. Last I heard Danny and his guys messed him up because they found out he helped us. I thought he was dead."

"So, you're saying that you didn't do this?"

"No, I didn't. He dropped us off at a Walmart about forty-five minutes outside of Chicago. He couldn't go any farther, he said. That's the last we saw of him. But is he alive?"

The cop watched me again before slowly nodding. "He's in the hospital. Just woke up from a coma. When he's ready we'll verify this story."

My heart exploded in relief. I leaned back and took in a deep breath. "You have no idea how happy that makes me. Does Ellie know? She needs to know. We've both felt so guilty. We thought Danny killed him."

"Not for lack of trying," the cop muttered. Then he took out a picture of Shazz. A very dead Shazz. I shuddered, the smile vanishing from my face. "What about this guy?"

"That's Shazz. I didn't touch him. I did steal his car, but when Ellie and I left, he was only knocked out. Not dead."

"You and Ellie took his car?"

"Yes."

"Only the two of you?"

I paused. The cop acted like he already knew the answer. Something told me not to lie about this. "There was a third guy, but he's innocent too. He came with Shazz to get me, and he left with me and Ellie. The three of us left Shazz and Danny at the accident scene, but they were very much alive."

"Who is this other guy?"

"D'Juan."

"And where is D'Juan now?"

"I don't know. He left us at the gas station. But he didn't do anything wrong either. All of us are trying to get away from criminals."

"Are you sure you're not the criminal?" He leaned forward and gave me a steely expression. "Stealing cars? Breaking into motel rooms? Carrying a weapon without a permit? People have ended up seriously hurt or dead, and they're all connected to you."

"They're all connected to Danny. Not me. I'm just trying to find Gil Godfrey because my mom asked me to. I'm supposed to give him a key because somehow my mom thinks it's going to get Baltagio off her back. That's all I know. And I've been running ever since."

The police officer left me not long after that, promising to come back with another cup of water. But I must have sat in that small room for what felt like hours. I eventually dozed on the table, jolting straight up when the door finally opened.

The same police officer from before entered, handing me a large water bottle. Another man entered. Tall and lean with broad shoulders and a chiseled chin. He looked right at me with sad eyes. Eyes that told me what he had to say I wouldn't want to hear.

"Gil Godfrey?" I asked, even though I knew the answer.

He sat across from me and gave a slight nod. "Drink some water."

"You're white."

He watched me with those sad eyes. "She never told you?"

My heart sank deep in my chest, and I felt my breath catch. I didn't know what I had expected. But not this. Not a white man who was clearly not my father. "She told me to come to you. To go to my father in Minneapolis. She gave me your name. Said you were the only one she could trust. Why would she put me through this? If you're not—which you're not—"

"Drink some water."

"I don't want water! I want answers!" But my throat was parched, and my hands itched to do something. I opened the bottle of water and guzzled.

He leaned back in the chair. "What do you want to know? Ask me, and I'll answer."

"Why'd she send me to you? Why this game of cat-and-mouse?"

"I think it's mostly what she said. She trusts me. We went very different directions after our break-up. But she knows I became a cop. Is she in danger?"

"I think so. She was in jail, but someone paid for her to get out. I don't know who. Mr. Langston told me that, but then again, I think they got to him."

"Charles Langston? The social worker? He went missing yesterday afternoon. I pulled up as many files as I could to try to help you figure this out." He indicated the small stack of file folders he brought with him.

My stomach rolled. "Not Mr. Langston." I remembered him in the alley, trying to defend me. "So many people getting hurt because of me."

"We don't know that he's hurt. When was the last point of contact you had with him?"

"Just this afternoon. I called him to get your number. He sounded okay, but strange. I knew something was up. Especially after I called the number he gave me. I talked to you—or whoever was pretending to be you—and he seemed only too eager to travel over thirty minutes to a small gas station to get me."

"That's why you stole the Saturn?"

"Yeah, and I'm sorry about that. But we've been in real danger. Especially Ellie. Some guy by the name of Danny is bad news."

Gil Godfrey rubbed his face and opened one of the files. "Daniel Pataki. Twenty-five years old. Dropped out of MIT his sophomore year. Investigated over a dozen times. Always comes out clean." He showed me a recent photo of Danny taken at the bus station. It must have been before I shoved him away from Ellie, because she was right beside him, her eyes widened in fright.

"That's him."

"And you can attest that he held a gun to Miss Elvis? That he tried to take her against her will."

"Yes and yes. He held a gun to me and bruised me up some at the motel."

"Is he working in connection with Baltagio?"

"You know about him?"

Gil lifted up the files. "I'm a quick read. I figured that's why you came out here to see me. Something about Baltagio. I told your mother eighteen years ago that guy was trouble. But he was charming, and I was a nerd."

"Ray Baltagio? So, what D'Juan said is true. My father is the son of a crime lord?" I shook my head, remembering Langston's warning. "He told me it was complicated. Why didn't anyone tell me that you're not my father?! Why make me come all the way out here just to look like a fool!?"

"Would you have come?" he asked. "Your mother must have been desperate. She needed you to have a reason to come. If you thought I was your father, curiosity would probably push you to make the trip. Which it did."

All my nerves and frustrations were turning into a hot, molten mix of lava directed at my mom. She knew I'd come. So did Langston.

Neither of them told me that Godfrey wasn't my father. Both of them knew. "The joke's on me," I said in a low voice. "And now I'm wanted for stealing and murder and God knows what else."

"You left a pretty clear trail," Godfrey said, reassuringly. "I don't think any of the charges will stick. Surveillance caught Danny several times too. Plus, I'm sure Ellie's story will collaborate with yours."

"It will."

"What did you come all the way out here for? What do you have to tell me?" Godfrey leaned forward, a perplexed expression on his face. "What about Baltagio?"

"There's a key that Mom took. I don't know why she took it, but it'll possibly implicate him. He knows she took it though, so she sent me to give it to you."

"What does the key do?"

"I don't know. Maybe it unlocks stolen money?"

"No, that wouldn't worry Baltagio." Godfrey rubbed his face again. "He's in a jam, especially with you being his ..."

I swallowed the hard lump that had formed in the back of my throat. "Grandson? This can't be happening."

"I need you to give me that key, so that we can investigate it."

The door opened, and another cop walked in. He set my duffel bag on the table. "Couldn't find anything."

"It's in the Children's Bible," I said. "Mom knew I wouldn't want to part with that one."

Godfrey found the Bible and flipped through it. "I don't find anything." He handed it to me.

Last night, D'Juan took off, leaving both my bag and Ellie's along the sidewalk. I didn't even have to look. Of course, the key would be gone. D'Juan had no intention of starting over. He only wanted to clear his name.

I flipped through the Bible one time, then set it down, and exhaled slowly.

"Where would it go? Is it in another book?"

"No." I refused to give him D'Juan's name. Even with him betraying me, I couldn't find it within myself to give up his name again. "Someone must have found it and taken it."

"I don't know how to tell you this, but without that key, we've got nothing on Baltagio."

"I know." I stared at my Children's Bible and wondered where in the world D'Juan went with that key.

Chapter Sixteen: Ellie

The Deal

I sat on the bench outside the police station, holding the key in my hand and feeling like puking. "You can do this," I said, opening my hand to stare at the key. I closed my hand quickly then searched the parking lot.

He said he'd be here. The longer he took, the greater the chance Jamison would find out. And he couldn't. It was bad enough that my heart knew I was betraying him, but if he ever discovered the deal I had made, he'd never forgive me.

A motorcycle zoomed into the parking lot and stopped right in front of me. The helmet was tinted dark, and I couldn't make out who it was. "Two blocks from here is a park. Find the picnic table across from the pond." He zoomed away before I could say anything.

I glanced back at the police station. This was it. Jamison wouldn't understand, but this was for the best. This would end the running. Both of us would be free from these bad guys. It had taken me until now to make the decision.

As I walked the two blocks to the park, I thought of my conversation with D'Juan at the first gas station. He'd waited for me outside the bathroom. After Jamison left us to go order some food, D'Juan handed me a card with a number.

"Think about it," he said. "Baltagio wants that key. He'll do anything for it. Anything. You can either keep running or you can make a deal."

I had shoved the card in my pocket, unwilling to even consider it. Until I knew that Danny was still alive. And Jamison was wanted for murder. At the police station, no one recognized me as a runaway. That meant my mother hadn't yet reported me. That had been my luck turning. When I got my phone call, I dialed the number.

"Make it all go away," I said to the guy on the other end. "I want Jamison left alone, and I want to be left alone."

"Deal. Bring the key outside. Wait for instructions."

I found the park and pond easy enough. Across the street, a tall, slim man sat atop the park bench, his feet resting on the bench's seat. He had on a black leather jacket even though it had to be at least eighty degrees outside. He turned his head, spotted me, then turned back to look at the pond.

My stomach flipped, and my feet slowed.

"Do you have it?" he asked.

I nodded. "Who are you?"

"That's not important."

"Ray Baltagio?" I remembered D'Juan's explanation. This guy fit the description.

"And you're the girl that's betraying Jamison," he said simply, without looking at me. "Do you have it?"

"I'm not betraying him." Though it looked like I was. "I'm thinking about him. I don't want him to run anymore."

"You don't have to lie to me. I really don't care why you're giving me the key. Just so long as you give it to me."

"But I'm not lying." I sounded like I was pleading. Stopping myself, I sighed. Enough of this. I made my decision. "So, it's going to be over, right? We can stop running?" When he didn't say anything, I pushed again, "Right? That's the deal."

He stretched his legs to the ground, then stood up. As he approached me, I saw the gun tucked in his pants. I looked from the gun to his face. There was no warmth or any expression that would encourage me that he would honor the deal. I suddenly felt a strong sense of foreboding and wanted to kick myself for thinking that striking a bargain with a

Baltagio could change anything.

"Here's the thing, girlie," he said real low, closing the distance between us. "Didn't your mother ever teach you not to make a deal with the devil?"

I followed his gaze as he nodded to someone—or someones—behind me. Danny stepped out of a Charger. He was banged up, and when his eyes met mine, he communicated easily that I would pay for it. And there was no one to help me. I was on my own. My mind worked quickly.

I turned fast to face Ray. "Listen, I don't have any more time to give to this crap. We had a deal. You broke the deal. You don't get the key."

He grabbed both my upper arms in a death grip. I yelped. "You don't tell me what to do. Now give me the key or I'll take it, and trust me, I'll take a lot more than just the key."

"It's not on me," I lied. "Do you think I seriously trust you? Especially after everything Jamison told me? I came here to make the deal, but the key is elsewhere. And if you want it, you have to get rid of Danny." I tried to make my voice sound menacing and believable, and I hoped that he couldn't hear the shaking in it.

"How about you take me to the key or I'll kill you." He took out the gun and pressed it against my stomach.

"Then kill me. And you'll never see the key." I stared him down, scared with every fiber of my being. But I needed him to buy my story. I had messed up big time. If he didn't buy my story, Jamison would never know I was taken. My life would be over. And more than that, I would have handed the key right to Satan himself. No. I had to get away. "Get. Rid. Of. Danny," I said through gritted teeth.

"Really?" he said with a sinister smirk. "A good girl like you wants me to what? Kill him?"

I hesitated. Is that what I wanted? But my hesitation cost me. He grabbed my arm and started pulling me to Danny. Knowing that I had to do something, I began to yank my arm from him and scream at the top of my lungs. There were a few people who littered the area but they were too far from us. I didn't care. I screamed for all I was worth, then

I kept screaming, "Help! Help! I'm being kidnapped!"

He slammed me against a tree so hard, I saw stars. "Shut up," he hissed.

But I pushed against him and brought up my knee as hard as I could. He swore and fell to his knees, as I moved to take off.

"Stay put or I'll put a bullet in your back," Danny said beside me.

"Never!" I yelled, running with all that I had. I braced myself for the bullet, ducking my head as I ran. He'd have to shoot at me because his leg was all bandaged up, so he couldn't chase me. "Help!" I screamed again.

Observers stopped and watched me warily.

"They're bad guys!" I yelled. "Help!"

I made it to the street. Only a couple blocks to the police station.

A black SUV pulled in front of me. The back door flung open.

"Grab her," someone ordered.

An ugly man with a face full of scars pulled me into the SUV as if I weighed nothing at all. He shoved me in the back cargo area, and I landed sloppily on top of a badly injured man. I pushed off him, apologizing and trying not to be grossed out. His face was a mangled mess. Both eyes swollen shut and black-and-blue with open wounds on his forehead, mouth, and left cheek. Oddly he wore a suit with a large Bart Simpson tie. The shirt had been ripped though and the tie hung at an angle.

The man with the scars on his face grabbed my shirt and pulled me to him. "Where's the key? I'm only asking once."

I couldn't hesitate again. "I left it back at the police station. I wanted to see if Baltagio could be trusted first. Obviously, he can't. So, no key. At least until his side of the deal is fulfilled."

"Search her," the older man in the front passenger seat said.

The scarred man slapped me with the back of his hand, and the right side of my face exploded in pain.

"Don't hurt the girl!" The injured guy in the suit pleaded. "It's unnecessary."

"One more word out of you and your brains will be plastered inside this car."

"No, they won't," the man from the front said. "This is a rental. No more blood in the car. Now search her."

I kicked and punched and screamed while the man's large hands roughly felt me up. "It's hard to search her in here," he growled. "Can you drive straight?"

"We've got company," the driver said. "It's that Charger."

"Just get us to the location. We'll take care of her there," the older man in the passenger seat said.

The ugly man left me alone, turning to face the front. I sat up. I must have been kicking the already injured man sitting on the floor of the SUV.

"Sorry," I whispered, removing my feet from his lap and bringing my knees up. I rested my head against my knees. This turned out horribly. The guy in the park—Ray Baltagio, probably—had it right. What did I expect? That making a deal with the devil would be fair? Now I was in serious danger. One group would stop at nothing to get the key, which luckily, I had tucked into my sock at the bottom of my foot, and the other group would stop at nothing to have me. Obviously, my plan of giving the one group what they wanted didn't turn out too well.

"Are you all right?" the man across from me asked.

I lifted my head and studied him. What had he done to be hurt so badly? Beneath the blood and bruises, he appeared to be a normal type of middle-aged man. His question brought everything to the surface of my emotions, so I merely shook my head then rested it on my knees again. My eyes welled up with tears, but I couldn't show any of these people. I couldn't be weak. I didn't want anyone else to know what a huge mistake I had made.

"How's Jamison?" he whispered.

His question caught my attention. "How do you know?"

"I'm Mr. Langston," he said so low I had to lean forward to hear him.

My mouth fell open and tears threatened again. Oh no! Jamison would be so upset if he knew that Mr. Langston was hurt.

"Hey! No talking!" The scarred man pointed a gun at both of us.

"What do you want me to do about the Charger?" the driver asked the old guy.

"Let him follow us. He only wants the girl."

The SUV maneuvered in and out of traffic so much that it didn't help my already nervous stomach. I feared Danny more than this bunch, but with Mr. Langston all beat up across from me, my fear was becoming equally distributed. More than fear, I felt anger. Mostly at myself. I was safe in the police station, but no, I had to try to fix things on my own. Why didn't I give the key to the police? Why did I take it in the first place? It was Jamison's, and now, when he found out, he would never speak to me again.

Because of my stupid decision, I was on my own with a bunch of criminals.

For the briefest of moments, I thought of home. Not the trailer where my mom would flop on the couch with her cigarettes and bag of chips, but my room. My bedroom was home to me. I'd lock myself in there and chat with Lauren via text or Facebook or Snapchat. I'd curl up in my bed and read whenever I wasn't working. Before Billy died we'd cook together. Spaghetti was our favorite. But home wasn't home if Hank had come back. To make it worse, I couldn't seem to escape him. Somehow, he had followed me, or at least his debts. Would I ever have a home again? A place where I could relax and kick off my shoes? Where I wouldn't have to worry about someone's motives or whether or not they were chasing me or out to hurt me.

Eventually, the SUV pulled off the expressway and slowed. Judging from the trees outside, we weren't in the city anymore.

Where are we going? I mouthed to Mr. Langston.

Motel, he mouthed back. *In the middle of nowhere.*

My heart sank even farther. No one would find me out here. If Jamison did come looking, he'd have no idea where I was. I closed my eyes tight and willed myself not to cry, but the tears didn't listen.

Okay, Ellie, stop and figure this out. You don't have Jamison to rely on.

I glanced around the SUV and wondered if I could escape. Mr.

Langston's hands and ankles were tied. Mine, however, weren't. They must have forgotten to do that when they grabbed me and threw me back here. The only problem was that Danny followed them. If I managed to open the hatch and jump out. I'd either get run over, or Danny would come after me. Then again, he couldn't run. His one foot had been badly hurt. Did he have someone with him? Yes, he had Ray. Somehow it made sense that they were together. But why would Ray Baltagio be with Danny and not his father?

If I jumped, I'd have a shot of getting away. Once they stopped at the motel, who knew what they'd do to me. The SUV slowed to a stop. Panic bubbled in me. I had to make a decision. I still had the key in my sock. They'd find it. I'm sure their search would be thorough.

Maybe I could hide it here in the car. But how would I get it back?

I'd run out of options. They were pulling into the motel. No one had checked on me in a while. If I was going to hide the key I'd have to do it now.

I eased the key out of my shoe. I tried to make sure not to get Mr. Langston's attention. At this point, I wasn't sure I trusted anyone but Jamison. And I had shot that relationship right through the heart.

Finding a slight tear in the carpet near the backseat, I worked on it enough to fit the key. I had to move fast because the SUV had stopped. I forced myself to keep my cool as I shoved the key into the tiny tear in the carpet.

The hatch opened and the old man himself pulled me out. It was now or never.

"We had a deal, Mr. Baltagio." From his tailored suit to the meticulous way he was groomed, it could be none other than Baltagio himself. "You get the key if you leave me and Jamison alone. Why can't you just follow the deal?"

"Nothing's going to happen to Jamison. He's family, after all." He seemed to watch me for a reaction, then he smiled. "Oh, you didn't know?"

"Gil Godfrey is his father." I refrained from asking how Baltagio had a black son. It seemed a moot point.

He chuckled. "One look at the guy we sent, and Jamison will know."

"The guy you sent? You're tricking him?"

Mr. Baltagio laughed in my face. "Look at you. All upset over a little trick. Honey, just wait. I can do a lot worse."

Danny's Charger pulled up to us. "Please don't make me go with Danny. Please. Jamison is my friend. He would be upset if he knew you let Danny take me."

"Why's that?"

"Because Jamison has spent this entire time protecting me from him."

"And yet, you so easily betray him." He stepped so close I could smell the mint on his breath. "I tire of women who turn on their men. Women who know no loyalty. If you think I'm going to do anything for you, then you are a very stupid girl."

"I'm not betraying him," I pleaded as Danny approached. "I thought if I gave you the key that you could help us stop the madness."

"You are a liar," he said. "You thought only of yourself. Be honest. You want me to handle Danny so that you can go your way."

The truth stung, but it wasn't entirely the truth. I really had thought about Jamison. But the time had come for me to switch tactics. "If you give me to him, then you'll never get that key."

"Yes," he said. "I will."

Ray Baltagio approached with Danny. "What are we gonna do with the girl?"

"We're going to search her thoroughly, and if need be, we'll persuade her." The dangerous glint in Baltagio's eyes let me know that their means of persuasion wouldn't be pleasant. "Ray, take one of the vehicles back to that park. When Jamison's released, that's where he'll go looking. Bring him to me."

"Done."

I watched Ray leave and would have done anything to warn Jamison.

"Don't mess her up too much," Danny said, bringing me back to the situation.

"No one tells me what to do," Baltagio said. "You get her when I get the key." To the scar-faced man, he said, "Take her to one of the rooms. Not Langston's. We're not done with him either."

"Mr. Baltagio," I tried one last time. "Please, I'll tell you everything. Don't do this."

"On that, we agree," he said. "You *will* tell me everything."

Chapter Seventeen: Jamison

An Unexpected Truth

For being in an interrogation room and feeling betrayed by D'Juan, I slept hard with my head resting on my arms on the table. I didn't hear the door open, and it took me a minute to fully awaken from someone shaking my shoulder.

"I thought you might be hungry." Godfrey handed me a ham sandwich in a plastic container and a can of Coke.

I rubbed my face and stretched out my neck and shoulders. "Thanks." I opened the can of soda and taking a swig.

"Sorry that took so long." He sat across from me again.

"How long has it been?"

He glanced at his watch. "Not quite two hours. You were knocked out for most of it."

"Yeah, I didn't sleep too great last night." I peeled open the plastic wrapping and bit into the sandwich.

"I contacted Detroit police. They're going to let your mother know you're okay."

"Mom? How do they know where she is?"

"She was taken into a rehab facility from the jail."

"Wait. Backtrack a second, my mother is still in police custody? Nobody came and got her?"

"Technically, she's in the custody of the rehab facility."

"Mr. Langston told me someone had signed her out of the jail." I took a deep breath and exhaled in relief. "So, she's all right?"

"From the sound of it."

I allowed the news to sink in. Why would Mr. Langston lie to me? Either he wasn't as squeaky clean as I thought, or they had already got to him.

"I got you cleared of all charges."

I stopped eating and raised my eyebrows. "You did? How?"

He shrugged. "You're innocent on most counts. The car theft wasn't too bright, but with some finagling, I got the girl from the gas station not to press charges."

"Thank you." Relief poured through me.

"We want to catch the bad guys too," he said. "Unfortunately, you got on their radar. So did that girlfriend of yours."

"Ellie? How is she? Can I see her?" We'd already been separated for a couple hours. I hoped she was okay.

"She's gone."

"Gone? Where?"

"We were hoping you could tell us. She was released a couple hours ago, and she made a phone call. She was observed walking to the local park a couple streets from here. Observers have come in to report that she was screaming for help and being chased. We've got a good look at two of the vehicles, but we're hoping you might have some info to help find her."

"She was screaming for help?" My stomach tightened. "What happened? Who was the phone call to?"

"I don't know. We traced it to this number." He gave me a sheet of paper with the number on it. "Look familiar?"

"No. But it's a Detroit area code."

"Exactly. And the number's dead. We're thinking she contacted Baltagio. Is that a possibility?"

"No."

"Then who would it be? She's not from Detroit, right?"

"I don't know." I stared at the number and tried to figure out what she had done. It didn't make sense. This was the girl who came right to me and begged me to pretend to know her. The same girl who was afraid of mice and wanted to sleep with the light on. She was alone. So, who would she call?

"The fact that the number is disconnected is a major red flag. Jamison, are you sure that she didn't work for Baltagio?"

The last piece of ham sandwich stuck in my throat. I coughed hard and swallowed the last of the soda. I shook my head. "There's no way she worked for him."

"You sure?"

"Yeah, I'm sure." Yet, I was upset at how unsure I was becoming. "I saw Danny try to take her. I know that she was scared. I saw it in her eyes. None of it adds up if she worked for Baltagio. She was in the motel alone with me. Why not take the key then?"

"So, it's possible she has the key?"

"She didn't take it."

"Are you positive?"

"My gut tells me it wasn't her. Ellie wouldn't have known what to do with the key. Plus, she wouldn't do that."

"She wouldn't give the key to Baltagio? She wouldn't try to make a deal?"

I paused, unsure of an answer. "Didn't you say that she was screaming in the park? That should show you that she wasn't a bad guy. She's obviously in some serious trouble."

"I can see that," Godfrey said. "What I don't understand is why she would walk to the park on her own accord and talk to them. Whoever 'they' are."

"All of this is confusing."

"I've been in this business for a long time, and I know a deal when I see one. Jamison, I think your girlfriend went to that park to make a deal. Something went sour, and now she's in serious danger."

The door opened and the older guy from before stepped inside. "A blue Charger and black Acadia were spotted going southwest on 35, taking exit 67. There's a motel over twenty miles away, a good distance off the highway. Unusual activity has been reported."

"Let's move." Godfrey stood up.

"The charges are dropped, right? So, am I free to go?"

"Release him," Godfrey said to the other guy. To me, he said, "Don't go far."

"I don't have a car to go anywhere."

Godfrey left, and the other guy uncuffed my wrist and led me back to the sitting area of the station. "Make sure to sign out before you step outside."

I went to the counter and signed out. They handed me my duffel bag. "Thanks."

Not knowing what else to do, I walked out the doors and watched as a set of cop cars zoomed out of the parking lot. I didn't understand why Ellie would meet with anyone, but I knew she wasn't working for Baltagio. At least, I was pretty sure.

None of it changed the fact that I was worried. No telling what any of them would do to her. My heart hurt at the thought of all the times my mom had been abused. She never talked about it with me, but I could see. And I could hear her crying in the bathroom.

I didn't want that for Ellie.

I also had no idea what I was going to do about it.

Godfrey might have cleared me of all charges, but I didn't think he would be too happy if I stole another car.

I walked out of the parking lot and onto the sidewalk, then paused, feeling like I was being watched. I scanned the area, not finding anyone around. Across the street, a guy sat on a motorcycle—well, it was more like a dirt bike—looking at his phone through his helmet visor. Why would he keep his helmet on?

"You're jumpy, man." I headed in the opposite direction toward the park. Maybe someone was still there, or there was some clue. Mostly, I needed to do something. Standing around wasn't going to cut it.

Once at the park, I began searching for a clue or anything out of the ordinary. But I didn't know what I was looking for, which didn't help. A car door shut near me, and I glanced up at a tall, lean black man who I'd seen before. I squinted and tried to place him. I knew him. With sunglasses on, he made it difficult for me to place him.

Maybe I should have run, but curiosity won out.

As he approached, I remembered the man who lived with us while we were in the trailer. He'd show up off and on until we were evicted for not paying rent. *Him.*

"Ray?" I asked, putting the pieces together. "Ray Baltagio."

"Hello, son." He said the word in disgust.

The truth fell at my feet like a heavy brick. Of course, my father wouldn't be a police officer, fighting crime, doing good, helping save people. Nope. My father would have to be a criminal. Someone who got my mom hooked on a lot of bad drugs. Suddenly, I became angry. Just once I wanted a fair shake. I didn't even bother greeting him. "Where's Ellie?"

"The girl who was trying to cut a deal?" He tilted his head. "The pretty one with the long, dark hair under a baseball cap? The one with the key?"

I opened my mouth to say something, but nothing came out.

"Yeah, she showed up," he said. "She called and said she wanted to meet and make a deal. She'd give us the key if we gave her money and got rid of some guy named Danny."

"No." I told myself not to believe it. "She would never do that."

"How well do you know her?" Ray approached me, but I didn't feel nervous. Even with the gun in plain sight, nervousness had left the building. "You just met her, right?"

I didn't answer. What could I say? I didn't know her very well.

"Listen, don't feel bad. Girls do crazy things when they're desperate."

"You're lying. I know it. She wouldn't do that. I was helping her."

"You know it's the truth, Jamison. You know that's where the police are headed. You know because you're here searching for answers."

I swallowed hard, trying to steady my breathing. I told myself it didn't hurt. I told myself that I should be glad to be rid of her. I told myself that Mom shouldn't have forced me to have the key. It wasn't my responsibility.

"Just leave me alone!" I snapped and started to leave.

"You have a right to be upset, man. That's why I took care of her.

Nobody messes with you. Nobody."

I stopped and turned around, my heart betraying my anger. "Y-You took care of her? What do you mean?"

"Don't worry about it. I'm here to take you home. I got my father to swear that he'll leave you alone. He just wanted that key. Your mother should have never taken it. That woman's gonna get herself killed one of these days if she don't watch it."

My head spun. He was throwing so much at me, I didn't know what to respond to first. *Answers. Get answers.* "What's with the key?" I decided to start there. "Why would Mom take it, and why did Baltagio's bodyguard point a gun at us?"

"I took her to a party, and my dad threw a fit. He doesn't like your mother. Sorry." He shrugged. "But we weren't gonna stay there long. Just until, you know, the good stuff got handed out."

I could feel the heat rise to my face. Mostly embarrassment. Did Mom realize this is what people thought about her?

"Then my wife showed up to the party, which surprised me, so Claire went to go hide. My wife don't like your mother."

"I get it. No one likes my mom," I said, more embarrassed than ever.

"I guess your mother overheard some business my dad was doing in his office. I'm not going to go into it, but she saw my father pocket the key."

"What's it for? Money? Weapons? What's the big deal about this stupid key?!" My voice rose with each question.

Ray stepped close. "I'm going to tell you because you're going to be one of us anyway. You might as well know. Counterfeit," he said real low. "Okay? Now lower your voice."

"So, the key could implicate your father?"

"Technically, your grandfather. Would you want him in prison?"

"What do I care?" All of it seemed off. Ray couldn't be my actual father. I was expecting some kind of connection. Something. But all I got were a lot of red flags going off in my mind. I felt as if I were still in the game. And they were playing with me.

"How 'bout a little respect? I kept you out of stuff for years, but I think it's time we come together. Father and son."

I scoffed and stepped back. "I don't have a father. I was raised by a single, drug-addicted mother—thanks to you—who ran me from one motel to another. And every time she tried to get better, who always showed up with more drugs? Somehow, I have a feeling it was you. While you got to go home to your wife and eat your dinner, I got to hunt down meals in restaurant dumpsters or steal food from stores. What kind of father does that?"

"Listen, I don't have time for this. Baltagio wants you there now."

"Is Ellie there? Could I see her?"

"Does it matter? That girl had no problem making the deal. She only started singing a different tune when she saw that Danny guy approach. Besides Baltagio's not gonna release either one of them. I'm sorry, kid, but you need to forget about 'em."

"Them? Who else is there?"

"You need to stop asking questions. I'm tired of playing this little game of pretend, all for you to give us the key." He reached for me.

I twisted away. "Who?"

"We need to go." He grabbed my arm. "If you make a scene, it won't end well. I promise."

"Who?" I shouted and yanked my arm from his grip.

"Walk with me, Jamison. Or else."

"Or else what?" I asked. "You gonna kill me? Do it. I don't care anymore. I'm done with this. All of it. So, if you want any cooperation from me, answer the question!"

"Langston," he hissed. "That guy had it coming, and you know it. He's been egging us on for a while now. But we got the last laugh. That's how we found you. Followed that idiot over here. He started singing like a canary the minute we busted his jaw."

"Mr. Langston?" My stomach rolled. "What's he ever done to you?"

"Don't worry about it. Now I told you. Let's go."

"What's gonna happen to him?" I thought of all the times he tried to help me. All the times he'd show up just to check in. And I'd treated him like garbage for most of it. And now, when he traveled to Minnesota to help me, he would suffer.

"That guy's annoying and a pain to most of the southside."

I might have been confused about Ellie, but not Mr. Langston. I knew what I had to do. "Yeah, I guess you're right," I said, hoping he'd buy it. "I just want to get out of here. Are we flying out?"

"You and me are gonna drive back. There's too much security at airports for me. I'm wanted on a few charges."

As we walked closer to the car, I knew I had to make my move. "Where'd they take them anyway? They gonna throw them over a bridge or something? I mean, I hope they treat them okay. They're not bad people."

"They know too much. And don't worry about where they went."

"Fine. I'll figure it out without your help." As soon as the words were out of my mouth, I swung my heavy duffel bag, loaded with my books, as hard as I could at him. He stumbled back, so I used the moment to shove him the rest of the way on the ground.

But he was quick. Too quick. He maneuvered himself fast, throwing me off of him. I tried to roll away, but he snatched my shirt and, holding me in place, pinned me to the ground.

I would have continued to fight, but he pulled out his gun and pointed it right at my head. "Stupid move, son."

Anger still licked my insides like flames from an uncontained fire. I spat in his face. "I'm not your son."

"No, you're not. You're some pathetic kid who needs to die."

"Go for it. Especially if you think I'd ever go anywhere with you voluntarily."

"I can't kill you here. But as soon as we're alone, you'll pay." Ray went to pull me up when someone from behind him knocked him across the head with a dead tree limb. Ray's gun skittered across the pavement.

He fell to the side, and I was staring at the guy in the motorcycle helmet. "We need to leave. Now."

I scrambled off the ground, grabbed my duffel bag, and on a whim, grabbed Ray's gun. I pocketed it and turned to follow the motorcycle guy.

It was then I saw him limping to the dirt bike. A limp on the left side, heavy on the right side. Trying to make it look like a saunter.

Relief rushed through me as I ran after my friend.

Chapter Eighteen: Ellie

Caught in the Crossfire

The motel door slammed shut, leaving me with Baltagio and the scar-face guy. Baltagio approached me slowly. I'd like to say I held my ground, but I inched backward, trying to keep my distance.

"I'm done playing cat-and-mouse," he said. "Give me the key."

"Keep the deal." I forced myself to act brave.

His left hand shot forward and back-slapped me so hard that my head hit the wall. Pain shot through the side of my face. I brought my hand up protectively and felt the trickle of blood on my cheek. I also tasted blood, and my tongue throbbed from biting down on it accidentally.

"I'm not going to say it again," he said.

When I didn't respond fast enough, he yanked off my ball cap and snatched my hair. I yelped as he pulled. "Don't forget how expendable you are." He dragged me to the chair by the window. He shoved me down, telling the other guy, "Tie her up."

I kicked and scratched, trying to maneuver myself away from his hands. He was built like a freight train and not easily deterred.

He yanked my arms and shoved them behind the chair, tying them tightly. I kicked and screamed at Baltagio, but my legs only kicked air as Baltagio watched me with a sick smile on his face. Scarface grabbed my flailing legs and duck taped my ankles. By the time he finished, sweat poured off me from the exertion while he didn't even seem fazed.

"Elvis, Elvis, Elvis," Baltagio said. "What a horrible name to give a girl. It screams 'white trash,' doesn't it?" He sat on the bed beside me. "And then your desperate, chain-smoking, chip-eating, couch-sitting mother chooses a felon over her own daughter. What a sad life you've lived."

I refused to look at him. I stared straight ahead and focused on not letting his words hit their target.

"I could kill you right here and right now, and no one would care. No one's looking for you. Your mother's relieved you're not home." He leaned forward and whispered, "There's no competition for Hank's affection with you gone."

I swallowed hard and tried to keep my breathing even, but it was becoming more difficult. Memories flooded through my mind. Ones I had hidden. Now, here with these bad men, the memories roared back like a hungry lion ready to devour my sanity.

"Here's what's going to happen. Leo here is going to search you. Thoroughly. When he finds the key, I'll send that Danny character in to finish you off."

As he made his way to the door, my tears couldn't be contained any more. "Why?"

"Why what?"

"Why are you such a bad person?" I didn't raise my voice. I didn't even look at him. "There's a special place in hell for people like you."

Baltagio smirked. "And I'll rule there too." He slammed the door behind him.

Suddenly Scarface had his hands all over me, running them up and down my body. "You won't find it on me."

I gritted my teeth to endure the worst. After everything with Hank, I should've been used to a man's uninvited hands all over me. But it felt dirty. Every. Single. Time. "Please God, please, please, please." The word grew in intensity as the search continued.

"Keep begging. I like it."

A car backfired outside. At least I thought it was a backfire, but Scarface stopped feeling me up and shot his gaze toward the window. Fear and urgency flashed across his ugly face. Then the door burst open and he jerked his head to the two men storming inside, guns drawn.

For a second, a surge of hope filled me. Maybe Jamison or the police found me. But then I recognized them. This wasn't a rescue. These were Danny's men.

Just as Scarface reached for his gun, a gunshot exploded in the air. Scarface fell on top of me, his blood splattering my face and soaking my shirt.

With my arms tied behind me, I could do nothing but gag and choke on the bile rushing up my throat. I screamed and squirmed but couldn't get the dead man off me.

The two men who entered the room dragged him away. I trembled, my entire body shaking in fear and horror. Scarface's blood was still wet, sticking to my skin.

Danny entered the room, took one look at me, and said, "Get her washed up. And hurry. The owner might have contacted the police before you killed him."

One of the men wet a washrag in the bathroom sink and roughly wiped at my face, scraping painfully where Baltagio slapped me. The other one did the same thing. I pressed my lips together in pain.

"What about her shirt. It's covered in it."

"Take it off her. We can't have any blood in the car."

Without releasing me, one of them cut my shirt off with a knife, revealing the tank top over my bra.

Danny grabbed my hat, limped over to me, and placed it on my head. "There," he said. "Good as new."

"Are they all dead?" My voice wavered.

"I was tired of waiting around," he said. "Besides we have a score to settle, and I always get what's mine. Get her to the car."

"Can you untie me?"

"No. Nice try."

"We gotta loosen her wrists. She's tied tight around the chair."

Danny exhaled in impatience. "Fine. Just free her hands. I don't want her running."

One of the men pulled me up and led me to the door. Outside

a couple bodies lay dead on the ground. My stomach rolled. I could still smell Scarface's blood. I could still feel it splatter against my face. Suddenly I became violently ill. I bent over and puked until all I could do was dry heave.

Death hung in the air, and it chilled me to my core.

"Come on," Danny ordered, pushing me out of the way.

My knees gave out, and I fell to the ground. I couldn't get in that car. I'd rather them kill me.

Just as one of them pulled me up, another gunshot pierced through the air. I screamed and fell back to my knees, holding my hands over my head.

A body hit the ground behind me. I slowly turned to see Danny down. In the midst of my terror, I almost felt relief.

"I can't let you leave." Baltagio said. Two more gunshots.

I screamed and cowered to the ground again. The men beside me fell with a solid thud.

Dead. Nearly everyone dead.

"Get up," Baltagio ordered. "Change of plans. Get in the SUV. I'll be right there."

He staggered to one of the other motel rooms, holding his right side. So, he had been shot. He paused and reloaded his gun. Then I remembered.

Mr. Langston.

I had made a terrible mistake with trying to make a deal. I would probably never see Jamison again. But I had to do this for him. He couldn't lose the one person he trusted the most.

I hastily tried to loosen the tape around my ankles, but even with Baltagio moving slow, I couldn't take any more time.

Finding my balance, I stood up and started shimmying toward him. He was nearly at the door.

Almost there.

He opened the door and stepped inside. He raised his gun.

Baltagio must have seen me out of the corner of his eye, but before he could aim at me, I threw myself at him, toppling both of us to the floor. The gun went off, but it fell from his hands. I rammed my elbow into his side, and he howled. But he was a tough, full-size man, and even with a wound, he overpowered me.

In seconds I was pinned. Suddenly Baltagio's gun pressed against my forehead. "I'll figure out another way to get the key."

I closed my eyes, said a prayer, my last thoughts of Jamison.

Chapter Nineteen: Jamison

The Great Escape

D'Juan moved in and out of traffic, flying by vehicles. I held on and tucked my head down. Without a helmet, I had already swallowed a few bugs.

As we whipped past our surroundings, I tried to put the pieces together.

Why would D'Juan be here? How'd he even know where I was at?

Because he was working for Baltagio.

I knew it, and I wanted to be angry. Did he tell them where we were? Did he try to convince Ellie that she needed to make a deal? All of these questions were even more confusing because he had once again protected me.

Unless he was taking me to Baltagio himself.

I might have considered ditching D'Juan. Somehow fall off the bike, but Ellie was in serious danger. It stung that she took the key and set up a deal, but I couldn't walk away. Not now. Besides, I needed to get that key back. My mom still needed help.

D'Juan took an exit and slowed down. I glanced up. There wasn't much around. Still, I studied signs and scenery to make sure I remembered the location. He turned right and zoomed down a small two-lane road. Several miles in, he made a left down a dirt path, zigging and zagging through thick trees.

Finally, he slowed to a stop and took off the helmet. "Help me push this in the trees, so no one sees it."

I helped only because I was at a temporary loss of words. We moved the dirt bike into the trees. D'Juan rested it against a dead log.

Then he faced me. "You okay?"

"Cleveland, huh?" I asked, ignoring his question. "Got some auntie? Got a place to start fresh?"

"I do," he said. "My auntie lives in Cleveland, but going there's not an option."

"Why not?" When he didn't answer, I pressed, "Why not?"

"You know why!" he said. "I'm sorry, man. I would have told you, but I couldn't."

"The whole time?" I asked. "The whole time you were working for Baltagio?"

"After Pastor Steve died."

"Leaving one gang for another? That's not moving up or out."

"I had to leave the reds. My own brother killed my pastor. At least with Baltagio, if I keep my head down and do his running, I have the gangs off my back."

"And if you stop doing his running?"

"Like I said, I don't have that option."

"So, why didn't you just take me to him? Why travel all the way here only to ditch us at a gas station?"

"Because for a little while, I wanted to believe that we could run. The accident was unexpected. Shazz's death was unexpected. None of that was planned. Baltagio said that if we brought you back, we'd each get ten grand, and Shazz could keep you."

"And you were cool with that?"

"No, man. I was gonna wait for a moment to get rid of Shazz. I didn't want you in a gang. I thought maybe I could convince you to work with me. Seeing that Baltagio's your family and all."

"Stop," I said. "He's not my family. You saw what Ray was willing to do to me. Family doesn't do that."

We paused for a moment.

"There's one more thing," D'Juan said quietly.

"What is this? Confession?"

"Yeah, sort of. I don't think I'm gonna make my twentieth birthday after all."

"Don't say that." I might have been hurt and angry, but I didn't want to think of him dying.

"Let me get this off my chest. I gave Ellie the number. I told her that Baltagio would make a deal. I didn't know if she would do it. And …"

"There's more?" No longer able to look at him, I turned to face the trees. I would have been more freaked out about being in some creepy forest if it wasn't for everything else going on.

"I'm the one who told Baltagio that Mr. Langston was coming to Minnesota to help you. I told him about Godfrey too. I'm not sure about Godfrey, but chances are Langston's dead."

"You betrayed Mr. Langston?" I turned back to face him, clenching my fists at the thought of Mr. Langston suffering because of me.

"Jamison, I'm sorry."

"What did you *do*?" I yelled, shoving him so hard he fell back. I jumped on him and started swinging my fists. "What did you do to him?"

"I'm trying to make it right!" he yelled while trying to block my punches.

"Make it right? You *caused* this!"

Suddenly, D'Juan pulled out a gun and pointed it to my chest. "Get off me!" he hissed.

"You gonna shoot me now? Might as well. You already betrayed me."

"No, I just wanted you off of me." D'Juan stood and brushed himself off. "I'm here to help. I'm done. It's not gonna end well for me, but I'll deal with it. I don't want to betray you anymore. When I saw you leave the police station, I wanted to grab you right then, but I kept talking myself out of it. It wasn't until I saw Ray nearly pull the trigger that I knew I could never live with myself if I didn't make this right."

"You just aimed a glock at me!"

"I wasn't going to shoot! I needed you to stop hitting me!"

"Whatever. I don't have time for this. Somehow, I gotta find Ellie and now I gotta worry even more about Mr. Langston. And then there's my mom, but at least she's in rehab."

"No, she's not," D'Juan said with a sigh. "Baltagio has Judge Blackwell in his pocket. He's going to throw the book at her for a long list of charges. Some true, most not true. She's going to prison, Jamison."

Any words halted in my mouth, as I stepped back. Mom? In prison? "So, all this for nothing," I said to myself.

"Listen, we're here because the motel is not far. We have to go on foot because they'll hear the engine. We have to move now if there's any chance of helping Ellie or Mr. Langston."

I nodded, still in shock.

D'Juan reached for me, but I jerked away.

"I was only trying to lead you north. That's the direction we're headed."

"Don't touch me, and don't ever speak to me again. As soon as this is all over, consider yourself dead to me." I pushed past him in the direction he indicated.

Anger ripped through me, leaving my heart in pieces. I would have collapsed right there and wallowed in it, but I had no time. Two people might be dead because of me. And because of my double-crossing, two-faced friend. And Mom? In prison? I didn't know what to believe anymore.

"Why help me now?" Not stopping, I moved through the terrain, shoving aside branches and brush. I even picked up a large, heavy limb and used it for beating the crap out of anything in my path.

"I'm trying to do the right thing," D'Juan said from beside me.

"Oh, shut up! I even gave you all my money."

"I'll give it back."

"*Shut up!*"

We moved through the woods until my feet got sore. Then we kept going.

"How far away is this place?" That's when I heard the gunfire. "Ellie!"

"Jamison, wait! We need a plan!"

More gunfire.

Soon the trees thinned, and I saw the scene in front of me. Ellie was on her knees, holding her head down. Bodies littered the ground.

Then I saw Baltagio. Fury erupted as I went to run toward him.

D'Juan stepped in front of me. "Don't be stupid, or you're dead. What's the plan?"

Ellie got up and wobbled toward Baltagio. It looked like her legs were tied.

I shoved D'Juan aside. "Get out of my way!"

Another gunshot didn't stop me from running. "Not Ellie," I prayed, my fist clinched around the limb as I pumped my legs. "Please."

In the room, Baltagio sat on top of Ellie, his gun drawn. I lifted the limb and slammed it against Baltagio's head. He fell to the side of Ellie. I hit him again in the head.

"Jamison!" Ellie cried, getting up and throwing her arms around me.

"We need to leave," I told her.

"My legs are taped up."

I tried to rip the duck tape off, but rage, fear, and adrenaline made my hands quake. If only the police hadn't confiscated my knife.

"Here," D'Juan said from behind me.

I took his knife and cut through the thick tape. I tried not to look at Ellie's face. Her one side was badly bruised with a fat lip. She had blood spots all over her cap and shoulders.

"Are you okay?" I asked, trying to keep my emotions together.

"I am now." She wrapped her arms around my neck again. "I'm so sorry, Jamison." She began to cry. "I was trying to make a deal. I thought I could get them to leave us alone."

On the other side of the bed, D'Juan said, "We need to get Mr. Langston to a hospital."

"Mr. Langston!" I released Ellie and went over to D'Juan.

My social worker lay on the floor with hands and legs tied. His face was almost unrecognizable. "Mr. Langston," I whispered, kneeling beside him. "I'm here, and I'm gonna get you help."

One of his eyes fluttered open. "Jamison," he croaked. "You cut your hair." He closed his eyes and laid his head back. I checked his pulse while Ellie called 9-1-1.

"We better move," D'Juan said, going to the door. "Just in case Baltagio ain't done."

"Help me get Mr. Langston to a car," I said. "We've got to get him to a hospital."

"They said an ambulance will take around twenty minutes." Ellie came around the bed.

"We can't wait that long. Besides, do you want to be here with all these dead bodies? It's freaking me out."

"Tell me about it." She shuddered. "I will never be able to get this out of my memory."

"I'm sorry you had to experience it, but if you hadn't made the deal—"

"Yeah, I know." She kept her eyes down. "I've made a lot of dumb mistakes."

D'Juan grabbed Mr. Langston's legs. "We've all made mistakes. Now let's go."

We lifted him up and carried him outside. Mr. Langston moaned in pain.

"We're taking you to the hospital," I told him.

Ray Baltagio stepped around a SUV. "No, you're not."

"Are you serious?" Ellie said, acting annoyed. "How many criminals are left?"

"We're not setting him down," I said to Ray. "He needs a doctor."

Ray looked over at D'Juan. "What are you doing? Didn't you have a job to do?"

"Yeah, and I did it."

"So, you have the key?"

"Not on me, but yeah. Jamison had it the whole time."

Ellie and I exchanged a brief glance, both knowing that D'Juan was lying to cover for us.

"Where is it?"

"At the dirt bike. It's in the small backseat compartment. Don't worry. The bike's in the woods just south of here. I'll take you there, but first you need to come clean to Jamison."

Ray glared at D'Juan and reached for his pistol. "It's time I shut your mouth for good."

"Ray's not your father," D'Juan said to me. "That was the big plan. Tell you that you were a Baltagio, so that you would join us. But it's a lie."

Ray sneered. "You're dead."

Before I could process what D'Juan just admitted, Ellie yelled, "No!" She let go of Mr. Langston to face Ray, blocking D'Juan from the line of fire.

I caught Mr. Langston's right side before he hit the pavement. But he was heavy.

"I'm tired of this!" Ellie extended her arms as if protecting us from the line of fire. But her hands trembled giving away her fear. "Put the gun away! None of us deserve to be hurt. Or killed."

Ray now aimed the pistol at Ellie. "I get to decide that."

Suddenly D'Juan dropped Mr. Langston's feet and threw himself in front of Ellie right as Ray pulled the trigger.

The screaming I heard was my own. Without thinking, I set Mr. Langston down and tackled who I thought was my biological father. But I felt no guilt as I charged. I took him by surprise because we both fell to the ground. I started clawing, hitting, punching, kicking as if all of my frustrations, worry, fear, chose that moment to release themselves.

Ray hurled me off of him, tossing me on the ground and straddling me. "You need to learn some respect, boy." He spat out blood beside my head. "But you'll learn. I'll make you learn."

Ellie attacked him from behind, hitting his head with a rock. I lunged for the gun. Ray knocked Ellie off of him and moved toward me, but I pointed the pistol at his chest. "Game over."

"You gonna kill your old man?" A grim smile played on his lips.

"You're not my father." I pointed the gun at his thigh, closed my eyes, and pulled the trigger.

Ray collapsed to the ground, howling in pain. I shakily emptied the pistol of its bullets. Then I ran over to D'Juan, lying still on the ground. I checked his pulse. It was barely there. But the blood. It surrounded him.

"I'll check the cars and see if there's any keys in them." Ellie left me with my friend.

D'Juan opened his eyes briefly. "I told you I wouldn't live to see—"

"Stop it," I ordered, tears falling off of me and onto him. "You're not dying today."

"Pray for me," he whispered. "Father God, forgive me ..."

I closed my eyes and begged God for a miracle.

And that's when I heard the sirens.

I paced beside the police car.

"They sent us on a goose chase," the officer barked into the police CB. He dropped the device and slammed the door, then turned to me. "You okay?"

He checked me up and down. Patted my shoulders. I'd never met this officer, but he acted so worried for me that I couldn't respond. I could only blink back desperate tears and stare down the road. D'Juan and Mr. Langston had just been rushed by ambulance to some hospital, and I was stuck here.

"I'll be right back," the officer said and squeezed my shoulder. He paused to study me before going with another officer to question Ellie. Then they wanted to question me. Not sure why that couldn't happen *after* I made sure my best friend and social worker weren't dead, but I didn't get much of a say.

The only thing good about staying back was watching them drag both Baltagio men to another set of ambulances.

After that, I couldn't stomach anymore of the carnage, so I settled on pacing. And praying. I didn't know what else to do.

The kind police officer approached me. "Ellie told us where the key is hidden. So, it's over. How you holding up?"

"Not good," I said. "I need to get to the hospital."

"I know. I thought we could talk on the way."

I nodded in relief. "Yes, so we can go?"

"Give me a sec to inform the other men. They'll be taking Elvis."

"Why can't we go together?"

"You can be together in a little bit. We just have to question you separately. Standard procedure."

"Can I say good-bye? You can be there."

He paused as if to think, then turned and waved a police officer and Ellie over to us. When she reached me, she hugged me hard and began to sob. We held each other in front of the men, both highly traumatized and full of anguish.

"It's my fault," she finally said, not letting go.

I didn't know what to say. I wanted to tell her no, to not talk that way. But I couldn't. The fact is that I didn't know how I felt about any of this. It would have been easier if I had never met her, but I couldn't imagine never knowing her. I wrestled with feeling hurt at her actions while still caring so much about her. Too many conflicting emotions. So, instead I hugged her back.

As she released me, she whispered in my ear, "I gave them the key." She stepped back and added, "I guess they got ahold of my mom. So, I'll be going back home. At least for another couple weeks."

"What about Hank?"

"I told the police about his ties to Danny, and they're going to investigate all that. The police say that with our past, Hank will not be able to live anywhere near me."

"Like a restraining order?"

"Yeah, something like that." Her eyes welled up with tears. "If I would have only gone to the police to begin with, none of this would have happened."

Once again, I couldn't say anything. I looked down at my shoes.

"I know you blame me. At least partly, and I hope that you can forgive me someday."

"There's a lot of blame to go around," I finally said. "And now we can be free. From Danny. From Baltagio. Let's focus on that."

She nodded. "So, I guess this is good-bye?"

"Are you not going to the hospital?"

"No, they need me to go to the police station to fill out a complete report, then I'm being escorted home. I hope they'll be all right. If there's any way you can let me know …"

"At least you'll be safe." There was so much more I wanted to say to her. But I didn't know how to say it. Instead I shut the door to my heart and said to the officer, "Are you ready? I need to check on my friends."

Ellie opened her mouth to say something, then shook her head.

I walked away first. I slid into the back seat of the cop car and stared straight ahead. Too many emotions. Nothing logical. Nothing perfect.

As the police officer started the car, he said, "You know, she might have tried to make a deal with them, but from when Jenkins interviewed her, she could only speak of you. How you protected her. How you risked so much. Seems to me like you both are victims of horrible crime sagas, none of which is your fault. Nor is it hers."

I looked out the window and met Ellie's gaze. So much hurt and guilt stormed in her eyes. I wanted to tell her I didn't blame her. That I cared for her. That I couldn't imagine my life without her in it. That she had been the game-changer.

But the words never came, and we drove away.

Chapter Twenty: Ellie

All That Matters

It was done. Then why did I feel like my heart had been ripped out of my chest?

Danny might be dead, but I didn't feel as much relief as I thought I would. Seeing Jamison's distrust reminded me that things were changed between us. And that bothered me.

I sat in an interrogation room. The same room as before. I'd already given my statement, and now I waited to leave. I rested my head against my arms, overwhelmed, brokenhearted, and exhausted. Reliving the events had completely depleted me. I could still hear the gunshots and the sound of a body hitting the ground. But Jamison. My mind kept going back to him.

The door opened and an officer entered. I didn't move. The same officer that escorted Jamison to the hospital walked in.

"Here." He set a cell phone down beside me. His voice was deep and kind. "You need to call your mother and make contact. Let her know we'll be leaving immediately to get you home."

I kept my head on my arms. "Any news from the hospital?"

"They're hopeful the social worker will make a full recovery. The young man is still in surgery. They're not as hopeful with him. I'm sorry."

A tear escaped, trickling onto the table. "I might have only just met him, but he saved my life."

"His actions were highly erratic. He worked for Baltagio. Was supposed to bring Jamison in. One minute he's helping, the next minute he leaves you high and dry, then he comes back. It's hard to figure that kid out."

"No, it's not." I sat up to better study the police officer. "He loves Jamison, but he also fears for his life and Baltagio's retaliation. I think that's why he kept going back and forth. But at the end of it all, he chose Jamison."

Pointing to the phone, he said, "Make that phone call."

The last thing I wanted to do was talk to my mother. Sighing, I picked up the phone and dialed the number. It rang several times until someone picked up. "Hello?"

But it wasn't my mother on the other end of the line. It was Hank. I froze.

"Who is this?" he demanded.

I disconnected and slammed the phone down, my hands shaking.

"What happened?" the officer asked.

"I-I can't go back." Everything boiled over at that moment. "How does anyone think that it's safe for me to be with that guy?" I took the phone and threw it across the room. It smacked the wall and hit the floor, the battery falling out.

The officer slowly walked to it, bent over and picked it up. But I wanted to throw it again.

"Just let me *hit* something!" I banged my fists on the table. "Let me pretend it's him!" I banged the table again, then stopped because it hurt. I slumped back into the chair and started to sob.

The officer sat across from me. He didn't say anything at first, letting me cry it out. Eventually, he asked, "Are you finished?"

I sniffled and wiped at my nose with my shirt sleeve.

"It's okay to lose it every now and then, so long as you don't break stuff or hurt yourself. But then you got to pick yourself up and move on."

I glared at him. "Thanks for the motivational speech. Let me tuck that away for a rainy day."

He gave a slight grin. "If you don't move on and keep living, then the bad guys win. Your mother's boyfriend wins."

I didn't have a witty comeback for that.

"Ellie, you are nearly eighteen. You have the whole world ahead of you. Don't let your past, or even these horrible events, change the trajectory of your goals and plans. Become wiser. Become smarter. But move on." He stood up and went to the door, the phone in his hand. "Do you have any family that you can stay with for a couple weeks? Until your birthday?"

"No one that Mom will let me stay with. I have a grandfather who I see occasionally and an uncle who lives close to him, but they're hours away. Mom refused because she takes so much from my paychecks. If I'm gone, then she doesn't get my money." But it was more than that. Not that I could tell him. But it wasn't only about Hank and my mother. Thoughts of Jamison rushed in my mind, and I found myself getting choked up. Him. I wanted him in my future. But I had ruined any chance of us.

The officer paused, studying me for a moment. Looking thoughtful, he said, "I'll see what I can do about Hank. His record shows that he's not to get close to you. So he's already violating his probation. I'll try to make something happen. In the meantime, stop throwing other people's phones."

"He trusted me," I blurted.

"You did what you had to do," the officer tried to reassure me, but his smile fell flat and his eyes said that he thought I betrayed him too. "I'm just glad you kids are all right. It could have ended a lot differently."

"Except for D'Juan." My mouth quivered as tears threatened again.

"Maybe he'll pull through."

"He was Jamison's friend."

"And he double-crossed him, yet Jamison is at his side right now. I'm sure Jamison realizes that desperation can make people do crazy, irrational things. Such as walk away from a young mother and son because you're too scared of what the future may hold."

His words confused me until I saw the sadness in his eyes. I'd seen that sadness before. In very similar eyes. "Wait, are you—"

"Gil Godfrey?" He held out his hand. "Nice to meet you."

"But, does Jamison know?"

He acted guilty. "I tried to bring it up on the way to the hospital, but he was so distraught, and in all honesty, I was a bit overwelmed."

"How'd you find out about the motel? About Jamison?"

"The guy who impersonated me didn't realize that I play racquetball with some of the officers from the precinct. One of them saw my name as the one interrogating Jamison, but when he saw who walked out, he knew that it wasn't me. So, he made a call."

"Were you scared?"

"Not at first. I didn't put it together who it was. And then when I found out Jamison was in danger, and it was, in fact, my son, I knew I would never live with myself if I didn't find him, help him. And say I'm sorry."

"You left him."

"Yes. And I have regretted it for nearly eighteen years. Claire told me to go, that the baby wasn't mine. But that's not an excuse. The social worker contacted me a couple years later. By then, I had a fiancé and was making a life for myself. It seemed easier."

I didn't know what to say. I couldn't put into words how much kids need their dads. How Jamison probably longed for him, the way I had always longed for mine.

"Anyway, everyone has regrets."

"Please talk to him. He needs to know."

"Yes. I know. I'm just trying to come to terms with the situation. He looks so ..." Gil tried to keep his emotions in check, but I could tell that Jamison's appearance had shaken him up. "Claire wasn't bad into drugs back then. She was vibrant. Fun. Happy. I'm not sure what's happened the last decade or so, but when I first saw Jamison and how malnourished he was, my heart crashed. Shoot, he's got two brothers. How can I explain all of this to him?"

"Can we go see him?"

"I need to talk to him, but it's already almost nine at night. You've been assigned to me, so I'll have to see if they will let us make a special trip."

Godfrey left me in the room by myself, which might not have been the wisest decision. My thoughts whirled from my dysfunctional relationship with my mom to the evident dysfunction between Jamison and his mom and dad. And every noise in the hall—from doors slamming to someone shouting—had me jumpy. I wrung my hands together and paced. If I could see Jamison—if I could tell him how I felt and how sorry I was and why I did it. I needed to talk to him.

The room seemed to close in on me. "Hello?" I called out. My heart began to race. A door slammed next to the room I was in. I jumped, my breathing accelerating. I tried the door, but it must lock from the outside. Panic and desperation and wanting to see Jamison so badly all merged into one explosive bomb, and I started pounding on the door with my fists and yelling for release. "Somebody let me out!"

I pounded until my fists felt filled with broken fingers. Just thinking of Jamison and our mothers and D'Juan and surgery and Mr. Langston and betrayal and bullets pushed me to shout louder.

The door flew open nearly smacking me in the face.

"What in God's name is going on?" Godfrey demanded.

And I collapsed. Right there. Fell to the floor like crumpled paper. I brought my pulsating hands to my chest and began to sob. "I need to see him." I sobbed. "It can't end this way."

I started to hyperventilate. Godfrey knelt on one leg and gently lifted my chin until we were eye-level. "You've been through a lot. What you're feeling is normal. It's a lot of emotions. A lot of unanswered questions, especially about the future."

"I need to see him," I begged. "I have to tell him I'm sorry."

"There's nothing to apologize for."

"Please, can we stop by the hospital? For closure?"

"It's past nine at night. Visiting hours are closed. We'd waste a lot of time if we waited until morning."

"But I can't leave without talking to him," I said. "Without making sure D'Juan and Mr. Langston are okay."

"If we left now, we'd get to Michigan tomorrow morning." But he rubbed his face and looked off to the side of me as if contemplating.

"It was hard for you to walk away from Jamison's mom," I said. "I can't walk away from him like this. Please."

Godfrey studied me for a moment, then nodded. "All right," he said. "I'll give you the closure you need. Then you're going home."

He helped me up and led me out the door. From that moment and through the entire drive to the hospital, I tried to come up with a thousand different ways to get Jamison to forgive me. I *needed* his forgiveness. I *needed* to know we were okay. I *needed* him to know how I felt.

Chapter Twenty-One: Jamison

Second Chances

Mr. Langston slept quietly in the hospital bed with the gentle beeping of the machines providing the background noise. He had been bandaged up and suffered from some broken ribs, a knife wound in the thigh, a sprained ankle, and some heavy facial bruising, but his prognosis was good.

I barely registered any of that though because of the war inside me. I had fought back emotion the last hour or so of being here. One minute I had to choke back fear and worry over D'Juan, the next I had to choke back hurt and worry and longing with one thought of Ellie.

But I couldn't think about her right now. Not with D'Juan fighting for his life in an operating room.

"There's a lot of bleeding," the ER doctor had explained, as other medical personnel rushed D'Juan out of ER and into surgery. "Internally, as well. We don't know where exactly the bullet is, but it missed the heart. It looks like it might be lodged in his spine, but we won't know for sure until we x-ray it."

"Lodged in his spine? That sounds bad."

"Well, if it's there, then yes, it would be very bad." The ER doctor—a young, Indian man—studied me for a moment before saying, "If I were you, I would prepare—"

"Prepare for what?" I demanded. But then someone was summoning him, and he left me there. "Prepare for *what*?" I called out.

Now I pushed myself up from the chair only to pace, check the hall, and sit back down again. No word from the surgeon yet about D'Juan. I had tried to pray, but my tongue stumbled on the words. How could I express what D'Juan meant to me? It seemed like words wouldn't be enough to show God how much I needed my friend. Or that he couldn't die because of trying to save the lives of both Ellie and me.

⸺⸺⸻

I woke up to hushed voices and a sore neck. Then I remembered where I was. A nurse talked quietly to Mr. Langston who was sitting up in bed. He glanced over at me and tried to smile, only to stop.

"Good morning," he said. "I'd smile, but it still hurts."

"Good morning." I got up and stretched, then stepped to the end of his bed. "How you feeling? Other than not being able to smile."

"I hurt," he said. "But I'm feeling better today."

His coloring did look better.

"What about D'Juan? Have you heard anything?" he asked.

"No, I haven't."

Mr. Langston turned his head to the nurse. "Could you check about a young man who went into surgery yesterday? His name is Day-Juan Hardy."

"D'Juan," I corrected with a small smile.

"Sure. I'll let you know what I find out."

As she left the room, a young woman came in, carrying a tray of breakfast foods. My stomach rumbled so loudly, she shot me a look that said *this ain't for you.*

"Want to share?" Mr. Langston asked, handing me a small container of orange juice.

"Nah, that's okay. You need to eat it and get better."

"I'm not a breakfast person, and the medicine is making me a little nauseous. I'm probably only going to eat the toast anyway. I'd hate to waste the eggs and oatmeal." He brought the small cup of tea to his lips. "Go ahead, drink the OJ. Eat the eggs."

I drank the orange juice, then ate eggs while Mr. Langston took small bites out of the toast. "Why'd you come out here, Mr. Langston? I would have never known if D'Juan wouldn't have taken me to the motel."

He set down the toast and sipped his tea again. "After your first phone call, I thought you might need help. So, I decided to fly out here to make sure Godfrey got the right information, and I wanted to make sure you got to him all right."

"I should have never come. It's been a mess, and now look what's happened. You know, if she had never said anything about it being my father, I probably would have stayed back in the D. What do you think?"

"You would have gone. Think about it. If she said, take the key to some guy I know in Minnesota, and never mentioned your father, would you have gone?"

I didn't have to think twice. "Yeah, I guess I would have. When have I ever not done something she's asked me to do? How many of her secrets have I kept? How many times did I cover for her at the door, so she could escape through the bathroom window?" I was getting worked up. "She didn't have to lie to me. For almost eighteen years she has lied to me."

"I know," he said quietly.

"And you know what else I don't understand? I don't understand how Ray could make sure the gangs didn't touch me, only to threaten to kill me himself!" My voice shook. "Explain that."

"I don't think he was keeping you from gangs to protect you. I think the expectation was that when you turned eighteen, you would work for Baltagio."

I thought about what he said. "So, it wasn't fatherly protection. It was keeping me in line until the right time came…"

"When your mother called me to come get you, she said that time was up, and she had to do something to protect you. I thought she was talking about getting herself in trouble somehow, but now I think it had to do with this. Maybe she knew that when you turned eighteen, she couldn't stop them from doing whatever they were going to do."

"If she would have cleaned up, we could have got of town. Something. So, she thinks protecting me from Baltagio and gangs is going to—what? All the while I'm walking the streets, trying to find her, trying to make sure she isn't dead."

"None of it really makes sense, but this one thing," Mr. Langston said. "You were protected. Look at D'Juan. You were spared. And now that you're older, you can make choices of your own. D'Juan, on the other hand, is tangled up in a lot of bad stuff. In that one sense, your mother spared you."

"What else is he tangled up in? Baltagio and Ray are arrested, and Shazz is dead."

"You think those are the only guys D'Juan's afraid of? It's like a festering disease in Detroit. Crime never really dies. If one goes, another steps up to take his place. D'Juan might be in more trouble now than ever. He still has to answer for what happened to Shazz, and I'm sure Baltagio is going to find a way to contact his crew and to tell them how D'Juan helped you." Mr. Langston paused, "That's why I've chosen to forgive him."

"Forgive him? You mean for tricking you?"

"He … Well, I don't know how else to say it. He set me up. Came into my office the day you left. Told me that he wanted to help you. He said Baltagio was going to have Shazz chase you down. Then he asked for me to tell him where you were, so that he could go protect you. I hesitated, knowing he worked for those guys. But he pleaded with me, promised me that he was looking out for you. 'They already know where he's going,' he said to me. 'But they won't tell me. They know I want to protect him.'

"Anyway, I didn't tell him right away. Not until you called that night. You were so scared, and I couldn't get ahold of anyone to help you. So, I called D'Juan. Made him promise that he would protect you. He said he had a car and would leave right that minute to go help you out. Something didn't sit right. So, I decided to fly out here, only they were waiting for me." Mr. Langston closed his eyes and grimaced, as if even the memory was painful.

My stomach felt heavy. "Mr. Langston, that's horrible."

"They were going to kill me." His voice caught. "But Baltagio told them to stop. He wanted to use me as bait. That was before they knew how much you liked the girl."

"D'Juan regrets it," I said. "I know it. He's torn. It's like he wants freedom, but he's scared. He went with Shazz to come get me, and then he helped me. A lot. I was mad when I found out that he went back to them. I yelled and said a bunch of stuff, but I get it now."

"I know," Mr. Langston said. "That's why I choose to forgive him. He's been nothing but a pawn for them. He is trapped, and I hope that if he makes it through this, that he won't be stuck in the same predicament as before."

"What aren't you telling me?"

His eyes darted from me to his tea. "What are you talking about?"

"You can't look me in the face. The last time you did that was when I was in your office, and you were keeping info about my mother and father from me."

"About that," he sighed. "I should have told you about Godfrey being married with two other children. At least to warn you. I was thrown a curve ball with your mother behind the dumpster. I feel bad that you found out that way. But, please know that it was a hard decision for him. He wanted to stay in your life, but your mother insisted that he go and not come back."

"You don't know?" I asked, surprised. "Gil Godfrey is not my biological father. He's as white as you are. Unless you're pretending you don't know about Ray Baltagio. He's Mr. Baltagio's adopted son. He runs all the illegal operations, and he's a real jerk. He told me he'd protect me so that I could follow in the family business. But you know what, I don't want to talk about him. He's no father to me. I've lived without a dad for almost eighteen years, and I'm just fine."

Mr. Langston's mouth literally hung open.

"What?"

"Ray Baltagio is not your father. Where are you getting this from?"

"From D'Juan. And from Gil Godfrey."

"You met Mr. Godfrey?"

"Yes."

The police officer from earlier stepped into the room. "I'm Officer Godfrey."

I looked from Mr. Langston to the police officer, standing inside the doorway. The same police officer who took me here yesterday.

"I'm Gil Godfrey." He walked over to me and extended his hand. "It's nice to formally meet you, Jamison."

I looked back at Mr. Langston.

"That's Gil Godfrey," he said.

"Then who was the guy at the police station?" I had yet to shake the man's hand.

"One of Baltagio's men," Godfrey answered. "He works at the Detroit precinct, so they didn't think twice about his story. One of the officers there, however, knew it wasn't me, and I was notified. Which is why I was at the motel."

I shook my head, not wanting to believe the truth even though it was right in front of me. This officer, Gil Godfrey, was a tall, slim man who had my eyes. Actually, if it wasn't for him being older than me and a shade darker, we would look a lot alike.

"You even have his deep voice," Mr. Langston said. To Gil, he added, "I've always thought Jamison would make a great radio deejay."

But Gil kept his eyes on me. "Hello, son."

I ordered myself to keep the emotions in check. Don't show this man one shred of emotion. Not to let him think I needed him. I had to clench my jaw to keep from making it quiver.

"I bet you have a lot of questions. But first, how are you? Are you all right?"

I shook my head furiously.

"Jamison, it's all right to talk to him," Mr. Langston said quietly.

I noticed the wedding ring around Gil's finger. "Married," I said. "Probably with kids. Kids who've never had to know one day of hunger."

Stupid, stupid tears. I blinked furiously. *Don't do it,* I ordered myself. *Don't show him you care!*

"If I had known—"

"What?" I raised voice. "What would you have done?"

"Claire asked me to leave. She had high hopes that it was going to work with Ray. At that moment, I was told that the baby wasn't mine."

"I saw Mr. Langston's files. He called you, and you signed off on rights."

"Yes, my circumstances had changed. It seemed easier." Before I could say anything, he kept going, "But it wasn't easy. I thought about you all the time. And I didn't know about how bad things had become."

"Because you didn't ask. You didn't ask if I needed school clothes every year, so instead I had to wear stuff from the church's charity! And you never asked if I needed a hot meal or a place to call home! Do you understand that?" I bellowed. "I've been looking for a place to call home my entire life! And here, this whole time, my father has been raising a family—"

The emotion exploded inside me like a bomb of bitterness. I shoved at him, hot tears blinding me. He let me pound my fists on his chest. I swung, and he blocked, and I swung again. Over and over, until he grabbed my wrists and stopped me.

"A million times over, son, I'm sorry. I can't imagine. I can't."

I didn't want to hear the emotion in his voice. "Do me a favor and stop. You don't get to decide to care."

"Just tell me what I can do to make this right."

"Go back in time eighteen years and don't abandon your son."

The door opened, and a doctor stepped inside. "Are you the family of D'Juan Hardy?"

"Yes," I said quickly, walking over to him. I wiped at my eyes, my mask back in place again. "Is he alive? Please give me some good news."

"The bullet was lodged just outside his spine. But the internal bleeding was significant. I can't say that he's out of the woods yet, but at least this morning, it's more hopeful than last night."

"So, he's alive?"

"Yes. Right now, he's in critical condition, but the bullet has been removed."

I pressed a hand to my heart and closed my eyes. He'd live. I knew it. "He's a fighter," I said. "And he doesn't want to die before he turns twenty."

"Every hour that goes by only increases his chances of complete recovery."

"Can I see him?"

"Yes, that's fine. One of the nurses will give you his room number."

I went to the nurse's station, got the information I needed, and headed to the elevators.

"Jamison!"

I stopped at Ellie's voice. She sat in a waiting room next to the nurse's station. She jumped up and ran over to me, throwing her arms around me. "Officer Godfrey asked me to wait here while he talked to you, but I have been sitting here, going out of my mind. I wanted to give you two time to talk, but I was about ready to come in there anyway."

"I-I can't do this right now." I removed her arms from my neck. I was so raw.

"You talked to Godfrey, didn't you?" Sadness filled her voice. "He was so nervous about talking to you. I had to give him a pep talk on the way over here. What can I do to help?"

"Please. Not now, okay? I need to focus on D'Juan." I walked away from her, my heart burning with desire and anguish. Any other moment I would have pulled her to me and not let go. But at the moment, I needed to get away and find a private place. Then go see my friend.

"Forgive me!" she called after me. "I was only trying to help."

I stopped and turned to look back at her. "I know. I'm not mad."

She smiled sadly, acting like she had more to say.

"I've got to go." I walked away before anything more could be said.

Instead of the elevator, I opted for the stairs and ran up the four flights. Before exiting onto D'Juan's floor, I stopped and sat on the top step. No one else was in the stairwell. I tried to even out my breathing, but just knowing that my biological father was here had me feeling weird things. It didn't bother me when I thought it was Ray. Maybe a little, but it gave me permission not to care. But this guy? A married man with kids. Kids who were related to me. A family that I never met. My heart screamed *unfair*!

I wanted that life.

I stayed on that step for a long time. Once the emotions were in check, and I had talked myself into being a rational human being again, I stood up and made my way to D'Juan.

Once at his room, I took a deep breath and walked in. There he lay, soundly sleeping. Or at least it looked like he was.

I moved the room's chair next to the bed and sat down. "Hey, D."

To my surprise, his eyelids fluttered open briefly before closing again. His mouth moved and he rasped, "You're here."

"Of course, man. Gotta make sure you don't die."

"Not before I'm twenty."

"Exactly. Next time I recommend not throwing yourself in front of a bullet. That'll help."

The corners of his mouth twitched in what might have been a smile. "I wouldn't have ever forgiven myself if anything happened to you."

"Yeah, well, I won't be able to forgive myself if you die trying to protect me and Ellie. So, don't die. Got it?"

"I'm not gonna."

"Good."

"I'm gonna change my ways."

"Good."

"Yeah … gonna be a preacher." He stopped talking, and his breathing became even as sleep overtook him.

"You're gonna be a great preacher."

I stayed and watched him sleep for another hour. When the hour passed, and he was still breathing strong, I stood up and let out a sigh of relief. Another hour down, which improved his odds.

I headed back to the second floor to check on Mr. Langston and to see if Gil Godfrey had left. Maybe if Ellie was still around, I would take that hug she had offered. Just knowing that D'Juan was improving helped my mood greatly. Maybe I could try talking to Gil Godfrey again and not act like I was losing my mind.

A nurse aide was walking out of Mr. Langston's room. "Hey," she whispered. I could see Mr. Langston was asleep. "You're Jamison, right?" When I nodded, she continued, "There's a letter that someone dropped off a little bit ago. I placed it on the bedside table. Also, an Officer Godfrey left me this card to give to you. He said that he would like to talk some more, but he had to escort someone back home."

"Thank you." I took the business card, sad that I didn't get a chance to properly say good-bye to Ellie. "I'll see that Mr. Langston gets the letter."

"Well, the letter is for you." She pointed at the table, then left the room.

I went to the table and picked up the long, white envelope.

For: Mr. Langston.
Please give to Jamison Jones (he'll be in Mr. Langston's room).

Ellie.
My heart quickened as I ripped the envelope. I only ever saw her write a few things down, but she always drew a heart over the letter "i" instead of a dot.

Dear Jamison,
I'm bummed we didn't get to say good-bye. I know you're worried about a lot of different things, but I needed to see you one more time and say good-bye.

Listen, I am so sorry about the big mess I made. I know you're upset at me, and I'll have to live with that. But I really was thinking about you when I took the key to make the deal. I wanted it to end. In my head, we'd get them to leave us alone, and then I could convince you to come with me to Wyoming. Yeah, I know. A girl's pipe dream not exactly rooted in reality. But, hey, this is the girl who wants to be a country singer, so reality is overrated. Honestly, I think deep down I knew our time together was coming to a close, and I was trying to stop it.

They're taking me back to my mom's in Grand Ledge. I guess Hank isn't supposed to be living there with me in the house. Since I'm technically underage for another couple weeks, he can't step anywhere near me. Would have been nice to know before running away, but oh well. I don't regret that part. If I hadn't ran away, I would have never met you.

And you're the best part of all of this.

If you can ever forgive me, come find me. On my eighteenth birthday I'm leaving for Buffalo, Wyoming. This time, I'm buying a plane ticket.

I hope to see you before then. Still hoping for a happy ending.
Love always,
Ellie

I read and reread the letter, hearing her say the words in my head. And I smiled just thinking about her. I couldn't be angry at her. That wouldn't be fair, especially when I had called Mr. Langston at the motel to pick me up, ready to leave her there. When I thought of her in Michigan, my smile faded. That seemed far from here. And Grand Ledge from Detroit? That might as well be to the moon when I didn't have any cash or a vehicle.

"One minute you're smiling, the next you're frowning," Mr. Langston said with a yawn.

"I've got a lot of things going on inside me. Don't judge."

"Not judging."

"Besides, it's not like you have a right to judge, considering your fashion sense."

"What's that supposed to mean?"

"It means that your wardrobe looks like it's straight from the eighties."

"I happened to like what I wear. Thank you very much."

"Which explains why you're single."

Mr. Langston acted so put out, I started laughing. "I go on dates!" he said. I kept laughing. "My dating life is no concern to yours, mister." He started to chuckle, then stopped. "Don't make me laugh, my face hurts."

"Yeah, it's killing me!"

Mr. Langston took a plastic spoon and threw it at my head. "Abuse! Absolute abuse in here!"

"Okay, okay, I'll stop." I pulled up a chair. "About what happened earlier, with Godfrey. I don't know what came over me."

"What you did was completely normal," he said. "You've had hurt buried for eighteen years. It all came out."

"I'm embarrassed."

"Don't be. He understood." We didn't say anything for a few minutes. "I think you should forgive him. Maybe not today, or even tomorrow. But I find that forgiveness is very freeing."

"I don't know. Maybe. It gets on my nerves that his other kids got to have a dad."

"Yeah, but you can't go back in time. What's done is done. But you now have a man who is wanting to come into your life. You'll be better for it."

"Maybe. I'll think about it. Right now, though, I want to make sure you and D'Juan get better and can go home."

"How's D'Juan doing?"

"Good. He talked to me. He said he wants to be a preacher."

"Really? Well, if he can help other kids not go down the same path, then I say go for it."

"You're pretty impressive, Mr. Langston. It's not many guys that can forgive someone who nearly killed them."

"I told you. Forgiveness is freeing."

"Yeah, yeah, yeah, don't you become a preacher too. Next thing I know, everyone's gonna want me baptized."

I opened the letter again and reread it.

"What's the letter say?"

I handed it to him.

"Grand Ledge?" he asked. "That's interesting."

"What's interesting about it? It's far enough away that I'll never see her."

Mr. Langston handed me back the letter. "Your grandmother—the one you were supposed to go to before you skipped out of town—lives just outside of Grand Ledge."

I stared at him, feeling the flicker of hope starting to spread throughout my entire body. "Please don't be joking."

"I'm not. As soon as I get out of here, we'll head home, and I'll arrange it. She's still waiting for you."

I closed my eyes and thought of Ellie. I thought of her eyes staring out from underneath that cap. I thought of her smile and the way her hand felt in mine. Maybe one day, when our hearts were healed, there'd be hope of something more.

Don't leave just yet, Ellie. I'm coming for you.

Chapter Twenty-Two: Ellie

Warm Welcome

Godfrey put the car in park and turned off the engine. He studied the dull brown trailer with the faded white trim. "This is home?"

"For another four weeks, six days, and"—I checked my watch—"five hours."

"If you have any trouble, call. I also gave you a couple numbers here in the area."

"As long as Hank is gone, I can handle my mother." But I still didn't move. I glanced over at him. "Thanks," I said. "Most men I encounter are really bad. For lack of a better word. But you aren't. It makes sense that Jamison is your son."

"Yeah? He's a good guy, huh?"

I spent the last several hours replaying everything that happened to Jamison and me. I explained what I knew about him and his mom. But it wasn't enough. Mr. Godfrey kept asking questions, as if seeing his son for the first time opened his eyes to what he was missing. "He's the best."

"I wish I could change the things that have happened, but I can't."

"You are Jamison's father, so don't stop pursuing him." When he raised his eyebrows, I added, "He deserves to have some goodness in his life. You two deserve to have a relationship, and he deserves to have a family. Outside of his mother, of course."

"It's hard to get ahold of him. He doesn't have a phone."

"I'm sure you'll find a way." Resigned, I opened the door. "So, are you heading all the way back to Minnesota?"

"I have family in the Ann Arbor area, and some college friends. I'll probably hang out for a few days. Stop and visit Claire. And Jamison."

"If you have family here, why'd you move so far away?"

"A little over eighteen years ago, I needed to get away from everything. I took the first police job I was offered and that was that."

I slid out of the car, grabbed my backpack from the floor, and said good-bye.

As I approached the steps, Mom opened the door. She walked out onto the small porch. A cigarette dangled from her lips, and they were turned down in a deep frown. My anger flared. I moved past her to go inside. "If I were you, I'd wave at the policeman and act nice. You don't want him to see the real you."

Once inside, I crinkled my nose and covered it. The living room and kitchen stank of stale food, mold, and cigarettes, and even a little pot. My eyes immediately filled with tears, and I hurried to my room. I slammed the door then sighed in relief. Nothing had changed in here. Then again, it had only been four days. Strange how much had changed for me in those three days, yet here in the trailer, everything had stayed the same.

Mom opened my door without knocking.

"Thanks for knocking. I'll have to remember to start locking it again."

She stood there, staring at me with that deep frown. A storm brewed behind her eyes, like she'd burst into tears at any moment.

"I know, I know," I snapped. "Hank can't be here because of me. Well, don't worry. The minute I'm eighteen, I'll be gone."

"He always told me that he never touched you," she finally said.

"We've talked about this before, and I'm not in the mood to be called a liar again."

"Even when he was in prison. Said that you lied and made the whole thing up because you were jealous."

I closed my eyes and counted to ten. "My room is my sanctuary. Please leave me alone."

"When he got here—after I picked him up from prison—and saw you weren't here, he started acting really weird. He got a call the next day from someone he knows, I guess, and I heard him. He closed the bathroom door so I wouldn't listen, but I heard anyway. He said your name. He said something about when the guy got done with you that he wanted you back." Mom's face crumpled. Her hands shook, and she acted like she didn't know what to do with them. "Everything you said was true."

"Yeah." I felt a little sorry for her. "Everything I said was true."

"So, he …" She sucked in a breath, her lower lip quivering.

"Yes. And it didn't matter if my door was locked. He'd unlock it somehow and come in."

"Why didn't you—" She started to sob.

"Tell you? I did. You refused to believe. It wasn't until I got scared and went to the school counselor that anything happened." Suddenly, I was furious. I no longer felt sorry for her. All of it was her fault. "Why are *you* crying? You're not the one who went through horror, only to have your mother not believe you!"

"You're right," she cried. "God, I've made mistakes, but this—I didn't know! He got furious when I brought it up. Told me you were a liar and jealous and to never bring it up again!"

"I was fourteen," I said through clenched teeth. "A child. Why would I lie?"

"I thought you blamed me for Billy's death. That you were getting back at me."

"Don't bring up my brother's name."

Mom's shoulders shook as she sobbed in the doorway of my room. A part of me felt relief that she finally believed the truth. Another part was peeved that it was only because she'd heard it through Hank's mouth. Eventually she stopped and said, "He's gone. You don't have to worry. I would have had him out the minute I heard him admit what he'd done to you, but I was scared. There was a real scary side to him. But then the cops came over and told him that he wasn't supposed to be anywhere near you."

"Good. I'm tired. I'm gonna take a shower then crash."

"For what it's worth, El, I'm sorry."

"Yeah, me too. But none of it's fixable at this point." I opened a dresser drawer and grabbed some clean clothes, then I walked past Mom to our tiny bathroom.

My entire body trembled from fatigue and memories. After locking the bathroom door, I turned the shower on hot and got in. For a moment I only stood there, wanting the water to relax me and erase everything bad from my past. As I washed my hair and scrubbed my body, my mind wouldn't stop replaying scenes that I didn't want to remember. Scenes from years ago, like Billy's funeral and Hank's greedy expression when he approached me ready to take what wasn't his. Recent events tumbled through my mind too and those were just as horrid. The motel, gunshots ringing through the air, bodies falling on the ground, Danny threatening me.

I sank to the bottom of the tub and sat there, the hot water still beating down. I would have never exposed Jamison and me to such danger if I had felt safe in my own home. *Safe.* What did that feel like? I wanted to find a home where I felt safe. Could I ever have that? Not here. There were too many bad memories in this trailer. And I wasn't sure my mother and I would ever have a good relationship. Too much had happened, and I wasn't at a place of forgiveness.

"Jamison," I whispered. Thinking of forgiveness got me thinking about the one I wanted to forgive me. Did he receive the letter? Would he come to me?

I hoped so. If not, I would go to him. I decided right then and there that I wasn't going to let our story go unfinished.

Feeling better, and no longer like a victim, I turned off the water and got out of the shower. I now had a sense of purpose. *Jamison.*

Once dressed, I grabbed the laptop I left behind and googled the hospital's phone number.

"Hello," I said to the hospital's call center operator. "I would like to be connected to a patient's room. His name is Mr. Langston. I don't know his first name."

The next thing I knew, the phone line was ringing.

"Hello?" a man's voice said.

"Mr. Langston?"

"Yes, who's this?"

"This is Ellie. We were together in the car and then at the motel."

"Of course. How could I forget?" he said.

"I know. It's definitely something not forgettable. Anyway, is Jamison in the room?"

"No, he's with Day-Juan right now. I mean, D'Juan. Jamison keeps telling me I'm saying his name wrong."

My heart sank. "Oh God, how is he? D'Juan?"

"The surgery was successful, and he seems to be getting stronger. At least that's what Jamison told me."

"You mean he's gonna live?" I felt an overwhelming sense of gratitude. It would have been hard to live with myself if I had been a reason D'Juan died.

"He's recovering slowly, but the doctors now think that there's hope."

"How's Jamison?"

"He's like the energizer bunny. Bounces from my room to Day-Juan's."

"I had left a letter for him. Did he get it?"

"Yes, and I think it touched him. That was a good idea."

"You think so? I don't know," I admitted. "I don't know if what I did was forgivable."

"Ellie, I realize the whole motel scene was very traumatic. And sure, your involvement was because of you trying to make a deal, but it ended. The bad guys lost. And it was because of you."

"It wasn't me," I said. "If Jamison hadn't shown up—"

"I would be dead if you hadn't charged at Baltagio. You are brave, Miss Elvis. Braver than you give yourself credit for."

"Really?" I smiled into the phone.

"Really," he answered. "And now it's time you start believing it." He paused, then said, "Hey, Jamison just walked in the room. Hold on a sec."

My heart began to pound. I wet my lips and held my breath.

"Hello?" His low voice hit my ears like a much-needed rain.

"Hey, Jamison. How are you doing?"

He didn't say anything at first.

"Jamison?" I said, to make sure he was on the line.

"I'm here."

"Will you ever forgive me? I can't—I mean, I need you to forgive me."

"I was mad at first," he said. "When I found out you stole the key. And really hurt. Like you betrayed me."

"I know, and I'm so sorry. I was only thinking about us being free."

"Yeah, I get that," he said. "I'm not really mad anymore, I just …"

"What?"

He paused again. "I just miss you."

I covered my mouth, but I doubted it hid my grin.

"I feel like you should be here, and there's a hole because you're not."

"I feel I should be there too," I said. "With you."

We both stayed quiet for a moment.

"How's everything at the house?" he asked.

"Okay. Hank's not here, and Mom finally believes what happened between us."

"Good. It's been hard worrying for four people. It's nice that you're okay. At least until I get there."

"Wait—what?" I asked, my heart pounding again.

"I'm coming for you," he said. I could imagine the grin on his face as he said it. "Mr. Langston told me that my grandmother lives close to Grand Ledge. I'll be staying with her, finishing my senior capstone project, at least until I turn eighteen."

"No way!"

"I know. I would have found a way to you no matter what, but I don't think it's a coincidence."

"You would have?"

"Seems weird, doesn't it? We only met a couple days ago, but now, everything's changed."

"Everything *has* changed," I said softly. "I no longer feel alone."

"Listen," he said. "I don't know when I'm leaving here. D'Juan is still in critical care, and Mr. Langston hasn't even been released yet. Then I got to get back to Detroit and visit my mom. I'm not sure how long all of this will take. Just … wait for me, okay?"

"I'm kind of a mess," I said.

"We can take our time. We've got a lot to get over. I get it. But maybe one day."

"Yeah," I agreed. "I'll be here waiting."

As I hung up the phone, I thought of Godfrey's words. There really were good people, and I just so happened to have met one of the best.

Chapter Twenty-Three: Jamison

New Beginnings

"**S**he's been writing a lot," one of the aides said to me as we walked down the hall. "It's been very therapeutic, or so she says."

I swallowed down my nerves, not responding. I didn't know what to expect. Not to mention, there was so much that needed to be said. I had been at the hospital an entire week, sitting by D'Juan's bedside. Each day he had made incredible progress. It was like he had a new purpose and a new determination to live. "I'm telling ya," he'd said. "You wait. I'm gonna be helping other people. Maybe even start a church. What do I have to do to start a church?"

"Don't you have to get like a Bible degree?"

"Then that's what I'll do."

Mr. Langston had made arrangements for D'Juan to stay with his aunt in Cleveland, but he wanted to go with me to see Mom. "I have to ask for forgiveness," he said. "I nearly got her son killed."

D'Juan's change had renewed purpose in Mr. Langston too. Especially when D'Juan sought forgiveness from our social worker. "You are an angel," D'Juan had said to Mr. Langston. "Helping kids and families in a community that doesn't act very grateful." That started a fire inside Mr. Langston to get working on saving kids from the perils of the street.

He wouldn't stop preaching forgiveness at me either. After Gil Godfrey got back from escorting Ellie home, he visited me every day at the hospital. At first, it was awkward, and I acted hostile. Until D'Juan observed me.

"You need to get over yourself. You have a father who wants to hang out with you. Don't be bitter, man."

"Thank you, *reverend*," I said with sarcasm.

"Just trying to save your soul from the flames of hell."

I rolled my eyes but laughed. When Godfrey came in that day with a change of new clothes for me, I remembered D'Juan's words and said, "Thank you. I need to change."

"I thought you might be tired of wearing the same outfit. Maybe after you clean up, we can head down to the cafeteria and grab some lunch."

Before I left for Michigan, I was invited over to his house for dinner. It was harder than I thought, being a part of the normalcy of my father's family. His wife, Lisa, was a soft-spoken woman with a beautiful smile and amazing skill in the kitchen. I had about five of her chicken fajitas. The hardest—and coolest—part was meeting my thirteen and nine-year-old brothers.

"This is Jackson and Dimeitri."

"You're our brother?" Dimeitri asked.

"Yep, it looks like it," I said. "It's pretty cool to have brothers."

"Until they take what's not theirs," Jackson said, looking pointedly at Dimeitri.

"Dad said we have to share Fortnite." Dimeitri stuck out his tongue.

"That's enough," Gil said.

"Do you play games?" Jackson asked me.

"Um, I play card games, but I haven't had a chance to play a video game. Well, other than at the arcade sometimes. My friend, D'Juan, and me would go and play some Street Fighter. It's an old game, but the arcade only had old games."

"Street Fighter is the best game," Gil said.

But throughout the dinner, I felt guilty as if I was betraying Mom.

"I'm glad you came over," Gil said, taking me back to the hospital. "You sure you don't want to stay with us. I mean my house is your house."

"Really?" I asked, shaking my head. "You don't even know me."

"You are my son, and you are always welcome in *our* house."

"I should probably hang out with D'Juan and Mr. Langston. They're releasing them soon."

"Then I will see you tomorrow. I'll stop by after my shift."

"It seems light years away from Mom, doesn't it?"

"She wouldn't have sent you this way if she wasn't willing for this to happen."

All of this was good. Each of these important people in my life had hope restored. But could the same happen for my mom? Or was she too far gone?

Now, as I stood outside the rehabilitation facility, I hesitated before entering. It seemed forever ago that she hid behind that dumpster, giving me my father's address. I put one foot in front of the other and walked through the double sliding doors. The air conditioning blasted, which was a welcomed relief. Mr. Langston's car did not have air conditioning.

"I'm here to see Claire Marie Jones," I said to the lady behind the information desk.

"Sure thing. Let me get an aide to assist you."

I waited in the lobby until a young guy not much older than me came out and called for me. "Are you here to see Claire Jones?"

"Yes."

"Please show me your pockets. To be on the safe side." After I finished, he said, "Lift up your pant leg please and let us check your socks."

"Do I need to step out of my shoes?"

"You should be fine. All set. Follow me."

He took me to the second floor. "How's she doing?" I asked.

"She's still suffering withdrawals, which might make her a little erratic." The aide took a couple turns, then led me down a long hallway, stopping at a room with a thick, locked door. "She'll only be in observation for another couple of days. Want to make sure that she's past the worst of it. Leave your shoes out here, please."

The aide opened the door, and I stepped inside.

Mom sat on a small bed shoved in a corner of the mostly empty room. There was a chair and a small bedside table. She was writing feverishly into a notebook. Her blonde hair had been pulled back into a ponytail, and her face was completely void of any makeup. But her coloring was good. Better than I'd seen it in a long time.

"Hi, Mom."

Her head shot up and her eyes widened. "Jamison!" She got up and ran to me, throwing her arms around my neck. "You're okay," she said in relief. "I've been so worried."

I hugged her back, letting my anger and hurt at so many of her wrong decisions dissolve a little. "I've been worried about you too. How are you?" I asked, releasing her.

"I'll make it," she said with a small smile. "And now that I know you're all right, I'm gonna keep fighting."

"Good."

"What's this?" she asked, rubbing my head. "Where'd it go? You look like a different person."

"My friend helped me cut if off. To make it not so easy to spot me. My Afro was a little hard to miss."

"It was, wasn't it? Well, I like this. You look so mature."

We stayed quiet a moment. "So," she said, moving back to her bed. "I take it that you met Godfrey?"

"Yep."

"He came by here a week or so ago. We had a good talk. I apologized and thanked him. He told me how brave you were. And everything you went through. I've been struggling since then because I sent you to him. Knowing … I only knew that I had to get you out of Detroit to save you. And me. He's always been a reliable guy."

"At first, Ray Baltagio told me that he was my father. Like a bad Star Wars episode. But when he pulled out a gun and pointed it at me, I was pretty sure he wasn't my dad. There was no hesitation either."

"He pointed a gun at you?"

"Oh, he did worse than that. He was going to shoot Ellie, and

D'Juan threw himself in her place."

"Trust me, I didn't want to send you," she said. "It was the only chance to break my agreement with Ray and his father."

"So, there was an agreement?"

"Yes," she said. "Baltagio wanted you to work with him. He liked D'Juan and wanted to train you too. Maybe he thought you would join his side if you thought Ray was your dad. But when I overheard Baltagio discussing counterfeit money and it being held in a safe deposit box, I saw my chance. I thought if I took the key and turned it in, they'd be arrested, and you wouldn't have them breathing down your neck."

"Well, I was nearly killed a bunch of times, and I found out my real father is a police officer in Minnesota with a wife and two sons. Yes, I have brothers I didn't know existed. And a grandmother. Seems you've been keeping a lot from me."

"Jamison," she started. "There is so much I regret. So much I'm sorry for."

"Like what?" I asked, letting my anger show. "The fact that I never really had a place to call home? The fact that I had to take care of you because of your addiction to drugs? Or is it the fact that I nearly went hungry so that you could use whatever money we had on whatever you wanted? I actually sat at my father's house with his family and ate a meal. And you know what I kept thinking? That I never had that! I have a grandmother who's never met me and has tried for eighteen years?"

Tears filled Mom's eyes. "All of it," she whispered. "I'm sorry for all of it. It was Ray who got me addicted to—"

"No, you don't get to blame other people. It's your body. You could have said no. A good mother would have said no!"

"You're right. After my dad died, I rebelled. Met a college guy named Gil. Ran away to be with him. Then I met Ray. A real smooth-talker. So nice and charming and rich. It didn't take long to discover I was pregnant. I chose to stay with Ray because he promised so many things. But things started to change. And fast. I found out that I was the girl he kept on the side. I was embarrassed at my life. That's why I refused to see my mother. When I ran away, I thought that Ray would take care of me. Instead, he got me partying a lot. Everything spun out of control. And it's embarrassing and shameful. It's not the life I wanted, especially not for you."

The aide opened the door. "Time's up," he said. "Visitors only have limited time on this floor."

"I'm heading to Grand Ledge right now," I said to Mom. "I'm going to meet my grandmother for the first time."

Mom smiled through the tears. "You'll love her. She was a good mom. Unfortunately for her, I was a pretty rebellious kid." She shook her head. "That doesn't matter anymore. I can only move forward and change things. That's what the counselor told me. Anyway, your grandma's gonna love you."

I sighed, not knowing what to say. There were still so many unanswered questions, but seeing Mom and her improvement gave me hope that we'd have time for answers eventually. "I'll tell her you said hi."

"Give her this for me," Mom went to her notebook, found a few pages and ripped them out. "It's a letter I wrote to her."

I took it but couldn't bring myself to leave. "I love you, Mom. I'm hurt and dealing with a lot of feelings. We've still got a lot to work out, but don't ever think you're not loved."

She threw her arms around me again. "I'm gonna make it right. I promise," she said. "I won't have to serve hard time. They're going to keep me in here. And I'm gonna get clean, and when I'm out, I hope to be the kind of mother you deserve."

I left the room, headed down the hall, to the elevators, and made my way outside. Mr. Langston and D'Juan sat in the car waiting for me. I opened the back seat and slid inside. Neither of them paid me any attention.

"You don't control my radio," Mr. Langston was saying.

"You're killing me with this country music," D'Juan said. "Put on some R & B, right, Jamison?"

I didn't say anything.

"Jamison?"

"Let's get going," I said.

Mr. Langston started the car.

D'Juan asked, "How'd it go? She a'right?"

"She looks better than I've seen her in a while."

"So, what's the problem?" D'Juan asked.

"Just a lot of questions, but none of it can be changed."

"Your future can be," Mr. Langston said.

"I know, but I'm talking about the past."

"The past is gone," D'Juan said, moving into his preacher voice. He'd been doing that a lot lately. "It's time to embrace your destiny!"

"Amen," Mr. Langston said.

I rolled my eyes. "Whatever."

"Don't 'whatever' me. You know it's true. What you need is some good ol' fashioned prayer."

I gave him a look that clearly told him I'd had enough. "I think the bullet shook something loose in your head."

Mr. Langston turned the car onto the highway. "All right, folks, Grand Ledge, here we come. You ready to meet your grandma?" He peered at me through the rearview mirror.

I shrugged. "I'm a little nervous, but I'll be cool. She knows I'm half-black, right? I don't want her to fall over from shock when she sees me."

"Of course …" Mr. Langston paused. "Um, maybe not. I don't know that I ever told her."

D'Juan started laughing again. "Some black guy walking up to her door, and she gonna come out with a shotgun."

"Ha, ha, ha," I said. "Very funny. But maybe, Mr. Langston, you should walk up with me. Just to be safe."

D'Juan laughed harder. "Bang! Bang!" he said. "Wouldn't it be ironic for you to have lived through Baltagio and Danny and that whole crime ring, only to be shot by your grandma?"

Mr. Langston started chuckling, then stopped when he saw me watching. "I wouldn't let that happen."

"You're still stopping at Ellie's first? Like you said."

"Yep. Does she know you're coming?"

"Yes and no. I told her I was coming, but that was the last time I talked to her over two weeks ago."

"I don't know what makes me more nervous." I stared at Ellie's brown trailer. "Seeing Ellie again, or meeting my grandma."

"Get out of the car and go get your girl," D'Juan ordered. "We didn't come all this way for you to chicken out."

"I'm not chickening out," I said, opening the door and stepping outside.

I took a deep breath, straightened my shirt, and moved toward the door. Two weeks ago, I wondered if we'd ever see each other again. My insides warmed just remembering our conversation on the phone. She had called *me*. She told me that she wanted *me*. What we experienced was a horrible ordeal, but somehow, I didn't regret any of it. It brought me to her.

Suddenly, the door flew open, and Ellie came out. I drew in a breath, taking her in. Her long dark hair now fell over her shoulders. She wore denim shorts and a hot pink t-shirt, but no cap on her head. Not that she needed it. I didn't remember her being this beautiful. She'd always been pretty, and if I admitted it, I was attracted to her the moment she approached me at the bus stop. But here. The worry and fear were gone from her face. She smiled, and it seemed to shine like a beacon. "You came," she said.

I tried to act cool. "I told you I would."

We stood for a moment, not moving. Then she ran down the steps and flew into my arms. "These two weeks have been lonely without you."

"I've been lonely too," I admitted. "But I couldn't leave D'Juan."

"I understand." She released me just enough to look at me. "Your loyalty is one of the traits I like best about you."

"Really?" My face warmed at the compliment. I wasn't used to having nice things said about me by pretty girls. Actually, I had very little experience in the girl department, not that I would tell Ellie that.

"Yes, but there are a lot of traits I like about you."

"There's a lot of traits I like about you too," I said.

"So …" She looked away for a moment. "You're not mad anymore? You forgive me for everything?"

"There's nothing to forgive. You were doing what you thought would help us. And in a way, it did. The criminals got what was coming to them, and we're finally free. Without you doing what you did, it might have turned out a lot differently."

She closed her eyes and sighed, then looked back up at me. "Where do we go from here?"

I swallowed back the nerves and said, "According to Mr. Langston, my grandma only lives about ten miles from here. Maybe a date?"

Ellie grinned and she gave a slight laugh. "YES!" she said. "I'd like a date. Preferably no bus rides. Or abandoned motels."

"Until I get my license, I'll have to take one to get here."

"Call Uber," she said, which made me laugh. "Or I'll borrow my mom's car."

D'Juan called out, "You two are killing me!"

Ellie released me and turned to D'Juan. "Hey! I'm so glad to see you made it out alive."

"Amen," D'Juan said, getting preachy. "By the grace of God."

Ellie looked over at me and raised her eyebrows.

"He's gonna be a preacher," I explained, pressing my lips together. "Just go with it."

She nodded. "Well, praise the Lord," she teased.

"You know, neither of you should take lightly this enormous gift we've been given," D'Juan said the words in melody.

"All we need now is the organ," I said. "To go with your sermon."

D'Juan stopped and gave me a look of annoyance. "Don't make me get out and punch that mouth of yours."

Ellie gasped. "Would a preacher do that?"

"I ain't a preacher yet."

She leaned through the opened window and hugged D'Juan. "I'm glad you made it out alive."

D'Juan hugged her back. "Yeah, me too."

"Hi, Mr. Langston." She pulled herself out of the window and stood up. "You look good without the blood and bruises."

"I've decided the color of blood doesn't suit me. Did everything work out here?"

"It's better than it's been in a long time."

"Good," he said.

"That's a relief," I told her.

She took my hand and gave me a piece of paper. "It's our house number and my cell phone number."

"Got it." I stepped closer. "As soon as I get settled, I'll call. Or maybe I'll just come over."

"I'm not sure what happens next. But I'm not scared anymore."

I glanced over at D'Juan, then to Ellie. "I'm not either."

Epilogue

Hey J-man,

I was gonna call you back, but I'm supposed to practice my writing in English class, so this counts as an assignment. Glad to hear things are going good with your Grandma. My Aunt Patty has been cool. She's going to school to be a nurse and got me enrolled in the GED-to-degree program at the community college. And her pastor, Reverend Duncan, has taken me under his wing. I've signed up to take young minister's leadership training. It's only me and two other guys, but it's something. Next month, I'll be giving a ten-minute exhortation at Sunday service.

So, you and Ellie, huh? For the record, I really don't need you to send me every pic you take of the two of you. I get it. She's your girlfriend. I don't need a play-by-play. And another thing, tell Ellie to kick your butt and make you apply to U of M. I don't want to hear none of this I'm-not-good-enough garbage. You know you're smart. And Detroit needs you. So, go become Doctor Jamison.

I'm supposed to write three paragraphs, but I don't know what else to write. I'm gonna text you in a minute to get your address so I can mail this. That's kinda funny.

Peace out,
D'Juan Hardy